Pane and Suffering

Pane and
Suffering

Cheryl
Hollon

KENSINGTON PUBLISHING CORP.
http://www.kensingtonbooks.com

KENSINGTON BOOKS are published by

Kensington Publishing Corp.
119 West 40th Street
New York, NY 10018

All Kensington Titles, Imprints, and Distributed Lines are available at special quantity discounts for bulk purchases for sales promotions, premiums, fund-raising, and educational or institutional use. Special book excerpts or customized printings can also be created to fit specific needs. For details, write or phone the office of the Kensington special sales manager: Kensington Publishing Corp., 119 West 40th Street, New York, NY 10018, attn: Special Sales Department, Phone: 1-800-221-2647.

Kensington and the K logo Reg. U.S. Pat & TM Off.

ISBN-13: 978-1-61773-760-2
ISBN-10: 1-61773-760-7
First Kensington Mass Market Edition: October 2015

eISBN-13: 978-1-61773-761-9
eISBN-10: 1-61773-761-5
First Kensington Electronic Edition: October 2015

10 9 8 7 6 5 4 3 2 1

Printed in the United States of America

To George
A bushel and a peck . . .

Acknowledgments

If it takes a village to raise a child, it takes a planet to support a writer.

For craft development, nothing has had more impact than the Sisters in Crime's online chapter, the Guppies (the Great Unpublished). There are hundreds of Guppies and here's a wave of the fin to you all. In particular, Guppies are stellar at coming up with book titles—Lisa Mathews, Mariella Krause, and Di Schultz, that's you.

Big bear hugs go to Joye Barnes who courageously provided that precise balance of encouragement and gently targeted feedback to nurture my early writing attempts. Without her support, I would not be a writer at all. Her warm circle of friends followed my arduous journey with interest and supplied adult beverages in generous quantities.

I have been wildly fortunate to host a face-to-face critique group—Amy Jordan, Christa Rickard, Sam Falco and Aaron Steimle. Filled with dread, I've entered the "cone of silence" while they pointed out continuity errors, awkward dialogue, and plot holes big enough to hide a planet. Thank you.

If you have a chance to attend Donald Maass' Break-Out Novel Workshop—do it. This is where you learn to take your writing to the next level. No, two levels! Organized by the extraordinary editor and author, Lorin Oberweiger, of Free-Expressions, I attended my first one in Santa Fe, NM, and another in Charlotte, NC. The manuscript I tortured in Charlotte captured my agency's attention. Seriously, just go.

This series is based on an actual neighborhood of St. Petersburg, FL, the Grand Central District that runs along Central Avenue and an actual stained glass store, Grand Central Stained Glass. I've taken an artist's license of changing the names of some of the businesses and the name of the church downtown. Locals will recognize Queens Head Eurobar and 3 Daughters Brewing as well as other eateries and landmarks. I reserve the delight to research them thoroughly and move them around to suit my book. I've simplified the name of the pub to Queen's Head.

Deepest thanks to cover artist, Bruce Emmett. For the unknown debut author, I believe a first-in-series book cover is the most influential factor in attracting readers. He absolutely nailed the look of Webb's Glass Shop and the ever adorable service beagle, Suzy.

The editor of my dreams, Mercedes Fernandez, has been my cheerleader, counselor, and champion in guiding the way through my novice year as an author. She has pushed me gently out of my comfort zone and into a better story.

I am deeply grateful for the skill, knowledge, inspiration, and confidence that my agent shared with unstinting cheer and encouragement. Thank you, Beth Campbell, of Bookends, LLC.

Thank you to my mother, Marcella, who blessed me with a wildly original upbringing that provided life skills taught with love and a critical amount of joyous freedom. Thank you to my dad, Wendell, who broke the local library age restriction rules to help me check out books from the adult stacks. He also taught me how to make impossible things (remember the completely handmade canoe we built in the attic?). This book is one of those impossible things.

I'm also very grateful for the loving support from my family in this long journey to publication. Thanks, Eric, Jennifer, Aaron, Beth, Ethan, Lena Rose, Mister, Pepper, Ricky, and Snowy for simply believing this dream would come true.

Chapter 1

Monday Morning

Savannah fingered the key ring her late father had used only a week ago. She knew each key by memory, having used them from babyhood up through borrowing his car with her newly issued driver's license. She clenched them in her fist and took a deep shaky breath. *Dad will never twirl them barely out of my reach again.*

Paint flaked off the heavy, fireproofed and double-bolted back door. *It's like Dad,* she thought, *well-worn, but strong and solid.*

How could her smart, funny, marathon running dad die of a heart attack?

Savannah unlocked the shop, stepped into his office, and keyed the alarm code. With walls built of salvaged barn wood, the tiny space awakened a vision of his shoulders hunched over a mountain of paperwork. The sharp smoky scent of his after-shave clutched her heart.

Stop thinking about him. The students will be here soon.

Forcing a slow breath, she dropped the keys onto the rolltop desk that had once been her grandfather's. Small pilings of papers, files, bills, and Post-it notes covered every available flat surface and all the pigeonholes were stuffed like magpie nests. Grandpa Roy had used the sturdy desk for the motorcycle business he'd started after World War I. In continuous use by her family since the 1920s, it looked at her with serious expectations.

I guess you're mine now. I'll do my best.

She ran her hand over the top and smiled when her fingers reached the dent caused by a wildly thrown toy rocket when she was five. Her dad had yelled at her.

He seldom yelled.

Startled by the ringing of the black wall-mounted phone, she cleared her throat and picked up the receiver. "Webb's Glass Shop. May I help you?"

"Oh my. I wasn't expecting a real person. I meant to leave a message."

Good guess. I don't feel like a real person today. "It's okay. I'm opening up. May I help you?"

"I wanted to know if class has been cancelled. I would completely understand, you know, because the funeral was on Sunday. It was so awesome—all those young men in military uniforms."

Savannah flinched, recalling the haunting echo

of *Taps* floating behind the gravestone that marked the final rejoining of her parents. She swallowed quickly. "Classes are being held as scheduled beginning today. Which one are you taking?"

"I'm in Beginning Stained Glass."

"It starts in half an hour. What's your name?"

"Amanda Blake. I signed up for more classes with John, I mean with Mr. Webb, last month, but I thought the shop might close."

"Hugh Trevor is taking over the classes for Dad. I mean Mr. Webb. I'll see you in—"

"Oh my goodness. Are you Savannah?"

"Yes, I'm—"

"I am so, so sorry. I saw you at the funeral. You must be devastated. Mr. Webb was so proud of you. He talked about you all the time."

"Thank you. I have to—"

"He was so proud that you were studying at Pilchuck Glass School on a special scholarship. He told every class about how you won the Spinnaker Art Festival on your first entry when you were only seventeen."

"How embarrassing. Every class?"

"Yes, it was always in his first lecture."

Savannah struggled to keep her voice from breaking. "It's going to be difficult to—"

"Your dad looked so strong, so healthy, and so positively vital . . . if you know what I mean."

"Yes, it was a shock."

"He was such an excellent teacher and mentor. How are you going to manage everything?"

"I'm not sure yet." Savannah's stomach fluttered. "Sorry, but I've got to go. I'll see you in class." Savannah clicked the receiver down before Amanda could continue.

You're not the only one who is confused about why he died.

Savannah finger combed her short, black hair, tugged up the waistband of her skinny jeans, and rolled up the cuffs of her classic white shirt. It was her basic teaching uniform. Calm, she focused on getting the shop ready for the day's business.

Shoving the key ring into her back pocket and picking up the waiting stack of student handouts, she walked into the classroom. Situated between the office and the retail area, the large classroom contained six sturdy worktables for students, each with a tall wooden stool. As she placed a large brown manila envelope on each of the worktables, she remembered how her dad had experimented with various table sizes, table heights, stool types, and the number of students per table.

He'd tried to rope in Hugh to help, but his long-time assistant had no empathy for a student's environment. However, the crusty Hugh could teach a mule about the beauty, art, and mystic nature of always-liquid glass. Her dad's meticulous research had resulted in the current configuration of three rows of two worktables facing a whiteboard on the front wall and an instructor worktable facing the class. He'd practically wiggled with joy after he'd found the perfect environment for his students to create great glass art.

She switched on the overhead natural lighting that illuminated the projects of former students displayed around the walls. Her heart wrenched when she noticed her dad had placed her first piece, the traditional green turtle sun catcher panel, on the narrow shelf of the whiteboard. He had been planning to use it for the first demonstration project. Tears immediately formed and she pulled a tissue from her back pocket to press them away.

In her mind's eye, she saw her nail-bitten child's fingers struggling with the pieces of green glass. She had desperately willed them to be nimble and sure as she assembled the little turtle under her dad's watchful guidance. It must have pleased him to no end to use it as an example for the class.

After switching on the task lighting lamp for each worktable, she walked to the room at the front of the shop facing the street. It served as the student display gallery and retail section. It was neat and orderly as he'd always kept it.

Off to her right, she looked at the closed door of her dad's custom workshop. They had spent many, many hours working on delicate restorations, complicated repairs, and amazing consignments from almost every church in the city.

Deliberately delaying opening up the workspace that held her oldest and strongest memories, she found the right key and unlocked the front door. *If I don't open the workshop door, I can imagine that he's still in there working on his latest project. I know it's childish, but I don't have to be a grown-up all the time.*

At twenty minutes before ten, it was a little

early to open the shop, but some students preferred to arrive early so they could lay claim to their work area. She looked out the floor-to-ceiling windows that ran the length of the storefront to see a short man with an elaborate comb-over getting out of a red BMW, then striding up to the door.

"Rats," she muttered. It was the owner of Lattimer's Glass Shop, her dad's competitor. She pushed down a rush of panic and put on her face reserved for welcoming customers. Savannah opened the door. "Hi Frank. What brings you down here to the Grand Central District? Your shop is still downtown, right?"

Frank pursed his soft lips into a thin line. "Good morning, Savannah. I see you're opening up. I thought we could talk about my offer to buy Webb's Glass Shop." He stepped closer, but she blocked him from entering.

"I'm not ready."

"What's to get ready? Why are you torturing yourself when you could accept my offer and be on your way back to Seattle?"

Not slamming the door in his face took willpower. "I'm on bereavement leave. My scholarship will still be there when I get back. Besides, I haven't worked out all the finances yet."

"You can trust me on this. It's a generous offer."

Savannah started closing the door, "Yours is not the only offer, you know."

"Oh sure, that land shark Smythe can mention a tempting figure," he said, putting a name to the corporate real estate tycoon who wanted to buy the block to build a Super Store. "But he has to work through his corporate office *and* get the other stores to sell along with you. I'm only trying to save you time and trouble. Come on, Vanna. Your dad would have signed in a heartbeat."

Savannah snapped, "That's a bald-faced lie. The two of you hadn't spoken in ten years."

"You know he was a good businessman. That doesn't necessarily mean he wouldn't approve."

"Approve? You didn't even come to the funeral. He would expect me to have thrown you out on your ear."

Frank was quiet and the silence between them grew large and heavy. He looked down. "I'm sorry. I was busy. We did have some pretty wide differences. But that's only natural between teacher and student. He really was a wonderful teacher. I never thanked him for all he taught me. Now it's too late."

Savannah looked at the floor and took a calming breath. "Look. I need to check the books. I'm not turning it down. Quite the opposite. I need to make sure everything is ready and that there are no financial surprises."

"No one was a better businessman. John would have approved."

"He sounded stressed the last few . . . Never mind. Let's meet downtown for lunch, say Wednesday at the Casita Taqueria just down the street. I promise I'll give you either an answer or a counteroffer."

"Fair enough." Frank nodded his head. "I'll see you then. Vanna, trust me. John would have approved."

She leaned out the door. "Don't call me Vanna," she yelled as an afterthought, watching him scrunch back into his sleek status symbol, screeching tires as he drove away.

She had been lying. She had no intention of selling to Frank. If all went well, she would leave for Seattle the next day and let Hugh handle everything else. *I should have told Frank,* she mused. *A little suffering would do him good.*

Closing the door gently enough not to jangle the bell at the top, Savannah slipped behind the retail counter facing the entry door and tentatively pushed the power ON button to the point-of-sale PC. She watched it nervously, her fingers crossed that it would start up. Pushing the button was all she knew how to do.

I hope Hugh is on his way. It's more than strange for him not to be here already. I better call again. We need to finalize the transition plan of ownership of Webb's. I also need him to teach this class.

Savannah picked up the phone beside the screen and ran her finger down the tattered list of contacts taped to the counter top, stopping at *Hugh Trevor.* She dialed the number and heard his answering machine message. "I'm out. You know the drill." *Beep.*

"Hugh, are you there? It's Savannah. I need your help to open the shop. I hope you're on the way. Please be on the way. Please. See you soon."

As she spoke, the doorbell jangled fiercely and a tall man dressed in black western boots, black jeans, and a French blue oxford shirt topped with a black string tie bolted through. "Don't touch it," he cautioned in a BBC-newscaster accent. "If the cash register starts up wonky, it'll be ages before it sorts itself out."

Savannah looked into his seriously green eyes and caught a faint whiff of Polo Black. He crowded her to the side and peered at the PC screen. As she was six-foot in stocking feet, not many men looked down on her.

She stretched around his back to hang up the phone. "I didn't want to start it, but I couldn't wait for Hugh any longer. Who are you?"

He peered into the monitor. "Good. Coming online and"—he looked for a certain sign from the monitor—"brilliant. It's happy." He pulled back, then turned to her. "I have the same system next door and I had a meltdown with mine this morning."

"Right, but who—"

The tinkle of the door opening interrupted Savannah's question. A plump young woman with wildly spiked pink and yellow hair entered the shop. Wearing a white peasant blouse and patchwork midi skirt, she shouldered through the door balancing a huge purse, a canvas bag of tools, a briefcase overfilled with glass remnants, and a large plywood square for mounting stained glass work.

Green-eyed man lunged to hold open the door. "Amanda, you shouldn't try to carry everything at once."

Savannah's eyebrows lifted.

Puffing like an espresso machine, Amanda said, "It's all right. Two trips would take too much energy. My aura has been weak since I heard the terrible news about Mr. Webb." She made a bee-line for the classroom.

Savannah scurried over to push the classroom door out of the way. She nudged a doorstop in place to keep it open.

Amanda grunted and plopped her bundles on the worktable in the first row. "I want to sit where I can see." She nudged her bold orange glasses back onto her nose. "Savannah! Oh my goodness. You're just as beautiful as John said." She clamped Savannah in a round tight hug, stepped back, and looked into her face. "And you have his cobalt blue eyes. I'm so happy to meet you."

"Thank you, Amanda. Welcome to class."

Savannah turned to stare pointedly at the green-eyed man.

Again, the doorbell jangled and two slender elderly women entered, wearing matching gray ruffled blouses with gray polyester pants over gray ballet flat shoes. They carried large gray tote bags. One carried hers over the left shoulder. The other twin carried hers over the right shoulder. Even their round, black glasses were identical.

Savannah gulped. *I'll never be able to tell these two apart.*

"Let's sit in the back. I don't like others to overlook my work," said one twin.

"Silly. Everyone walks around and looks at each other's projects. It's how we learn. Let's go for the front so we can hear properly," said the other twin.

The first twin put her materials on the far back

worktable. "It's my turn to pick the seats. You chose for the pottery class."

"Very well. But don't whine if you can't hear the instructions."

"It's my turn."

Savannah turned to Green Eyes and whispered, "Have they been here before?"

His eyes crinkled, and he leaned closer and whispered, "The Rosenberg twins, Rachel and Faith, are addicted to craft classes."

"So, they're good?"

"Let's just say they make everyone else feel above average. They take classes for the sheer joy of criticizing each other. And they lie. About the quality of each other's work, about who made what mistake. They lie when there's no need to lie. They're the biggest liars in the district."

The bell announced the arrival of a deeply tanned couple. He was brown-haired with brown eyes wearing khaki cargo shorts, a closely tailored navy golf shirt, and Topsiders without socks. She was blonde with sky-blue eyes wearing a perfectly tailored khaki skirt with a teal sweater set accented by a single strand of pearls. They were perfectly on trend and looked more like they should be boarding a cruise ship rather than attending an art class. They slipped into the remaining open row of worktables.

The early-forties trying to look late-twenties woman looked around as though welcoming them into her living room. She smiled at each person until she caught their eye, and when she had everyone's attention, she said, "Good morn-

ing, y'all. We're Mr. and Mrs. Young. I'm Nancy
and this is my groom, Arthur. I've called him my
groom since the day Daddy announced our en-
gagement. I'm the Director of Programs at the
Museum of Fine Arts and my groom plays third
chair cello for the Florida Orchestra. We're so
happy to be here taking this wonderful class with
y'all."

Green Eyes grinned a wide smile and turned to
Savannah. He caught himself and the smirk disappeared behind an uncomfortable cough. He
shifted his weight slightly foot to foot. "Look. I
wanted to offer my sincere condolences. I think
the loss of your father is one of life's most devas-
tating events."

"That's very kind, but who—"

"Most of us along this street were at his funeral.
I stayed behind to run the pub so most of my staff
could attend. John made such a difference in
standing up for the small businesses on this
block. We'll miss his advice and experience in negotiating with the mayor and city council."

"Thank you so much. I appreciate it."

"I've got to get back to the pub." He walked
out, then turned to lean back through the front
door. "If you need anything, I'm right next door
or you can call. My number is on the list under
Edward, Edward Morris. I own the Queen's Head
Pub. Welcome to the Grand Central District." He
quietly closed the door with a small click.

Savannah smiled and let out a sigh of relief.
She was glad he was right next door. It looked
like she might have more on her plate than she

originally expected, especially if Hugh made a habit of running late. She checked the list of contact numbers and there was Edward's number standing out clearly on the smudged list. She plugged it into her cell.

Checking her dad's roster, the five registered class members had all arrived. She frowned. Where was the sixth and even more worrying, where was Hugh? She glanced at the large plain clock on the wall. It said 10:00 sharp as did her watch.

I'm going to have to start teaching his class until he gets here. I haven't taught beginning stained glass since I left for Seattle. Yikes, that's over five years ago. I hope it's like riding a bicycle.

She softly stepped behind the instructor's workstation and cleared her throat. "Good morning. I'm Savannah, Mr. Webb's daughter." Her voice shook at the mention of her dad. Ducking her head, she covered her mouth with her fist to clear her voice and stabilize it to a lower tone. "Welcome to Beginning Stained Glass. Each class will be structured roughly the same. First, a short lecture followed by a skill demonstration. Then you'll practice on a small piece to reinforce the skill. Hugh Trevor will be your instructor. He's a master glass craftsman who—"

Amanda's hand shot up into the air. "What's the project?"

"A small sun catcher panel." Savannah picked up her little green turtle sun catcher and held it high. "It's a simple design, but looks complicated. You will learn the skills of cutting glass, applying copper foil, soldering, and bending zinc came."

"What's that zinc cane stuff? I thought we were learning to make proper leaded stained glass," said Nancy.

"Good question." Savannah turned and wrote *C A M E* on the whiteboard. "Lead is a heavy metal that can, over time, leach into your skin. The new came is a preformed miniature U-shaped channel of zinc that can be bent to follow the edges of the panel. Modern knowledge sometimes overtakes tradition."

She looked at the door once again. *Hugh better have a damn good excuse for not coming in today.*

"Now, for a quick history lesson. Honest, I do mean quick. As a material, stained glass is colored by adding metallic salts during its manufacture. In ancient time, the colored glass was crafted into windows held together by strips of lead and supported by a rigid frame. The oldest known—"

A scraping shuffle and the jangle of the doorbell turned all heads to the front of the shop.

Thank goodness. That must be Hugh.

A gangly blue-jeaned young man with a black backpack over his shoulder rushed through the display room and into the classroom. He stopped cold in front of Savannah. "Sorry, I signed up for this class," blurted the pale-faced teen. He looked down at the floor. "Mr. Webb told me I could attend this class. He promised me his apprentices don't have to pay."

Okay, here's the last student. How on earth could I forget about the apprentice? This must be Jacob. Dad was wildly enthusiastic about his talent, raving in fact.

He said Jacob reminded him of me at eighteen. But, really, where is Hugh?

Savannah pointed to the remaining vacant work space. "It's no problem. You see we have plenty of room."

"I've been working with Mr. Webb and Mr. Trevor." The young man's eyes widened to owl-sized intensity.

"You must be Jacob. Mr. Webb told me so much about you, I feel like we're already friends." She pressed her hand over her heart. It was so like her dad to take this awkward fledgling under his wing as an apprentice. "My name is Savannah Webb. I'm Mr. Webb's daughter."

He gulped and nodded vigorously, then stepped forward to solemnly shake her hand. "My name is Jacob Underwood. Pleased to meet you."

She smiled. "Dad's apprentices are always invited to classes. Go ahead and get yourself settled." Savannah guided him to the remaining worktable.

"Where's Mr. Trevor?" Jacob perched on the work stool with his feet resting on the bottom rung and placed his backpack on his lap without letting go of the straps.

She moved back to the instructor station. "Mr. Trevor is delayed and I'm filling in until he arrives. Now, where was I?"

Amanda launched her plump hand into the air like a rocket. "You were telling us about the origins of stained glass."

"Yes. As I said, they crafted the colored glass

into windows or objects held together by strips of lead and then supported by a rigid frame. The oldest known stained glass window was pieced together using ancient glass from an archaeological dig."

"What did she say?" One of the twins leaned into the other's ear, whispering loud enough for everyone to look back at them.

Faith flushed from her throat to the roots of her white hair and whispered even louder, "Turn on your hearing aid, Rachel. You've forgotten again."

"Oops," muttered Rachel, turning the tiny volume control up with her polished blood red fingernail until there was a high-pitched squeal.

Gotcha! Rachel wears nail polish. Faith doesn't.

"Now, it's too loud!" Faith frowned. "Turn it down and be quiet."

Rachel adjusted the volume and ducked her head in a sheepish grin to everyone. "I'm ready now."

Savannah started again. "First things first. Before we start learning to cut glass, make sure your work surface is clean and clear of debris. If even the smallest glass chip is under your work, it will break in the wrong place and ruin your day. The best thing is to use a very soft brush on the entire work surface before you start anything. A well-worn paintbrush works great, but Dad always used an old drafting table brush."

He gave me mine when I took my first class. It's back in Seattle. She swept her worktable clear and spread newspaper on the work surface.

"I want everyone to take out their clear windowpane glass for scoring and breaking practice." She held up a small nine-by-nine-inch square piece for everyone to see. "The green piece of glass is for your project. Just put that aside."

"Ouch!" Arthur dropped his practice pane onto the worktable in a shattering crash. "I cut myself." He squeezed his thumb until a large drop formed, stuck it in his mouth, and began to suck the blood.

"Don't, honey bunny. It'll get infected. You have to be ready for the next concert." Nancy dived a hand into her purse, hopped off her stool, pulled Arthur's thumb out of his mouth with a soft *pop*, and pressed a tissue onto the cut. She looked around and eyed Savannah. "Is there a first aid kit?"

Savannah crossed the room to the large Red Cross first aid kit attached to the wall. A quick rummage produced a square compress pad and some ointment. She handed them to Nancy who was right behind her.

"Let me see," said Amanda, leaning over Arthur's hand. "I'm a trained caregiver, you know. I work in a nursing home."

Ah, she must liven up that atmosphere considerably. Savannah edged in between the women to get to Arthur. "I've got this, ladies. I can't even begin to tell you how many cuts I've dressed here and in Seattle. I've a finely tuned judgment for stitch count." She gently removed the sodden tissue, refolded it to expose a clean section, and then pressed it firmly onto the cut. "Good, it's small. No stitches."

Nancy fanned her face, "Thank our lucky stars, Arthur. You know that second chair cello player is unreliable." She mimed that he was a drinker. "You must be prepared to step into first chair at any performance."

Amanda peered over Savannah's shoulder. "It is quite small, but glass cuts are the evil older brother of paper cuts—so much blood for such a tiny nick."

"Miss Savannah, Miss Savannah." Jacob hugged his arms around his chest and rocked his weight from side to side. "I need to get my tools."

"Of course." She softened her voice and tilted her head. "Where are they?"

"Mr. Webb let me keep 'em in the workshop."

"No problem." Savannah pulled the key ring from her back pocket and handed them over to Jacob. "Go fetch them, please. It's the blue key." She turned back to deal with the Arthur situation.

"No need, Miss Savannah," he returned the key ring. "I have a set of my own."

Nancy wedged her body between Arthur and Savannah. "Excuse me. I can take care of my Arthur, thank you. Just hand over everything I need."

Amanda flushed a bright hot pink and returned to her seat, struggling to control her trembling lip.

Savannah used her teacher voice. "I'm sorry, ma'am. I'm the only one present who is authorized to give first aid in this shop. If you want to treat him yourself, that's fine, but you'll have to leave the class." She looked from Nancy to Arthur's bleeding finger then back to Nancy. "Both of you."

The woman pressed her lips into a thin scarlet line. "Very well. Of course, I didn't understand that. We have similar rules at the Museum of Fine Arts."

The class watched silently as Savannah removed the tissue, applied an ointment, and taped the sturdy bandage to Arthur's wound.

As one, the class looked up at Savannah.

"Okay, first blood goes to Arthur. Well done. Amanda is right. Glass cuts bleed like fury, but by their nature, the cuts are clean and normally heal quickly."

"Miss Savannah," shrieked Jacob, his voice breaking. "Miss Savannah, please come quick!"

Savannah nearly jumped out of her skin, then bolted through the door of the classroom, ran through the gallery and into her dad's workshop. Amanda was on her heels.

Jacob was pointing to the far wall of the custom workshop behind a long workbench. "Mr. Trevor won't wake up."

Savannah saw Hugh lying on his side with his face toward the wall. "Uncle Hugh, Uncle Hugh!" She could hear her voice shriek as she struggled to roll him over onto his back. His kind face was ash gray and he had been sick on his clothes. The sour smell was sharp and fresh. His chest was still and he wasn't breathing.

"Amanda, call 911!"

She was aware of Amanda's sharp gasp and heard her feet pound steps toward the phone. Sa-

vannah straightened him as much as possible in
the tight space. Making a fist with one hand and
the other hand wrapped around it, she started
chest compressions to the rhythm of "Staying
Alive" as her CPR coach had taught her. She didn't
know that she was crying until the tears dropped
one by one onto her forearms.

No way was she stopping. Uncle Hugh was all
the home she had left. He needed to stay alive.

She dimly heard the ambulance arrive and
numbly got to her feet when the paramedic gently lifted her up from the floor by her elbow.

Uncle Hugh can't be dead, too.

Chapter 2

Savannah and Jacob stood on the sidewalk in front of the shop and watched the last police department vehicle turn toward the station and drive back downtown. No sirens. No flashing lights. Only silence.

The business card that Officer Boulli had given her cut into her palm as she squeezed it into a crescent shape, released it, and squeezed it again. The last words he said were echoing inside her head. "Just give me a call if anything else comes up, Miss Webb. Thank you for your time." She looked at the card once more and slipped it into her front pocket.

She'd thought the nightmare was over with her dad's funeral. Now Hugh was dead. Her plans to sell him Webb's Glass Shop were dead, as well. She ached from the top of her shoulders down to her elbows. The gentle warmth of the spring sun began to seep its way through her shirt as a reminder that time passes.

Jacob peered down at his shoes. "Mr. Trevor was a great old guy."

Savannah looked at Jacob. His neck was flushed and he stood statue still as if trying not to breathe.

"Did you help Hugh and Dad with their latest project? The one that's in the custom workshop?"

Jacob nodded yes with his eyes still focused on his shoes.

"It's strange that I don't remember anything about that project. Lately, Dad was constantly chattering about his students and the classes. I guess I was so caught up in telling him about the struggles I was having with my own pieces, I didn't notice that he'd stopped talking about his projects." She smiled down at Jacob. "He did tell me he was training a gifted apprentice."

She felt like a horrible daughter. Her last visit had been over two years ago, but even when she did visit, it had been too short to manage anything but spending time with her dad at the glass shop.

I should have gotten him out more.

"Do you know what they were working on in the custom workshop?"

"I was painting some of the glass pieces, but I don't know anything else," Jacob paused then mumbled into his chest. "They said I was good at it. I don't want to stop."

"You're not in trouble, Jacob. I just realized that I don't really know what was going on."

And now it's only me.

"I've never seen a body before. Mr. Trevor was a good teacher. I am going to m-miss him." He gulped a short breath. "Can I go home for lunch now? I'll come back, like normal. Okay?"

Sensing that he was desperate to continue his normal routine at the glass shop, Savannah softened her voice. "Of course. I could use your help."

He turned, walked down the street and around the corner without looking up.

"How are you holding up, luv?" Edward appeared at her elbow and handed her a white chunky ceramic mug.

"I'm not thinking straight at all. I must be in shock."

"Not at all surprising."

"Thanks for taking the class into your pub. I didn't know what to do. Hugh has—I mean *was*—always a grumpy gus with Dad and me, but he was passionate about teaching stained glass. He was also a restoration genius. They have been—I mean *were*—partners in all things glass for over twenty years. I can't believe they're both gone." She sipped the warm drink. "What is this?"

"England's solution to all upsets. A hot cup of strong sweet tea."

Savannah sipped again. "And what else?"

Edward lifted his eyebrows. "Great lashings of Irish single malt."

"My dad told me how excited he was about your pub. He felt it was the perfect addition to the district." She looked down into the cup. "That is, when I stopped talking about myself long enough for him to get a few words in edgewise."

"Queen's Head is happy to help its neighbors. When we were just opening, everyone was grand and supported us in the best way possible—by spending their cash with us." Edward cleared his throat. "Are you going to close up for today?"

She looked deep into the cup. "I'm going to hang around for a bit. Sort through some papers. Calm down, I hope."

"You sure know how to make things interesting."

"I would say this is a good deal more than interesting." Savannah ran a jerky hand through her hair. "Dad raised me to be suspicious. Before he started the glass shop, he worked for the government. Two heart attacks within a week in one tiny glass shop? Hugh was dad's most experienced journeyman. They've been working difficult pieces together for years. This doesn't make sense."

"Are you saying you suspect foul play?" When she didn't answer, Edward said, "That's quite a leap in logic. You might be overreacting or just plain exhausted." He looked straight into her eyes. "You need to get some rest." He lightly touched her arm. "Really, luv."

She gently moved her arm away, pleased and confused by his touch. She had just broken up with her long-time boyfriend and studio partner, Ken. She would have to deal with him in a new professional way when she returned to Seattle and didn't need kind touches from a British stranger to further tangle her already stressed emotions. She was still reeling from the effects of the final breakup with Ken.

"You're probably right. I've cancelled the afternoon session. Good thing, too. I'm teaching now, and I need to brush up. I'm so unprepared."

"When's the next class?"

"Tomorrow morning. I don't understand why Dad scheduled so many classes. I haven't gone through his books yet, but I don't think he needed the money."

"He was a victim of the same program I fell for. Some of us in this neighborhood signed up for one of those online group coupons. It seemed like a very good deal." Edward pulled a slim bunch of keys from his back pocket.

Why didn't Dad tell me about this? "How does it work?"

"For the pub, we offered forty dollars' worth of food for a thirty-dollar coupon. We make most of our margin on drinks, so we benefit from the new customers. I've started running an offer every month. Unfortunately, your dad didn't put a limit on the discounted classes, and the response surprised him."

"I glanced at the calendar in the office. He's got classes booked for the next six months solid. I don't know what I'm going to do about that. It's insane."

"Yes"—Edward frowned—"but he was looking for help. Didn't he tell you about the interviews?"

"No, but that explains a few things. Once people signed up, he would feel obligated to see that each student had a seat in one of his classes. It wouldn't help that he firmly believed that six students was his maximum class size."

Edward looked down. "Yes, he was a man of his word. Old school."

"Maybe the paperwork for the coupon will help me decide what to do. I need to go through his desk anyway. I've been dreading it. It's such a personal invasion. I don't know how I'll manage his bedroom."

"I can't imagine. The additional classes are one of the reasons he took on Jacob. You must be aware of his Asperger's syndrome. It seems the quiet routines are helping him. His parents are delighted with his keen interest and new level of focus."

"I didn't know about the Asperger's. I wonder why Dad didn't tell me." She scrunched her brow. "That explains a few more things."

"I can't imagine denying Jacob's mother anything. Frances is a Juvenile Court Judge so she is used to wielding significant power." He fiddled with the keys. "I need to get a few emergency groceries for Chef before the evening shift starts. I'm going to shove off, luv. Take it easy."

"Thanks. You've been so helpful." Savannah watched him climb onto an antique Indian motorbike. It was old, finished in the original cream and white, along with hand-painted pinstripes.

"I'll stop by later and make sure you're on the right foot with the point-of-sale monster." He smiled.

"Thank you." She smiled genuinely for the first time in many days.

She was pleased he pulled on a helmet. She didn't need anyone else getting hurt today.

He waved a salute and drove away.

Savannah watched until he disappeared. She tipped the cup and drained the last drop of the spiked tea. *Rats, I didn't give him back the cup. No matter, I'll return it when he comes back.* Steeling her nerve for the sad ordeal of going through her dad's papers, she forced her heavy feet back to the office and stood in front of the rolltop desk. *Maybe a session of ordinary paperwork will carry me out of this anxious funk.* The ancient office chair squeaked a routine protest as she sat down and stared at the jumble of overstuffed cubbyholes, shelves, and drawers.

She started with the left side and the first thing on top was a business-sized envelope from Lattimer's Glass Shop containing Frank's offer for Webb's. Her mouth fell open at the number mentioned in the document. *This is a pretty big number.* She searched through the same pile and found a considerably lower offer from the main office of Smythe's corporation. She sat back in the chair for a second before sorting and filing the whole stack. She slipped the two offers into her backpack.

On top of the right hand stack by her elbow, she picked up a green short-order check pad in the greasy spoon restaurant style of the fifties. In her dad's nearly illegible spiky hand, the last entry was listed.

> Item: Last Supper Panel 8—Splendor
> First United Christian Church
> Contact: Reverend David Kline

She scratched her temple. *Funny, there was no sign of repairs at the funeral service yesterday. All the stained glass windows were fine. Beautiful as ever.*

She dialed the number listed on the pad and a cool voice answered immediately. "Reverend Kline, United Christian."

Irritated with herself for not planning what she was going to say before calling, Savannah cleared her throat. "Um . . . good morning, Reverend. This is Savannah calling from Webb's Glass Shop. One of your stained glass panels is here under repair, and I need some information about the work."

"Savannah? I'm surprised to hear from you. I thought you were going to sell the shop and return to Seattle later this week."

"Yes, Reverend, that was the plan, but there's been a horrible, horrible complication. Hugh Trevor was found dead in the workshop."

"Bless you, Savannah. That is horrible. How are you?"

"I'm all right for the moment, but now I need to teach the ongoing classes that Hugh was going to handle. Then I'll need to find another glass artist to help me finish the projects my father and

Hugh were completing. I thought I could get everything done this week so I could get back, but now I don't know how to get it all wrapped up."

"Oh, of course you would need to bring things to a sensible closing. It's so distressing when a small business just closes the doors without giving any indication to their clients. As your father's daughter, I am not surprised that you want to close it in an orderly manner."

"Thanks. I'm so glad you understand. I'm evaluating the offers, but in the meantime, I'm trying to clear up the works in progress. Your name is listed in his order book. It says Last Supper Panel Eight, then there's a dash followed by the word *Splendor*."

"No, no. That's a mistake."

Savannah picked up the pad. "Oh, maybe I have an old order pad." She squinted closer at the date. "The order was placed two months ago."

"I'm sorry. We do have an open account with Webb's since we have so many windows, but I don't recall any recent repair orders."

"There must be a mistake, because it's—"

"No." His chuckle turned into a smothered cough. "No, Savannah. How silly of me to mislead you. It's not a repair. It's part of the duplication project for our most vulnerable panels. There was a fierce competition from Frank Lattimer for the contract, but Mr. Webb won over the committee as he is an excellent craftsman."

"I thought it was a repair."

"Your dad repaired and maintained our panels for many years. In fact, he was training his apprentice to take over some of the maintenance. The mistake is that he is duplicating panel three, not panel eight. Panel eight won't be duplicated for several years down the road. I'm sorry about what has happened. I would like to encourage you to participate in bereavement counseling. Just call for an appointment. I hate to rush, but I must go now. "

"But—" Savannah heard a soft click followed by the dial tone.

Well that explains why Frank wanted to finalize the purchase so quickly. He wanted the duplication job. His wish may well be granted. She looked at the order pad again turning it around to look at it from several angles. The panel number could be either a sketchy eight or a sloppy three.

She pulled at her hair with both hands. What was going on? *There's no way both Hugh and Dad could accidentally die within a week of each other. No way.*

She went into her dad's custom workshop and automatically stared at the section of floor where Hugh had been. There was still a sour smell. It hit the back of her throat with a stomach-churning threat.

She walked back to the office and opened the storage cupboard. She grabbed a spray bottle of cleaner and a torn strip of T-shirt to use as a rag.

Back in the custom workshop, she sprayed and scoured the area with enough vigor to make the room smell like a pine forest. She got back to her feet satisfied with her efforts and tossed the rag in the trash.

She stowed the cleaner back in the storage cupboard in the office and returned to the custom workshop, staring at the large double-sized worktable. She lifted the corner of the sheet of white cotton that completely covered the large panel.

She hesitated. *Why didn't he tell me about this?*

She pulled the sheet completely away from the project. It was the central panel of *The Last Supper*. It was nearly complete, but Jesus had no face.

Chapter 3

Monday Afternoon

Leaning over the large stained glass panel, Savannah reached up and switched on the overhead work lamp. Its beam focused on Christ's missing face.

After folding the sheet into a tidy square to store under the table, she found several smaller areas in the panel that were missing, as well. From the look of it, the pieces were areas of the panel that were hand painted, then fired repeatedly in a kiln to achieve a three-dimensional illustration effect.

What was Hugh working on in here?

She leaned down to peer at the craftsmanship and admired the clean lines of the design, the perfect color choices. She ran her finger down the soldered joins that held the glass pieces together. Their velvety smoothness was the hallmark of a true craftsman. It was a stunning work of art. "There must be more written down somewhere. Dad was meticulous about documenting the progress of an important work."

Savannah went back to the desk and repeated her search through each drawer and storage space, sorting, filing, and straightening as she went. Nothing.

Where could the paperwork be? Why isn't it here with his other project notebooks? Is this another secret? She pushed back the chair and studied the desk. If he were going to hide something, where would it be?

She pulled out one of the two small drawers nestled in the cubbyhole section and emptied its contents onto the desk. The underside of the drawer was clean and there was no sign of a compartment inside the cavity. She tidied the contents as she was putting them back, then dumped the contents of the second drawer onto the desk.

A small brown envelope had been taped to the underside of the second drawer. There was something small inside. She removed the tape and turned the envelope over. A cold chill zipped down her spine. Her dad's spiky writing scrawled across the front.

Savannah, if you find this, I've been murdered and you are in danger.

She dropped the envelope like a hot potato and stood up. *He's been murdered!* Her hands were shaking, but she clasped them together and tried to think clearly. *I should call the police—that officer that came today.*

In her front pocket, Savannah found the card that the police officer had given her that morning. The name on the card jumped out. "He said to call." She dialed the number, listened to the directions, and punched in the extension number.

"Officer Boulli."

"Hello, my name is Savannah Webb. I met you this morning at the glass shop in the Grand Central District. We had a man who had died in our workshop. You said I could call you if I had any questions."

"Yeah, I remember the EMTs were saying that he died of a heart attack, right?"

"Yes, but I've found something in my dad's office that might change that."

"Found what?"

"I found an envelope from my dad. The writing on the outside said he had been murdered and that I was in danger." Savannah knew she was making a terrible impression, but she couldn't calm her nervous voice into behaving like a rational adult.

"An envelope?"

"Well, so far. I haven't opened it just in case you wanted it as evidence. I'm reporting this to make sure that you know that Hugh's death might not be a heart attack. My dad's death might not be a heart attack, either." Hearing the shrill shake in her voice, she swallowed and took a short breath. "My dad used to work for the government and I think he found some information that got him killed."

"Wow, little lady. That's a huge leap. So, you think that because your dad left you a note, we should open a murder investigation?"

Savannah reacted as if freezing water had been thrown in her face. *Little lady?* "My father was a senior cryptographer specializing in cold war ciphers and surveillance. There must be some basis behind his suspicions. I don't know why else he would have tried to warn me." She stood up and began to pace as far as the phone cord would permit.

"I think you've got your Nancy Drew imagination working overtime. I don't think you've got any reason to feel threatened." The officer sounded bored and annoyed.

She formed a fist and waved it at the phone. "Is there anyone else I can talk to?"

"Whoa. No need to get snippy. I'll report this up the chain and see what happens . . . but I seriously think you need to dial back your imagination and just accept that old guys die of heart attacks."

"I'm not imagining this. There's an actual envelope in my hands! Doesn't that warrant an investigation?"

"We'll get back to you if we have any questions." A solid *click* was followed by the dial tone.

Savannah replaced the phone handset. *Dad, I tried. I really tried.*

After plopping back into the chair, frustrated with her trembling fingers, she picked up the small brown envelope, turned it over, and pried open

the brass clasp on the back. She drew out a thin
tan Moleskine notebook. The cover was neatly labeled THE LAST SUPPER—SPLENDOR.

Savannah had been holding her breath. Exhal-
ing in a short huff, she drew in a calming breath
then opened the notebook.

GURAR KGVFP NPURQ VABHE SVEFG

She felt a familiar fury. He was playing yet another code game. *Why can't he play it straight and
just tell me what I need to know? What is wrong with
that?* She clapped her hand to cover her open
mouth.

*This is his last game. Maybe he was working on it for
my next visit? He loved giving me these puzzles so that
we could work them out together. It was the highlight of
my visits. Have I falsely called the police based on one of
his games?*

Savannah cleared a space on the desk by taking
the piles of paper and making neat stacks off to
the side. *Ugh!* She frowned as she shuffled and
sorted. *At least I don't see late notices in the piles.* She
pulled out a lined tablet and grabbed a pencil.

At the jangle of the front door, she dropped
the pencil and held her head in both hands. *Now
what?*

A low professional voice called from the front.
"Miss Webb? Hello. Are you here, Miss Savannah
Webb?"

She took a deep breath and tried to pull herself together. A quick glance in the mirror over

the sink confirmed that she looked reasonably neat and not at all frantic. She walked to the front of the shop to find Jacob standing outside in front of the door with a smartly suited woman at his side holding the door open.

"Hello, Savannah. I'm Frances Underwood. I thought it was time for us to meet. Especially after Jacob's alarming experience this morning." She held out her hand.

Savannah was surprised at the firmness of the grip. "Oh, you're the judge. Hi. It's nice to finally meet you, as well. I've heard a lot about Jacob from my dad. He believed that working in glass would be helpful for his . . ." She looked over to Jacob.

"His Asperger's? We don't mince words around his condition. Jacob is an expert about his syndrome and is comfortable hearing it discussed. John explained what positive effects a creative art might have on Jacob's behavior, and I've noticed an increase in his self-calming abilities. I will do anything you need to make sure that he can continue studying here." She looked up at her son and a tiny smile wavered on her perfectly glossed lips.

Savannah followed her glance to Jacob.

He held his head down, looking at a small beagle on a bright red leash wearing a blue service animal pack with a pocket on the side. He shifted his feet from side to side. "This is Suzy. She's my service animal." He looked over to his mom. "I think the service she is providing is peace of mind for Mom. I have a severe form of asthma and Suzy has my asthma inhaler in her pack, so she'll stay with me all the time."

Savannah bent down. "Got it, Jacob. Suzy is absolutely adorable." She presented the back of her hand to Suzy for sniffing and scratched the little dog behind the ears. "Mrs. Underwood, I'm not sure this is a good idea. We're not set up for a service dog."

"Please call me Frances. We were lucky that Suzy was available earlier than we planned. Jacob is nervous because I've insisted that she must be with him at all times and that if you aren't able to accommodate her, he will not be able to return to his glass studies."

Jacob continued to focus his gaze on Suzy. "You said I could return to be apprentice, but I can't work by myself." He patted Suzy, then lifted his eyes to look at one of Savannah's earrings. "I am just starting and there is more to learn."

Resisting the impulse to hug him, Savannah replied, "I'm not going to work on the Last Supper panel for a while, but more important, we have to find somewhere for Suzy to stay. She can't walk on the floor because there might be glass shards. Pick her up and follow me."

Jacob took Suzy into his arms and his fidgeting stopped immediately. He calmly stepped into the display room and waited patiently for his mother to enter and for Savannah to close the front door.

Savannah raised her eyebrows in appreciation of Suzy's immediate calming influence. "I will make this work. I'll do whatever it takes."

"That's just what I was expecting to hear from John's daughter." Frances glanced at her understated Rolex and pulled a set of keys from her bag, "Thank you, but I can't come in. I'm due in juvenile court for a hearing in just under half an hour." She shook Savannah's hand once more. "Thanks for helping Jacob through this." She blew a kiss to Jacob. "I'll see you at dinner."

Shaking her head slowly, Savannah led Jacob and Suzy back to the office and pulled some old T-shirt rags out of a basket. "Let's put these down here by the back door. Will she stay here?"

Jacob gently placed Suzy on the pile and extended a hand, palm out. "Suzy, stay."

Suzy circled twice, then lay down in a sphinx pose looking at Jacob with her head tilted and eyes alert.

He looked to Savannah. "Is that good?"

"That's perfect. Every time you come to the shop, this will be Suzy's place."

He nodded solemnly, then glanced sideways at the desk, noticing the open notebook with the scrawled scrambled letters. "The offset is thirteen."

"What did you say?"

He pointed to the nonsense letters. "That's a Caesar cipher. To solve the code, you write out the cipher alphabet as a plain alphabet rotated by thirteen positions."

"How do you know that?"

Jacob looked over at Suzy. "Mr. Webb liked to work puzzles and he showed them to me. He said because I notice things, I was a cipher wizard."

Rubbing the furrows that had exploded between her eyes, she grabbed the pencil and sat at the desk. "That makes perfect sense. My lucky number is thirteen."

Pointing to the brown envelope laying next to the notebook, Jacob frowned. "That's from Mr. Webb."

"Yes, it is."

"Why would he say that he was murdered? He never lied. This is bad for you. Very bad." He started breathing rapidly and looked over to Suzy.

Savannah nearly told him not to worry, but felt that would be wrong for him. Only the exact and precise truth would mean anything to him. Otherwise, he would never trust her. "It's definitely a message from Mr. Webb."

"It's a warning."

"Jacob, I don't know what he meant by leaving this cypher. I think if I solve this it will tell me what Mr. Webb wants me to know. It may be nothing but a game. Remember, he liked to play code games."

Jacob looked at Suzy again and his breathing returned to normal. "Can I help?"

Savannah grinned. "You know, I think that was the plan."

Below the coded message, she wrote out the alphabet in one continuous line. Then she wrote an *N* under the *A*, an *O* under the *B*, a *P* under the *C* and continued until each letter had a letter beneath it. "This is good, Jacob. Each letter is accounted for."

Jacob looked at Suzy and started shifting his weight from foot to foot.

Savannah put a new letter under each one in the message as she referred to the key. She propped her chin in her palm and studied the result.

THENE XTISB ACHED INOUR FIRST

Jacob piped up. "The spaces are not in the right places."

"Okay. Let's have them make sense." Savannah regrouped them to reveal her dad's intended message.

THE NEXT IS BACHED IN OUR FIRST

"This makes no sense at all."

"You made a mistake. The code letter *P* means *C*." Jacob took the pencil from her hand and changed her decoded letter *B* in *BACHED* to a *C*. "Now, it is correct."

THE NEXT IS CACHED IN OUR FIRST

"The next? Oh, he must mean the next clue. So, this is going to be a Dan Brown's *The Da Vinci Code* adventure?" She read it aloud. "The next is cached in our first."

Jacob walked over to Suzy. "Can I hold her? I won't let her feet touch the floor."

"Yes, of course." Savannah's head was still bent over the translation.

He picked up Suzy. She licked his chin and his manner magically transformed from nervous little fidgets to standing perfectly calm and composed. "First what?"

She stared at the cipher. "First cache."

"What's a cache?"

"It's a hidden storage space where you squirrel away things like food or supplies or even weapons for outdoor sports."

Holding Suzy securely, he asked, "What outdoor sport?"

"Oh my goodness, I remember, now. We played a kind of search game with latitude and longitude readings. There's an organization for that. What was it called?"

Jacob hugged Suzy up in his arms to kiss the top of her head.

Savannah rapped her forehead with a knuckle, forcing her brain to find the word she wanted. "Okay, I remember. It's called geocaching."

"Geo what?"

"Geocaching. It's like a grown-up treasure hunting game with some high-level navigation thrown in. Look here," she turned to the office computer on the table next to the desk and typed www.geocaching.com into the search icon and clicked on the website. The main screen played a video of people of all ages finding weatherproof boxes, film canisters, and disguised containers hidden in trees, under benches, and among flower beds.

"Mr. Webb was interested in that?"

"I remember that Dad joined the organization

and used a global database to keep track of our finds. He created a few by himself. This clue leads to our first geocache back when I was only ten. I think that's where he wants me to search."

She stood and placed her hands in the small of her back and stretched. She already missed the strenuous activity required of a glass blower. One of those boot camp workouts would feel very good. Sitting with paperwork and standing around teaching—not good if she wanted to keep herself fit.

"I'm not exactly sure what it means right now, Jacob, but I'll think about it."

Now what?

She thought back to how excited her dad had been when he'd discovered the game of geocaching. It seemed a perfect way to introduce his motherless daughter to an outdoor activity that also exercised her brain. That first cache was created to keep her grounded and active in the aftermath of her mother's long fight with cancer.

She felt a smile tickle her face and enjoyed the bittersweet memory of her dad's excitement when she found his first geocache. "That's where he means for me to go. The next clue is at Crescent Lake."

Chapter 4

Savannah's cell phone rang to the tune of ABBA's "Super Trooper." It was the ring tone for her roommate.

"Ivy! Oh, thanks for calling."

"What's going on? I just got back from New Orleans and found your message on the machine. I'm so sorry I was out of town when I heard about your dad. What a horrible thing and I wasn't around. I'm sorry. How are you holding up?"

"Hang on just a second." Savannah sheltered the phone against her heart and looked over to Jacob still holding Suzy. "Excuse me, Jacob. I need to take this call. If you need me, I'll be in the classroom."

He nodded.

Walking slowly out of the office, she replied, "It's so good to hear from you."

"I'm so sorry I couldn't come to the funeral. That stained glass conference was a breath of fresh air. Well, except for one dolt. Anyway, I'm completely inspired to try some new techniques. Luckily, the financial grant I just snagged covered the entire expense. Anyone who tells you that New Orleans has a recovered infrastructure hasn't actually tried to use that infrastructure. It was miserable. Even worse, my cell phone went belly up after the second day so I had no coverage for the whole week."

"I miss you. It's good to hear your cheery voice."

"Bull. You miss our apartment and your glass studio. *Hovel* would be a better description, but it is ridiculously quiet around here without you and your Ken drama."

Savannah's stomach sunk into a black pit at the thought of her ex-boyfriend. "I am *not* a drama queen. You know that."

"I know. I just couldn't resist riling you. Sorry. I shouldn't have done that. You already know I have no sense of social awareness. Anyway, I am truly sorry about your dad and the funeral and all that stuff. Really."

Savannah choked up. "Yes, I know."

"What?"

"Yes, you're right as usual. I miss Seattle." Savannah wandered around the classroom and perched on one of the student stools.

"So how is selling the business coming along?"

Savannah sighed deeply. "Things have gotten complicated."

"What? How?"

"Dad's long-time associate, Hugh Trevor, was found dead in the custom workshop this morning."

"Oh no. Savannah, that's horrible. That's unspeakable. What can I do? Do you need me to come out there and—"

"Hold on." Savannah took a long breath. "I'm okay for now. It's a shock and I'm not sure if I'm thinking straight."

"You? You're the straightest-thinking person I know."

"Apparently not when I lose my dad and Hugh in the space of a week."

"Oh, right. Didn't you leave a message that Hugh was going to stay on? At least during the ownership transition?"

"Yep. He wanted to keep on teaching so I was going to symbolically hand over Dad's keys to him tonight after class. I really thought I would be on my way back sometime tomorrow."

"That's crap in a handbag."

Savannah shook her head and rolled her eyes. *Only Ivy can get away with using phrases like that.*

"I've got a lot more to figure out now. How to sell the shop. How to teach this week's workshop. How to . . ."—*figure out if my dad was murdered*—"Never mind. As you say, crap in a handbag. The list is getting longer."

"Well, if anyone can juggle all that without getting a hair out of place, it's you. Hey, Ken was asking me today if I knew when you were coming back. Are you two in the falling-out or falling-in phase at the moment? It does get confusing."

"We are most definitely in the falling-out phase and well planted into the never-getting-back-together-*ever* phase. Trust me. It's over. We will have to act like real grown-ups and cooperate professionally since our exhibit opens in two weeks."

"Just because a guy looks good doesn't mean he *is* good. Anyway, call him. He'll want to know why you won't be back this week to set up the show and I can't lie. You know that. I'll spill the beans in a New York minute."

"Sorry, sorry. He shouldn't be bugging you. I'll send him an e-mail right away. Thanks for calling, Ivy."

"Now, I really mean it. If you need me to come down to sweaty old St. Petersburg, I'll do it. But just because it's you."

"You're the best. Bye. See you soon, I hope."

Savannah slowly walked back to the office door thinking about how drastically things had changed for her in just a matter of days. *No Dad. No Ken. No Hugh.* At least the familiar workings of the glass shop grounded her.

Jacob was sitting in front of the computer with Suzy in his lap searching the geocaching site. She calmly looked to him with the apparent intention to wait forever, for whatever was next.

She spoke softly. "Can you show me what you were working on with Dad and Hugh? Until things are settled with the shop, I think we should continue with your apprenticeship. At least for now."

Jacob nodded, stood, and snuggled Suzy up to his cheek, then placed her carefully back on the pile of old shirts. "Stay," he said.

Suzy circled the rags twice, then plopped back down into her sphinx pose. Her big brown eyes followed Jacob like a laser guided missile.

He turned and led the way into the custom workshop. He walked to the front wall to stand at a worktable that had a stool tucked underneath. On the wall above the table, a mounted spice rack held small containers similar in shape to those little white glue bottles found in most elementary schools. They were placed upside down and instead of written labels, each bottle had a small glass square taped to the front, representing the fired color of the liquid.

At the right side of his working table, Jacob had placed a small clear plastic cup of water along with a tiny spray bottle full of water, and a rag that was used to dry any of the four brushes that stood bristles up in a coffee cup. The brushes varied in size from an inch to a super fine brush of only a few hairs.

Because they weren't white, but a soft gray-brown, Savannah presumed that they weren't synthetic, but might be squirrel or mink. No expense had been spared.

Laying beside the brushes was a twelve-inch-by-twelve-inch square of glass that had been edged with duct tape and on it was a palette knife. In the center of the workspace, lay a clear piece of cathedral glass placed over a full color copy of the hand of Jesus. A single base coat of flesh-colored paint had been painted on the glass.

"Jacob, as part of your training, have you been duplicating the hand-painted panels for *The Last Supper*?"

"Yes, Miss Savannah. Mr. Webb helped set this up for me. He wants me to copy all the painted images for the panels."

Savannah raised her eyebrows. "Have you finished any pieces, yet?"

"Yes, Miss Savannah."

"Where are they?"

"Mr. Webb put them in the kiln over there." Jacob pointed to the corner at a large white kiln placed on a layer of bricks. With the lid closed, it looked like a square claw-foot bathtub. A large chrome handle was fastened to one side of the kiln and the adjacent side had a red LED display that was flashing FINISHED.

Savannah struggled to lift the heavy lid. In the bottom, a thin coat of fine powder obscured the details of a painted oval piece. That was the normal result of the firing process. Each piece rested on a specially coated shelf paper that protected the bricks as well as the fired glass in the bottom of the kiln.

She gently slipped her fingers underneath and carried it over to the industrial sink in the other corner of the workshop. She turned on the tap, adjusted the water to a warm flow, and slipped the piece of glass beneath the gentle stream. After softly rubbing it with her fingers, the colors began to show through the dusty film and a perfect image of the face of Jesus looked at her with kind eyes.

"Jacob," she called. "Come over here and look at this, please."

He looked over Savannah's shoulder into the sink. "It has to match the original picture. That's what Mr. Webb told me. It has to match the original picture."

Savannah grabbed a T-shirt rag, dried the painted face, and took the piece over to the worktable. Jacob followed on quiet feet and even quieter breath.

"This isn't the first time you've painted glass, is it?"

He shook his head. "No, Miss Savannah. I started glass painting a few months ago. I've been painting at the art center for a long time, but it got too noisy. I like it here much better."

At the far end of the worktable, taking up the full width, was a full-sized color collage of the painted pieces. She compared the fired piece with the image of the face of Jesus. "They match perfectly. If anything, your painted image has better eyes. It's subtle, but they are definitely more expressive."

Jacob stood by her side looking at the two pieces. "That's what Mr. Webb said. It has to match the picture."

Savannah blinked and shook her head. *He doesn't realize his talent.* She understood why the duplication contract had been awarded to her dad. The glass painting technique alone was reason enough, let alone the combined skill of Hugh and her dad.

How will Jacob handle it when the shop is sold?

"Jacob, who worked on the glass pieces of the panel?"

"Mr. Hugh worked on cutting and shaping the glass pieces. Mr. Webb was supposed to start working on the structure stuff."

Savannah sat on the tall work stool by the panel and let the enormity of the glass contract sink into her skull. She had been reasonably good with stained glass when she was growing up, but she had been working as a glass blower for the last few years and they were completely different skills. Stained glass is cutting and shaping cold glass into rigid designs. Glass blowing involves inflating molten glass into a bubble with the aid of a blow tube, then working the glass with a torch to form glassware.

Am I still good enough? She wondered to herself.

"Well, Jacob"—she got up, found a worn work apron, put it over her head, and tied the strings around her back—"now is the time to find out if I can still cut glass."

He looked at the door and back at Savannah. "May I check on Suzy, please?"

"Of course. Make sure that you are free of any glass bits before you pick her up. Understand?"

"Yes, Miss Savannah." Jacob vigorously scrubbed his brush along his arms, chest, and legs, making a little humming noise as he worked. He practically skipped from the room.

She turned back to the duplicate panel, thinking *little Suzy is a gift.*

The panel was nearly complete. Under the worktable on the shelving underneath lay more than enough cathedral glass to finish the project. Even if more than one attempt was needed for each of the remaining pieces, at least she wouldn't have to worry about color matching the expensive glass with another order from the manufacturer.

Savannah selected a piece that consisted of about eight square inches and only one curve. She tore a piece of butcher paper from the vertical cutter on the far wall and put it in the center of the worktable that Hugh had used.

Not yet ready to stand in her dad's place, she traced a template of the piece onto a small piece of butcher paper. She cut the paper with an X-ACTO knife and pasted it to the glass with a glue stick. Next, she protected the edges of the paper with wax. She moved over to the cutting section of the workbench and made the straight cuts with no problem. Picking up her dad's cutter, she placed it precisely on the curve and began to score.

"Miss Savannah?" Jacob appeared at her elbow.

Savannah flinched and the cutter threatened to veer off the line, but she pressed her lips tight and continued to guide the cutter off to the edge of the glass. *Well, that proves I need practice.* She turned to Jacob and smiled.

"Did Hugh tell you about when you should talk and when you should wait?"

"Yes, Miss Savannah, but—"

"It's important to wait until I'm finished cutting a piece of glass. I haven't looked at the invoice, but I think this is German glass and it's quite expensive. I could have ruined the whole piece." She stopped as Jacob began to breathe loudly and faster.

He looked down at his shoes. "I'm sorry, Miss Savannah." He gulped in a new breath and blurted, "There's a man outside."

"What? We're closed. I know I turned the sign around to CLOSED." She went out of the workroom and stopped just at the front of the display room.

A man was pointing a small black device up to the roofline of the shop. He was quite short in a sharkskin gray suit with a black shirt and cartoon tie featuring Felix the Cat. It was not a local look. His hair was so thin that he must have faced a daily decision whether to comb it over or shave it clean.

Savannah opened the door and stepped out onto the sidewalk in front of the shop. "May I help you?"

He smiled with brilliant white teeth that nearly glinted in the bright afternoon sun. "Good afternoon." He reached into the inside pocket of his jacket and handed her a business card. "Are you Miss Webb?"

She took the card without looking at it. "Yes, I'm Savannah. May I help you?"

"I'm Gregory Smythe of the ACME Land Development Company. That's *S-M-Y-T-H-E*." He enunciated each letter, stuctched out to shake her hand, then cleared his throat. "It's the European pronunciation handed down from my British relations."

"You must be the developer everyone's talking about."

He smiled like a Cheshire cat, then immediately frowned. "I'm sorry for the loss of your father."

"Thank you." *No, you're not sorry at all.*

"I'm looking at the properties on this block in the interest of the corporation. We are interested in making a fair market offer for your building. I believe we have already sent an offer to Mr. Webb."

"Yes, I found the offer letter on his desk earlier."

"That's great. Can I come in for a minute and discuss it with you?"

For a fleeting second, Savannah considered refusing, but in truth she was curious. She virtually towered over the pudgy little man—he was no threat to anything but her temper.

Nodding, Savannah walked back into the shop with Smythe following. As soon as he entered, he looked up at each corner in the ceiling and poked his head into the classroom and tried to peek into the other rooms.

Not subtle, she thought. She stood behind the sales counter with her arms folded. "What's your pitch?"

"Do you know the construction details of this building? Do you have any architectural drawings?"

"There might be some in my dad's older papers. I'm not sure, but I think he still has all the original drawings that were used for the construction of this building. Why?"

"I'm trying to estimate the cost of demolishing the individual properties on the block. The amount of concrete in each foundation is a critical cost factor in determining the effort required to remove the debris. It's part of my report to the corporate office."

Savannah dropped her chin to her chest. *If I sell out, then I sell out. I'll have no business to complain about after the sale.* She looked back at the slimy excuse for a real estate developer. *If I don't agree, he'll pester me until doomsday.*

"I'll look into the shop's records, but I'm not making any promises. I have your card. I'll contact you if I find them." She guided him to the door and opened it for him to leave the shop.

"Thanks for your time," he said, absolutely oblivious to the effect he had on the owner of a business that he was callously measuring up for demolition. Savannah watched as he moved over to the building next door and began pointing his laser at its roof.

She turned back to the workshop and saw Jacob deep in concentration working on painting the next piece. She addressed the errant cut she made and split the glass along the impromptu tangent. Then she scored the curve again using a lighter hand. She split the glass again and took it over to the panel and trial fitted the new piece. It was nearly perfect. Maybe she could do this.

The bell on the front door jangled again.

"I thought I locked the door." She dashed into the display room and nearly bumped into Edward who was carrying a tray with a plate of cranberry scones along with two cups.

"You need to eat something, so I thought you should meet up with my scones."

"They smell heavenly. Come on back to the office. She raised her voice. "Jacob! Mr. Morris has brought us some scones."

Jacob peered around the corner of the workshop door and glanced at the tray. "I've eaten lunch, Miss Savannah." Then he disappeared.

Edward shrugged. "His diet is strictly controlled by his parents . . . and also himself by that token. Food issues have an unusual interest as one of his obsessions. One week he refused to eat anything but blueberries. His lips turned *Smurf* blue."

"Exactly how long has Jacob been here?" Her father had told her when he took Jacob on, but she couldn't remember how long ago that had been.

"Only a few months, but I understand he's doing quite well." Edward set the tray down on a little table against the wall of the office. He lifted both to a spot near the desk and moved a gray metal folding chair next to the desk. He picked up one of the cups and placed it in Savannah's hands. "Now, tuck in."

She sat in the desk chair, took the cup, and sipped the tea. She looked up. "Bold?"

"Oh, yes. It's my version of English Breakfast. I mix all the teas for Queen's Head and we get some very fussy customers, indeed. I still don't have the Earl Grey right. The occult bookshop owner keeps telling me it's too mild."

"Did you bring scones to Dad every day? This looks like a regular routine for you."

"Well spotted." Edward grinned wide. "We had a breakfast coffee and afternoon tea ritual going on since I opened Queen's Head three months ago. He reminded me so much of my pa back in London. He missed you as well. I think it did us both good."

"I'm ashamed that I didn't know that. He mentioned the pub. Said I would like the beer."

"How's the exhibit coming along? John mentioned that it would be soon, right?"

"Very soon. It opens two weeks from tomorrow. I need to call my partner today and let him know things are a little more involved here."

"Partner?"

"Um, not in that way at the moment. Ken Silverhawk is co-artist for the joint exhibit. He's also my assistant when I'm creating a large piece in the glass studio and my ex-boyfriend. It's complicated." She shrugged and took another sip of tea as she glanced at Edward. Should she tell him about her dad's note? Could she trust him?

Dad had apparently liked Edward. I should trust that.

"I found a note from Dad."

Edward sipped his tea and looked up at Savannah over the rim. "I'm not surprised. He was worried about something but wouldn't talk about it."

She turned to the open desk, pulled out the

envelope marked SAVANNAH and handed it to him. He glanced at the warning, pulled out the notebook, and scanned the writing. His eyes first widened to saucers and then narrowed in concentration. "What does this mean?"

"After the warning is a cipher that Jacob helped me solve. Well, honestly, he solved it. It tells me to go to a location that only Dad and I knew about. I expect to find something there, as well."

Edward put his cup down on the little table. "This puts everything in a new light. You need to call the police and tell them that you found this."

"I called right after I found it. Dad was a bit paranoid. I think it was mostly because of the work that he did for the government years ago. But it's only a note—not really much of anything."

Edward handed Savannah a scone. "You really do need to eat. I mean it. You're not thinking straight. He meant for you to protect yourself."

Savannah munched on the scone and looked into those green eyes again. "I know you're right. There was always an edge to him after Mom died. I mean I still carry a Swiss Army knife on me because he said you never knew when you might need it."

"What did the police say? What are they doing?"

"The officer who was here when Hugh was found took down the details. But I have so little information. I don't think they're taking it seriously. My suspicions sound childish, even to me."

"Okay. But what if this is a real threat? How do

you feel about Hugh? Is it possible he could have been saved if you'd found the message sooner?"

"Good point." She looked at Edward. "It was humiliating. The officer treated me like a crazy child."

"You had to call. It was the right thing to do."

"Okay. Again, you're right." She picked up another scone. "Look, I know I'm starving, but these things are ridiculously good."

"Thanks. I enjoy bringing them. They're my favorite comfort food."

He looked a bit uncomfortable as the moment of silence between them stretched into a minute. Clearing his throat, he finally said, "We need to think about how to protect you. Your dad gave you a pointed warning. We should take it seriously." He let the words hang in the air. "I've got to get back to the pub and see what needs doing before the dinner crowd arrives. Let's get our heads together tomorrow and figure out what we can do. Cheers." He waved and scooted quickly out the door.

After Edward left, Savannah made herself sort through the papers and put them into two stacks. One short stack of drawings for the demolition estimate and another stack of last year's tax return and this year's financial statements from her dad's accounting program. The remaining papers were filed into the four-drawer oak filing cabinet right beside the desk.

She slowly read through the statements. According to the reports, the shop was doing quite well even before the profits from the church windows were projected. The reports indicated that her dad made most of his money on commissions but also a surprising amount on the materials that were purchased for the classes. This could actually grow into quite a nice living if she decided to stay.

Stay? Where did that come from?

She grabbed a sheet of notebook paper and began to calculate the total net worth of the business. She labeled the columns and then found herself staring at them through sand-filled eyes as if the figures had just turned into dancing Sanskrit. Her watch said 4:30.

My brain isn't working. It's still early, but I'm dead tired.

She tidied the stack of papers in preparation for completing the evaluation tomorrow, got up, and went into the custom workshop. "Jacob, it's time to clean up and put everything away and close up the shop. We've had a busy day."

And I have a lot of thinking to do.

Chapter 5

Monday Evening

Savannah pulled her dad's van into the attached carport of the family Craftsman house in the Euclid/St. Paul neighborhood. It was about ten blocks east of the Grand Central District and close to the downtown section of St. Petersburg. Most of the surrounding houses were built in the twenties and thirties, but many of them had been transplanted to these quiet streets from other sections of rapidly developing early St. Petersburg.

Her parents' Craftsman was one of the originally built two-story houses on a double lot, and her dad had been a founding member of the local neighborhood association. As an active and supportive group, they welcomed all new owners with a personal invitation to a monthly porch party. The association was determined to defend its eclectic charm of brick streets and giant live oak trees. Each tree was still circled with the traditional bright purple azalea plants that thrived with the constant falling of the acidic oak leaves.

One of the things her parents were most pleased about was when visitors remarked, "What a charming home. It feels so comfortable here."

Maybe I should go find the clue from the cipher. It's not far, and I know right where it is. Standing on the porch jingling the keys, she heard a short yip. That settled it—it wasn't fair to keep her dad's Weimaraner puppy out of the action. Rooney needed exercise and as her sore back testified, so did she. Besides, if she found the clue she might have more to tell Edward . . . and the police.

She walked up three steps and across the wide porch that contained a porch swing and two comfortable white wicker rockers arranged to look out over the street and entice neighbors to stop and chat. Her mother had always kept a pitcher of iced sun tea on the glass table in front of the window. Her dad had continued the small custom and it became an unspoken invitation to all that he was ready for visitors.

The barking from inside the house increased in volume and pitch. It was a fearful sound and one of the reasons she was uncomfortable about spending much time away at Webb's. She pulled a doggie treat from her backpack, then unlocked the door to find Rooney crouching by her dad's recliner rumbling an uncertain growl. At nine months he was still pretty much a puppy with long gangly legs and big feet that he hadn't grown into yet.

"It's okay, Rooney." She bent down low to reach out the treat to the trembling dog. "It's me. It's Savannah. You don't have to be afraid of me."

He stopped growling and lifted his head to sniff up in the air to catch the scent of the treat. Legs tentative, he took a tiny step forward, sniffed again, then another tiny step. Savannah stood and held the treat a few inches from his nose. He gently took the treat, and with a crunch and a gulp, it was gone.

The ghostly grey wiggling mass finally greeted her by placing his paws on her shoulders and licking her face sticky wet. It was a puppy response and she hadn't had the heart to begin training him to wait for a greeting until after she had put down her backpack and keys and motioned to him to approach.

She sighed. "Maybe I'll leave that to your next owner. I don't have room for a dog in my little apartment in Seattle. Down, Rooney."

He immediately returned to the recliner and sat with his head cocked and amber eyes alert.

The next step in her routine was to check the house for signs of Rooney's disobedience. Her dad's bedroom was untouched—no issues there. She thought she had left her bedroom door closed, but must have left it ajar, because it was now wide open. Rooney had found his way inside. Her heart sank. *My shoes!*

Her fears fully realized, well-chewed dress heels were lying in the middle of her bed. The tatters were strewn everywhere as he had apparently shaken the life out of them. She picked one of them up and groaned. "Rooney!"

His head appeared around the edge of the open door, but he didn't step inside.

"Why on earth do you only chew on left shoes?"

Rooney lowered his head and lay down flat, eyes looking up.

"You know this is wrong. Bad dog!"

He tried to sink even lower on the floor, looking more pathetic and adorable.

"I know. I can't stay mad at you—but really, only left dressy shoes?"

No movement from him.

"Let's go for a walk, yes?"

Rooney's short tail wagged a staccato beat in enthusiastic agreement and he whirled over toward his leash on the Stickley table by the door. Snapping it to his harness, Savannah set the alarm, grabbed her keys and phone, and they trotted out the door. The sidewalks were made of original hexagon paver stones. They were beautiful, but extremely high maintenance and worse, dangerous if not maintained properly. Her dad and his neighbors had found a specialist to make repairs twice a year and split the cost among them. As a result, the blocks were beautiful and safe.

At the end of the street, Rooney performed as expected and she made like a responsible pet owner and cleaned up after him. Back at home, he tolerated the removal of his leash, then returned to the recliner. She wanted to get things settled with her ex before going after the cipher clue.

Pulling out her cell phone and selecting Ken's number from the recent call list, she checked her watch. The three hour time difference worked to her advantage as it was still late afternoon in Seattle.

"Hello."

"Hey, Ken. It's Savannah."

"Where are you? I've been waiting for your call. Are you back yet? We have a ton of stuff to do before the exhibit opens."

She took the phone from her ear, looked at the displayed image of Ken looking absolutely smoking hot, and realized that he had not uttered one word of sympathy, not one. She pressed her lips into a tight line and put the phone back to her ear. "I'm still in Florida. Things have turned out a good deal more complicated with my dad's shop."

"I thought you were going to sell it to Hugh."

"Yep, that was the plan. Hugh died yesterday."

"What?" Ken's voice rose to a high pitch.

"I've got to stay a little longer and get things sorted." *How did I not see how self-centered he is?*

"What about the exhibit? We still have two pieces to create to complete the—"

"Ken, you need to find another partner to help you with those last two pieces. It won't be me."

"Who am I going to find at this stage? The studio time is reserved, the material is already ordered. Everything is all set."

"Ken, my dad is dead. Why do you not understand that?"

"Yes, I know, but—"

"Listen carefully. I won't be back in time for the exhibit. Do you understand?"

"I can't believe you would abandon the exhibit. It's taken me over a year to get enough pieces for an individual show."

"It's not an individual show. We were supposed to be co-exhibitors."

"Okay, but—"

"Ken, at this point, I don't care about the exhibit. Get a new partner." She punched the END CALL button on her cell, momentarily nostalgic for the satisfying feeling of slamming down an old fashioned handset.

It took me way too long.

As she passed the oak glass door bookcase handed down through her mother's family, she saw the family Bible on the top shelf. *One more chore I've been putting off.* She pulled it down, wiped a thin coat of dust off with her hands, placed it carefully on the dining table, and then opened the beautiful volume. Great-grandmother Adams signed the first pages using pale blue fountain pen ink. The year recorded was 1866. The Bible had been a rare and cherished wedding gift.

The last time she held the book was when her dad had entered the date of her mother's death. It was now her turn to enter the date of her father's death. She tilted her head from the left to the right several times to reduce the tightness in her shoulders. Then she got up and searched for the nicest pen stuffed in the coffee cup by the phone in the kitchen.

Carefully, she added the date of her dad's death and wondered who would be around to update it for her when she died. A chill crawled up her spine. *Stop that. Morbid thoughts are not helping.*

Looking over to the table that held the phone, she saw the red light blinking on the old-fashioned answering machine, the type that had a cassette tape inside. She punched the PLAY button and Edward's voice announced, "Hi, Savannah. I'm calling to see if you're doing okay after today's—well, you know what. Give me a call if you need to talk. I'm told I have a great shoulder to cry on."

Savannah pressed her lips together in a slight smile. "That was really sweet. Don't you think so, Rooney?" She looked down into the confused amber eyes. He tilted his head and looked up expecting an explanation.

It's too soon after breaking up with Ken.

"I don't think I'll call just yet." She reached down with both hands to waggle Rooney's head, but he cowered down into the recliner trying to disappear. "I know, I know. I'm not Dad, but right now, I'm all you've got. Time to eat?"

He scrambled off the recliner into the kitchen, toenails clicking on the wood floors.

She fed Rooney in the kitchen and made herself a peanut butter and blackberry jam sandwich on sourdough bread. She poured a glass of milk, wrapped the sliced sandwich with a paper towel, added a snack bag of chips, and put them on a small tray. On her way to the living room, she looked at her dad's fancy recliner. He'd bought it last year for his aching back. Glass artists were prone to back problems. She looked around.

What on earth was she going to do with this big house and all the furniture? She put the tray on the coffee table and settled in her usual place on the comfy sofa. As she was about to take a bite of the sandwich, the doorbell rang.

Rooney galloped in from the kitchen, barked once, and sat by the front door.

Savannah put the sandwich down and peeked out the security peephole. It was Mrs. Webberly from across the street holding a large dish wrapped in aluminum foil. She was a tall, loose-jointed yoga instructor who had been looking out for Savannah since her mother died.

Lately, she looked in on Rooney several times a day. Savannah exhaled quickly and relaxed her shoulders in preparation for the nosy grilling that was certainly coming her way.

That's mean. Mrs. Webberly was like family. She's the old maid aunt I never had.

She pasted a friendly smile on her face and opened the door.

"Hey there, Savannah. I've brought you a nice casserole so you don't have to cook." Mrs. Webberly stepped into the living room and spotted the tray. "Oh, another sandwich. I know you've never been much of a cook, but it's nice to have a hot meal after a stressful day. I'll just pop this in the oven for a few minutes."

"Please don't trouble yourself, Mrs. Webberly. I'm just fine with my sandwich. I don't feel like eating anything heavy. I had a shock today and I'm not over it yet."

"Oh, sweetie, it's no trouble at all. I understand

completely." She talked over her shoulder as she went into the kitchen. "I'll just put this in the fridge for you so you can heat it up later tonight or even better, tomorrow."

"That's very kind, but I really don't need—"

"I find that most of my casseroles are so much better the next day." She found room in the refrigerator, returned to the living room, and plopped herself into the comfortable recliner with the satisfied look of a zealous parishioner who had satisfied a moral obligation.

Savannah's mouth opened to protest and then she snapped it shut. Her dad really wouldn't have minded and the sad truth was that he wasn't coming back to use it.

"What was your shock today? Hugh was there to help with the class, right?"

"You haven't heard?"

Mrs. Webberly sat straight up in the recliner, "Heard what?"

"We found Hugh in the custom workshop. The police think he died of a heart attack."

Mrs. Webberly went pale as she cupped both hands over her mouth. "Oh my goodness. That's both of them gone."

"Are there any relations that I should contact?"

"Well, the last I heard, his only cousin died last year. He did have a financial manager, though. I have his name and phone number." She stood and stumbled forward a step. Savannah hopped up to catch her by the arm, but Mrs. Webberly had already regained her balance. "Goodness, how clumsy. I'm sorry but this is a horrible shock.

Hugh was a dear friend of mine. He would come by for supper and well, company, at least once a week."

"Are you okay?"

"I'm going to be just fine. Eat your sandwich, dear. You need your strength."

Savannah returned to her seat. "I didn't know that he didn't have anyone. He was like an uncle to me and he was around for all our holidays. I know he lived close by, but I've never been to his place." Savannah took a bite of her sandwich.

"He lived in a small garage apartment near the glass shop. It was all he needed and he didn't want to own anything that would require any trouble."

"I need to check up on that tomorrow. Can you give me the name of his financial manager? I'll give him a call in the morning."

"Oh, I know just where it is. Let me pop into my kitchen and get it from the bulletin board. That's where I keep it." Mrs. Webberly bolted out the front door, leaving Savannah and Rooney staring after her like the chorus in an opera.

As she said, she was only gone a minute and returned with a small yellow index card in her hand. She handed it to Savannah and stood with one hip canted and her arms folded across her stomach.

"Have you thought about funeral arrangements for Hugh? Since he was completely alone, there really won't be anyone but his business contacts."

"Um, not yet. I've just started to deal with Dad's

affairs and haven't even thought about Hugh.
Are you sure that there's no one at all?"

"It strikes me that I should really be handling
Hugh's affairs." Her voice began a watery trem-
ble. "I mean, we were quite good friends and now
that he's gone . . ." Her gaze slipped far away. She
sighed deeply and cleared her throat. "You're in
quite a pickle with the shop. It's too much for
you."

Savannah felt a huge weight slip from her
shoulders like a heavy coat. "Mrs. Webberly, that
is enormously kind of you. Are you sure?"

"Of course, I'm sure. At my age, I've more experience arranging these things and"—she reached
into a pocket, pulled out a wadded tissue, and
sniffed loudly into it—"he was a very close friend."

"I'm sure he would be pleased."

"He was an easy man to please. Enough of that.
Now, tell me. How are you coping?" She settled
back into the recliner. "Your dad's heart attack
was a surprise to us all. He was such a dedicated
jogger and he was training Rooney to run with
him. Did he tell you about that? Well, I'm sure he
meant to, but he was always telling me how busy
you were."

That was a direct hit to Savannah's guilt. She
should have paid more attention to what was
going on in her dad's life. Their weekly Skype
conversations mostly consisted of her chattering
away about the new works she was attempting. He
had so much more going on than she would have
ever expected. *I should have known.*

She reached down and attempted to give Rooney a small pat on the head. His low growl caused her to snatch her hand back. "Rooney is not coping very well. I think he will need a new home. I can't take him back to Seattle. Do you know anyone who would like to have him?"

He heard his name and looked up at her, but returned his gaze to Mrs. Webberly.

"You can't be thinking of giving Rooney away. It's too soon for that. You need to make sure that you don't need him first. He's a wonderful companion, don't you think?"

"He doesn't much like me. At the moment, he thinks I'm the reason Dad isn't around. He tolerates me, but just barely."

"It will just take time," Mrs. Webberly said while gently stroking Rooney's head as he looked up to her like a punished teenager. "He's still a puppy and he's confused."

"I know how he feels."

"It's bad. The only person in his life is missing and he's just waiting until John comes back. He doesn't understand that he's not coming back."

Rooney turned away and shuffled over to sit on the floor right beside the sofa. He had obviously been trained not to jump up on the furniture.

"One thing you can do right now is feed him every morsel he gets. That will make a positive bond for you both."

"I can do that."

"Another thing is to take him for his walks so that he will look at you as his new pack leader.

Dogs are not really very complicated. And our master Rooney here is young and smart. Once he sees you as his provider, he will change."

"Did Dad seem like anything was bothering him over the past few months? Now that I'm looking back, he seemed a little stressed."

Mrs. Webberly pursed her lips, "Actually, now that you mention it, Hugh seemed a little strung out as well. But then, neither of them were much for chattering about feelings and such." She sniffed noisily, "I'm going to miss them."

Finally, Mrs. Webberly left. Savannah cleared away the few dishes, set the kitchen up for her morning coffee, and sat back down on the living room couch. *I'm going to have to get involved in the investigation.*

Chapter 6

Late Monday Evening

Although it was getting dark, Savannah felt that she needed to find the hidden message at Crescent Lake as soon as possible. If her dad suspected murder, he must have had some evidence to lead him to that conclusion. Just because he was paranoid didn't mean that he was an alarmist.

Savannah clipped Rooney's leash onto him and jogged out the front door heading toward Crescent Lake. The cache was on the far side of the park from her house in the corner of what was now a dog park. Rooney would be the perfect cover. A complication was predicting the actions of a puppy. She wasn't sure how he would behave and even worse, if he would pay any attention to her at all.

In the early days of geocaching, the hidden

containers were created out of military ammunition boxes, but they'd progressed to smaller more easily concealed weatherproof containers. Her dad had chosen a Hello Kitty pencil box as the perfect geocache to make a small girl excited about finding others.

The pencil box was completely unsuitable for becoming an official cache. Given that a pencil box isn't exactly rugged or expected to be used for more than carrying a little girl's whimsies around in a backpack, he had chosen to hide it in a sheltered spot. He had probably been checking on it while exercising Rooney.

Rooney behaved perfectly until they approached the dog park and he began to get excited and pull strongly on the leash to hurry Savannah toward the entrance. Thinking that he wouldn't be calm enough for dog interactions, she decided to take another mile loop around the lake, hoping against hope that it would burn off some of his puppy energy and he would listen to her.

She was right. The next pass proved to be better, and Rooney was curious but calm as they approached the double gate to enter the large dog pen. She unclipped his leash and he looked up at her with sad eyes that said, *"Only my daddy brings me here. I don't want to be here with you."*

He was reluctant to leave the gated enclosure and stood stiff-legged, eyes wide. "Come on, Rooney. You know you love this place." A small pat on his head broke his stance and he followed Savannah into the dog park. As soon he entered, several dogs came up to greet him with sniffs and circles. He stood still and shyly returned sniffs and then he hop-jumped in playful joy and ran with the dogs in a game of chase and see who runs the fastest.

Savannah scanned the people benches and saw several clumps of doggy parents sitting together along with two groups standing together. It looked very much like a coffee shop kind of gathering. From their friendly greetings and comfortable chatter, it was obvious that most were regulars. Angling eye contact to avoid getting trapped into conversation, she wandered over to the back of the park to a small magnolia tree. It was a good deal larger than it had been when she was ten. Although it looked like a dwarf species specially selected to be slow growing and low maintenance for parks, it had been a good many years since they'd hidden their geocache.

She started scanning for the Hello Kitty pencil box from a distance. She vaguely recalled that it should be on a low branch about ten feet up the tree. She started the painstaking search for the camouflaged Velcro fasteners that kept the box well hidden if you didn't know where to look.

There it is.

It wasn't remotely within reaching distance, but still there.

Why would you do this? You could have instructed Burkart to hand over in complete privacy after the funeral whatever information you wanted me to have. We've known the people at Burkart's Financial Services for a long, long time. You could have left something with Mrs. Webberly. Why this fuss? Oh, right. I remember. You're paranoid.

Moving to the side of the tree sheltered from view, Savannah grabbed the lowest limb for leverage and placed her foot on the trunk of the tree. She froze. *Oh, no.* She dropped her foot and released the limb. There was no way to reach the little box without actually climbing the tree. Suitable limbs were in place to make it easy for a normal person . . . a normal person who wasn't petrified by climbing a few feet. The nausea she always experienced when faced with heights returned to sap all determination. *I can't do this. It's too high. I can't.*

Pulling out her cell, she dialed Edward.

He picked up and Savannah could hear the bustle of the pub in the background. "This is Edward. What's up, Savannah?"

"I need your help. Can you come down to the dog park at Crescent Lake?"

"Dog park?"

"Yes, I need you to climb a tree."

"Really? Have you gone crackers? Now? Right Now?"

"Yes, please. Right now. It's vital. I'm deathly afraid of heights. It's about Dad's message. He's hidden it in a tree too tall for me to climb."

There was a pause. "I'll be there as quick as I can."

While waiting, Savannah played fetch the stick with Rooney and admired his athletic grace. He didn't tire of the game and it was a useful means of keeping away from the other doggie parents.

It took about ten minutes until she heard the smooth rumble of Edward's motorcycle pulling up. He dismounted and strolled their way looking savagely handsome.

Savannah cringed in embarrassment but felt relief as Edward quickly climbed up the few limbs and ripped the box from its Velcro holders. He jumped down like a kid and handed it over to her. "Is this what John's code revealed?"

"Yes, this is it," she acknowledged, turning the small pink box over in her hands. "Our first geocache. Exactly what the message said."

Rooney was waiting a little distance from the tree, head cocked to the side. He walked up and sniffed the box in her hand and began to whine. Tears sprang to Savannah's eyes as she realized that it must smell of her dad.

"I've got it, Rooney." Looking around to make sure she wasn't being watched Savannah pushed the small box under his nose. "Here, you can smell him, can't you?"

He stopped whining.

She ruffled his floppy ears. "Now go and play."

Rooney wiggled his stubby tail, looked at the box again, then turned swiftly to join the other dogs playing chase at the far side of the dog park.

Motioning for Edward to join her, she sat at a deserted bench near the back of the park and opened the pencil case. She gulped a quick breath. On top was an old tattered envelope that she recognized. She picked up the creased, brittle envelope and carefully removed the yellowed sheet of ruled notebook paper. Unfolding it, she recognized her third-grade rounded cursive writing in thick pencil.

> *Mommy,*
> *Why did you leave Daddy and me?*
> *I promise to be extra good.*
> *I promise not to throw toys in the house ever ever ever.*
> *I promise not to draw on the walls.*
> *I promise to clean my room.*
> *I miss you.*
> *I Love You,*
> *Vanna*

No one else can ever call me Vanna.

Savannah lost her closely guarded control and began to sob in great gulping heaves into her hands. Edward gathered her gently into his shoulder and let the tears soak into his cotton shirt.

After a bit, she dragged a tissue from her backpack, dried her eyes, blew her nose, and regained her composure. "Thanks. I didn't know the letter I wrote to my mom would be in the box."

"Perfectly understandable, luv."

"Even in my earliest memories, my mother was always sick. For the longest time, I thought if I was the perfect little girl, she would get better, that the cancer would leave her body. She knew that and encouraged me and my dad to find adventures without her long before her condition kept her in bed. I learned to fish, surf, snorkel, camp, and hike trails. My dad and I were outside all the time. She was a wise woman. I think about her every day."

"Oh, Savannah. I'm sorry. Anytime you need me, I want you to call."

"I appreciate that." She looked into those green eyes and felt warm and safe.

"Do you know why John wanted you to find this box?"

She sorted through the box and found an assortment of meaningless little items. "No, I don't see anything that strikes me as meaning anything important. There must be something here, though. I'll study them at home under a magnifying glass."

He glanced at his watch and jumped up. "This is retched timing, but the assistant cook called in sick tonight so Chef is by himself. Even on a slow night, it's a brutal workload. I've got to get back to the Queen. Are you good?"

She nodded.

"Are you sure?"

"I'm sure."

"Catch me up in the morning."

Feeling better, she smiled, snapped the lid, and slipped the pencil case into her backpack. She watched him helmet up and ride away on the low purr of the Indian.

She looked around carefully at each person in the dog park. Could any of them be involved in what her dad warned her about—*if* the conspiracy wasn't just paranoia?

None of them looked particularly interested in her.

Rooney bounded back and nuzzled her calf,

then whined a bit. "Okay, fella. Let's get home
and figure out what these things mean."

She led Rooney out of the dog park and they
walked calmly back to the house. Opening the
door, she keyed the alarm code, removed Rooney's
leash, and checked to make sure he had water.

She took the backpack into the dining room
and removed the Hello Kitty pencil box. Setting
aside the letter, the box held an array of small
items that she placed on the table one by one.
They were:

a small green plastic snake
a guitar pick
an individual packet of Off! insect repellent
a worn wooden nickel
a gray plastic elephant
a logbook
a pen

Next to those, she placed the remaining items:

a letter to her mother
the Hello Kitty pencil box

She picked up the logbook. It listed the names
of the people who had located their Hello Kitty
geocache and when they'd found it. There were
multiple pages of entries that were spread errati-
cally over the prior year, but the last entry was
about a month ago. She felt a shock as she realized the last entry was in her dad's handwriting.

She figured that he had probably removed the location from the organization's global database before visiting the cache so that no one would look for it after that. The membership practiced compliance about rules like that.

So, he had been worried for a while. In order for her to access the geocache database, she'd have to become a member. She could renew her membership and sign into the database to find out when he had removed the cache, but knowing him it was likely only a few days before the last entry.

Savannah looked at the collection.

Damn! None of these is a puzzle or clue that I can make out. What was he thinking?

She glanced over them again and ran both hands through her hair. She grabbed a small flashlight out of her backpack, then picked up each piece to look for hidden clues.

There must be something here that he means for me to decode.

The little green snake was only about three inches long and was a little brittle from being in the box. It was a typical Florida green snake with no evidence of tampering or hidden compartments.

The guitar pick was a typical red marbleized plastic and completely unremarkable.

She picked up the insect repellent and used the flashlight to see if it had been opened then resealed. It didn't look like it had been tampered with. She set that aside as well.

The wooden nickel was fairly new and displayed the logo of the Queen's Head Pub on one side and an old-fashioned five-cent imprint on the reverse.

Maybe Edward knows something about this one.

The little elephant was a child's molded plastic toy with no marks, scratches, or obvious tampering.

She threw it back on the table and leaned back. Her eyes brushed over each object, then she had an idea that maybe they were just distractions.

She picked up the logbook again. It was another tan Moleskine notebook that her dad favored. It was a little misshapen, probably because it had been in the little box. Anyway, she used the flashlight to examine the little notebook and found a small nick on the inside of the back cover.

Dad, you are the clever one.

She carefully slid a fingernail under the nick and pulled gently. The back cover was a double thickness and between the layers, she found a folded piece of onion skin paper. She hadn't seen a sheet of onion skin paper in ages.

I didn't know onion skin was still available. Well, Dad, you would have saved some for just this purpose.

Slowly unfolding the thin sheet, Savannah spread it on the table. It was a little larger than a half sheet with tiny punched holes in random patterns all over the place.

She leaned back in the wooden dining chair. She looked down at Rooney's upturned face. She took his face in both her hands, and peered into his warm amber eyes. "Rooney, I'm absolutely lost. This is a new one for me. I don't have a clue how to decode this. Do you?"

He cocked his head to one side trying to figure out what she was saying.

"Maybe Jacob will know," she mused. She might not be able to decipher the code by herself, but she was sure this was serious. Her dad and Hugh had been murdered. Her dad's games never had been played with more than one code at a time.

She stretched a great yawn and wasn't sure if it was fatigue or tension. Either way, it was time for bed. She let Rooney outside into the fenced backyard and gave him a treat when he barked to be let back inside. He wandered down the hall and stood by her dad's door.

Remembering a program she saw on the Animal Channel last month, she went into her dad's closet and pulled a couple of his work shirts out of the dirty laundry hamper and spread them out on the floor right next to the bed.

Rooney groaned a gentle whine and rolled his head on the shirts, then turned over onto his back to rub the scent all over himself. He sat upright and looked at Savannah, his crystal-amber eyes reflecting a grateful thank you.

Rooney settled himself to sleep and didn't rouse even when the mosquito spray truck swooshed through the quiet moonlit brick streets.

Chapter 7

Tuesday Morning

Detective David Parker looked up from his display screen and frowned deep enough to cause him to rub his forehead. He could hear clumping footsteps echo down the hallway of the St. Petersburg Police Station. They were marching relentlessly along to his office.

It was one of the few private cubicles—if you could call a half-height cubicle *private*. It was counted among his peers as an early reward for setting a new record for attaining the rank of detective. He was proud of gaining it so quickly in what he hoped was a long and successful career.

He recognized the distinct footsteps as those belonging to eternally-on-probation Officer Boulli. He was famous for spending more time and energy avoiding work than if he had just done the work.

The only perceived skill he possessed was an encyclopedic knowledge of Pinellas County labor and employment laws. He was an expert in each of the detailed steps outlined by the flowchart of actions called out in the employee termination process. David couldn't count the number of times Boulli had flirted with the final steps of termination, raising the hopes of city management everywhere only to be reinstated to full employment status at the last minute.

One of Detective Parker's newest goals was to become an encyclopedic expert in those very same termination regulations and he had been using his precious novel reading time to study them carefully.

It was never good when Officer Boulli felt the need to stop by for a chat. David relished the peace of his office and Boulli spoiled the carefully crafted environment simply by stepping across the threshold.

Even though the small office was barely big enough for a desk, an office chair, and two guest chairs, David had arranged the limited standard issue furniture to be the most effective use of intimidating power and comfortable ease.

His office chair was behind the desk and the desk faced the metal cubicle door that featured a large pane of glass in the top half. The guest chairs were pushed against the walls so that any guest would have an awkward view and not feel inclined to linger. That was a key element in having the office to himself most of the time. It also encouraged electronic communication rather than conversations that could never be correctly recalled. Electronic data lived on forever.

A small, low bookcase was tucked behind David's chair and stacks of files were neatly stored on its shelves. The desk's surface was clear except for an open file folder with papers perfectly aligned within, and a ceramic coffee mug on a beer coaster. The only personal item was a lone African violet plant on top of the bookcase. It was in lush bloom.

The computer flat screen was angled just enough so as to not block his view, but ensured that no one could see what was on the screen. That was all.

David loved his office.

"Good morning, Officer Boulli. Have you lost your way to the break room?"

"On my way, sir, but I thought I would hand this weird call off to you. You seem to be the solver of strange cases, so I thought of you right away."

"I'm stunned that my case load has broken through to your attention. Thank you for thinking of me."

"No problem, sir." He grinned like a schoolboy and handed Detective Parker a small scrap of yellow paper raggedly torn from a ruled tablet. "This girl called to say that her dad had left her a coded message that her life was in danger."

"Girl? You mean a little girl called 911?"

"No, sir. She wasn't a little girl. I meant to say that she was a woman. She was a very tall full-grown woman. Anyway, she thought that the dead guy in the glass shop had been murdered."

"What did you think?"

"I think she's crazy. I mean to say that it doesn't make sense. I answered the 911 call about this old guy who was found dead in her glass shop. His name was Hugh something, I think. It was obviously a heart attack. The paramedics thought it was probably a heart attack."

"Did you formally report it?"

"Uh, no. I don't think there is anything to it. We answered the call yesterday morning if you want to look that up in the database."

"And . . ."

"She said her dad had worked for the government as a kind of cold war spy."

"When did she call?"

"Late yesterday afternoon. I got a last-minute reassignment to assist in a traffic emergency but I remembered the call this morning."

"Give it here. Which agency did her dad work for?"

"She didn't say, but she seemed positive that the information he left her would put her in danger. She sounded cranky, by the way. So you might want to record everything in case she gets pissed off."

Detective Parker walked around his desk and snatched the scrap of paper from Officer Boulli's outstretched hand.

"Hey, I was handing it over."

"I'll take it from here, Officer. Thanks for dropping by." David closed his office door on

Boulli who backed up quickly to avoid the advancing door.

David sat down and typed a few words into the search command line of his desktop computer. He stared at the results. He rubbed his smoothly shaven chin. Her dad had indeed served as an analyst in the government, but there were no details about the kind of work he'd done. David would have to submit a special request to get more information.

He opened the bottom drawer of his desk to select a brand new manila file folder. He placed the torn scrap of paper in it and began a new case file by writing *Glass Shop* in bold letters across the file tab. He placed that folder on his desk and lined it up with his three other open cases.

Tapping a few keys, he looked up the information on yesterday's incident and saw that the body had been taken to the city morgue awaiting release to a local funeral home. An autopsy wasn't scheduled and the case was awaiting assignment of an investigation officer so that the next steps could be processed.

He leaned back in his chair. His caseload was light at the moment, although it didn't look like it from the status of his records. He had solved them, but didn't have the finalized reports to close his current caseload. Those reports should be on his desk within the hour—all he had to do was wait. Waiting wasn't his strong suit.

This could be just the thing to do while he was waiting for the last information to clear. Closing four cases in a day would be a record that would not easily be matched by even the most experienced officers. He e-mailed his supervisor to ask if he could check out the young woman's tip that the two recent deaths in her glass shop were suspicious.

The e-mail reply bounced back almost immediately. **You already have three cases assigned to you. You can have it if you think you can handle it, but please see me at the end of the day to review current progress on your open cases.**

That was exactly the response that David was looking for. He anticipated telling his supervisor that not only had he closed his current caseload, but that he had resolved another one, as well.

He closed down the active window, waited a few seconds, then reopened the case file and noted that he was assigned as the investigating officer.

Reviewing the records of the two deaths, it did seem an extraordinary coincidence for two heart attacks to occur so soon in one small business. Maybe it would take a little longer than he thought.

He called Officer Boulli and miraculously found him at this desk.

"Officer Boulli."

"This is Detective Parker. On that case we just talked about—"

"Which one?"

Parker grit his teeth and reminded himself of the higher goal of his department—to investigate cases, not actually murder city employees. "I'm sure you remember. The unattended death of a man found at Webb's Glass Shop."

"Okay. Yeah. What do you want me to do?" There followed a pause not quite long enough for Parker to challenge. "Sir."

"Drive out to Webb's Glass Shop and verify the circumstances that the woman has reported."

"Today, sir?"

David noticed a decided reluctance on the part of Officer Boulli to make the short five-minute drive straight down Central Avenue. It was practically within walking distance of the police department building. "Do you have any other tasks that have a higher priority, Officer Boulli?"

"No, sir,"

"Then what is the problem? It's a necessary part of the investigation."

"It's probably a waste of time. It'll be a heart attack like the paramedics said when I was standing there."

The whiny tone nearly threw Parker into a fury—nearly. He took a slow breath. "Just do it. It needs to be done and should have been done immediately after she called. I hope we don't have to justify the delay in sending out an officer to verify the situation."

"It just didn't seem that important."

"I don't understand why you are not in your patrol car right now. This is an official request to verify her call. You are not deliberately refusing to take this assignment, are you?"

"No, sir. Not in any way. That would be considered a serious breach of duty to refuse an assignment. I am on my way immediately, sir."

"Good. I wouldn't want to have to file a report." Detective Parker hung up the phone then searched the database, bringing up records for Hugh Trevor. He discovered that both men had been analysts during the cold war years. Like John Webb, most of his information was also not visible.

David pulled up the form required to access the detailed government records and filled in information required to request access to the records for both men. He sent it up the signature chain and hoped it would go through the approval process quickly.

The few facts he had were beginning to pile on top of each other, looking more and more suspicious. It appeared to be a case of three too many coincidences. The first was two deaths within ten days in the same small business. Second, the two men were intelligence analysts of an unknown type. Third, one of them had left behind a warning to his daughter.

He quickly ordered an autopsy with primary focus on a toxicology analysis for the glass shop victim. He could report it as natural causes, not wait for the toxicology report, and take credit for closing four cases in one day, but that didn't feel right.

Setting a new case closure record would ensure his position on the fast track, but a haphazard effort would erase his efforts in one fell swoop.

In his experience, when the circumstances didn't feel right, it was usually because the circumstances weren't right. One of the reasons he had been promoted so fast was because his instincts were usually smack dab on target.

No shortcuts just for a record count. He closed the report folder. He'd wait for the toxicology report.

Chapter 8

Setting up Webb's Glass Shop for the second day of class felt easier, but still hollow. Hugh would never walk through the door with a cheery, "Hi Kitten." Savannah forced her swirling brain back to positive thoughts. Today's teaching plan included learning to solder safely. The awkward, pointy, scary hot irons presented a teaching challenge that required serious concentration on everyone's part.

She pressed the ON key on the cash register and noticed that one of the ceiling fluorescent bulbs had burnt out.

Perfect, perfect, perfect. Start the morning wrestling with ladders and light tubes. I've got to conquer this ridiculous fear of heights. Do it now. Don't wait. Do it before you think.

She fetched the long package of replacement

bulbs from the supply cabinet in the office and placed them on the counter, then returned to get the heavy wooden six-foot stepladder. She opened the ladder and checked to make sure the hinges were locked. Checked them twice, then once more. She put her right foot on the bottom step. The plan was to bring down the burnt out bulb first, then take up the new bulb so that she always had a hand free to grip the ladder. She placed her left foot on the bottom rung, paused, then followed with the right foot.

I can do this. It's not as tall as the tree last night. I've got to overcome this fear.

Holding her breath, she took the next step in the same rigid manner, and finally the third. Both hands were beginning to ache with the death grip she clenched on the sides of the ladder. The bell jangled, and she froze.

Edward stepped inside the front door with a smile and a tray that contained a French press filled with dark coffee, floral bone china cups and saucers, and matching cream and sugar containers. "I've brought strong coffee. I guessed you might need a little lift after . . ." He looked up at the ladder "What's the matter with you? Are you going to be sick? You've gone white."

Savannah gritted her teeth and moved her head the tiniest fraction down. "I thought I could manage my fear of heights."

"It doesn't look like it's going to plan." He put the tray on the counter and with deliberate slowness, stood on the second step on the ladder. "I'm right here behind you. You can't fall. Put your left foot on the step below. Good. Now your right foot. Good." He stepped off the ladder.

"Just one more step. Left foot first. Good. Now right. Now step onto the floor."

Savannah wiped the cold sweat from her brow with the back of her hand. "Thanks a bazillion. I'm sorry. I thought I could do it myself. I was wrong. I'm really glad you were here. Thanks."

Edward waved a Vanna White gesture at the coffee tray. "I thought you might need a strong wake up."

Savannah smiled as the warm scent of the scones filled the shop. She reached out and wiggled her fingers. "Oh, gimmie, gimmie, gimmie. You're a mind reader."

After he handed her a scone, he looked over to the cash register and then back at Savannah, eyebrows raised.

"I've gotten brave enough to push the ON button," she said. "Crabby Cash Register is whirling his gears. He looks happy."

Edward squinted at the boot-up process scrolling quickly up the cash register screen. "So far, so good. It should only be a minute or two before we know. How are you this morning?" He casually climbed up the ladder and using both hands removed the burnt-out light tube. "Here's the bad one. Hand me the replacement."

Savannah removed the new bulb from its paper sleeve and handed it up to him. "Still a little stunned by the whole situation, finding Hugh dead yesterday, closely followed by that message from

Dad." She took the burnt-out tube and slipped it into the paper sleeve. "I'm so grateful you came to the dog park last night."

"Not an issue. I can see now that you wouldn't have been able to get it." He installed the new bulb with a little twist. It flickered and light flooded the display room. "Did you figure out the message from the pink kitten box?"

"No, this one is really a puzzle. It took a long time to find it. All those little items were a distraction. The message was hidden between the binding of the notebook. It's a slim sheet of really old onion skin with a random—to me at least—pattern of tiny holes."

"What did it say?"

"I wish I knew. I'm going to show it to Jacob. It could be blatantly obvious to him, but I'm absolutely baffled."

"Good plan. Jacob might be able to solve it just by looking. You might show it to Amanda as well. I'm continually surprised by the various skills she's acquired holding down dead-end jobs. Ready for class?"

"I'm feeling better, and oddly enough, looking forward to continuing the class. It's a familiar routine that doesn't leave time for dark thoughts."

"That's good. Have you talked to John's accountant yet about Hugh?"

"That's one of my horrible tasks today. It puts a hamper on my plans to go back to Seattle quickly. Burkart will have some good advice. He's quick on his feet, but he needs to know about Hugh."

Have you heard anything from the police department?" He picked up the spoon in the sugar bowl. "Sugar?"

"Yes, and plenty of cream." Edward put sugar and cream in both cups, stirred them and handed one to Savannah.

"Thanks. You're a prince." She sipped the rich brew. "Not a word from the police. I think I'm being treated as a crank call."

Edward peered at the cash register. "Ah, it's happy again today. Good." He started to fold up the ladder.

"No, don't touch that. I can put it away easily. At least I'm strong, even if I need to stay at ground level."

"Sure. Anyway, the police force in St. Petersburg suffers from staffing shortages like any other business."

"Really? I didn't get the feeling that I would be welcomed with open arms. But maybe you're right. If they don't call back by the end of today's class, I think a visit to the station would be the next step. Now that I have more to go on, maybe they'll take me seriously."

"Would you mind if I went along?"

"Mind?" Savannah grabbed his arm. "I'd really appreciate it." She noticed her grip and removed her hand. "Are you serious?"

"Quite. I'll be free any time after four. Is that a good time for you?" He transferred the dish that held the scone to the counter, placed the French press, the sugar and the creamer on the tray he balanced with one hand, just like a waiter.

"I could use the support. I don't feel like I'm being taken seriously at all."

"No problem." Edward stood in the open door. "I'll check back with you this afternoon. Enjoy."

"Hi Edward!" Amanda appeared in the doorway, took advantage of the open door, and bustled her bags and bundles into the classroom.

Savannah smiled and scooted over to the classroom door to hold it wide for her. Amanda performed some acrobatic moves to get everything she was carrying onto the worktable. She walked over and stood in the doorway in front of Savannah.

"I meant to tell you yesterday, but things did get a little crazy, you know, after Hugh." Amanda turned her mouth down like a lizard. "Anyway, I just love your earrings. They match your outfits perfectly. Do you make them?"

"Yep. I can't stop either. They're quick and use up the various bits of glass that I have lying around from other projects."

"They're gorgeous. You should start a side business selling them."

"Then it wouldn't be fun."

Amanda looked from Savannah and Edward, around the rest of the empty shop, and then back to Savannah. "I'm not too early, am I?"

"Nonsense," said Savannah. "I'm already open and just getting the materials ready for today's lesson."

"Good. I don't want to be a nuisance. Some of my patients at the Abbey don't pay attention to what's happening around them most of the time.

They just stand in the middle of the hallway and talk up a storm while blocking the way for everyone else to get by."

"Excuse us, excuse us," Faith and Rachel spoke in unison. "We need to get through."

"Oh, of course." Amanda flushed up pink to her ears as she returned to her workstation and rearranged her parcels back and forth across the work surface.

"This is not right. Which side were you on?" said one of the twins as she scooted into the last row.

"You're on the wrong side. You were over here. Move out so we can switch."

"What difference does it make?"

"You know I'm left handed and need to be on the other side so our elbows don't bump."

"Really?" The twin smirked. "I keep forgetting." The twins shuffled their places and sat down.

Savannah looked at their hands. The nail polish identified Rachel, so it was Faith, the left-hander, who wanted to sit on the outside worktable.

"Good morning, Savannah. Are we going to make up for missing yesterday's class?"

Feeling the tightness in her chest, Savannah resisted the urge to tell Rachel—at volume—that was a callous thing to say after Hugh's death. Instead, she pushed the anger down to a quiet place. "Good question. As soon as we're all here, I'll make an announcement."

The bell jingled and she went to the front door to greet the newlyweds.

"Good morning," said Nancy. "I'm rather hoping today will be quite boring." She led the way into the classroom with Arthur following with a dreamy look on his face. "We're going to be very careful, aren't we, dear groom?"

Jacob sat next to Amanda. He had already settled and his eyes steadily focused on a blank page of his notebook.

"Jacob, I didn't see you come in. How did you get in?" Savannah asked, returning to the classroom.

"I have a key, Miss Savannah. Mr. Webb gave it to me last month. Do you want me to return it?" He spoke quickly with a hint of tremor in his voice.

"No, no, Jacob. I was just surprised. Where's Suzy?"

"Suzy is in the office. I brought a real bed for her. I bought it for her yesterday. Is that okay?"

"Of course. That's perfect." Savannah opened the door to the office. There by the back door was Suzy, all cozy in a little plush dog bed with a small bowl of water next to her.

She looked up at Savannah and her tail thumped hello on the side of the bed.

Savannah left the door slightly open and went to the front of the classroom. "Welcome back to Beginning Stained Glass. Just a few announcements before we get started. Jacob has brought his new service dog, Suzy. It's important that she stay in the office as all other parts of the shop may have glass shards. Jacob, when you're ready,

I'm sure each class member would like an individual introduction."

"Oh, that's wonderful!" Amanda shot her hand into the air and peered over her shoulder at the crack in the office door. "Can I be first, please? I love animals. This is way, way cool."

Jacob stiffened and began to breathe faster.

"Not today," Savannah said quickly. "Let's give Suzy a chance to become more comfortable with her new surroundings."

Jacob stopped gasping immediately and quieted.

"Now for some announcements and decisions. We have lost some class time and we need to decide how to make up for it. I have two choices for you. One, we stay an hour later each day this week. Two, we return on Saturday morning. Any questions before I ask for a show of hands?"

Nancy raised her hand in a queenly little wave. "What about a third choice to not make up the schedule at all?"

Savannah bobbed her head. "Good idea. We'll make that choice number three. Anything else before we vote?"

Everyone looked at each other, but no one spoke.

"Okay, then. Who wants to stay an hour later each day?"

Rachel raised her hand.

"Who wants to come on Saturday?" Amanda, Jacob, and Faith all raised their hands. No one moved.

"Choice number three—who wants to ignore the lost time and keep to our original class meeting times?" Nancy raised her hand and looked pointedly at Arthur who quickly raised his.

"Well, that's a majority for making up time on Saturday morning. Thanks. I'll change our posted schedule. Now, let's pick up cutting glass where we left off yesterday."

She picked up the black whiteboard marker and walked over to the classroom board. It was chock-full of posters for local events, conference announcements, glass art exhibits, classified ads, and the master class schedule. She added Saturday's class to the schedule and noticed that some were out of date.

Jacob leaned over to Amanda and whispered loudly, "Mr. Webb left Miss Savannah a scary letter. I saw it."

Amanda glanced around at the other students and leaned over, as well. "What did the letter say?"

Alarmed, Savannah quickly leaned between them as Jacob opened his mouth to tell Amanda. "Quiet, you guys. We'll discuss this after class."

Noticing something strange in Savannah's voice, Amanda looked up at her with a mixture of concern and curiosity.

The doorbell jangled and Savannah turned to greet the visitor. "I'll be right back. Continue cutting all the straight pieces you're going to need. Then we'll move on to curves and arcs. It's better to cut accurately so that you don't have to spend a lot of time grinding it to shape."

She went through to the display room. Officer Boulli was standing just inside the door of the shop with his thumbs tucked into the belt that was way south of the normal waistline. He turned to Savannah and removed a full-sized clipboard that he had wedged under one armpit. He removed a clipped pen from the clasp, shifted his weight to a wide stance, and tilted his head to one side. Pen poised above a form, he asked, "Are you Savannah Webb?"

"Yes, Officer Boulli. We met yesterday."

He made a small check on the form. "Humph." He moved his pen down the form and read carefully. "Are you the owner of Webb's Stained Glass Shop?"

"Yes, sir. I'm taking over the shop from my dad. He died last week."

He made another small check on the form. "Did you call in a suspicious death on Monday?"

"Yes, Officer. You took the call. Don't you remember?" She could hear the irritation in her voice, but couldn't dial it back.

He made a final check on the form, slipped the pen back onto the clip, tucked the clipboard back under his armpit, and held out his right hand. "I'm Officer Boulli of the Homicide Division for the St. Petersburg Police Department. I spoke with you yesterday and I'm here to verify your statements."

She shook his outstretched hand. "What does that mean?"

"It means what I said. I was ordered to verify the statement you made yesterday at"—releasing the clipboard from his armpit, he drew a finger down to one of the filled-in slots—"fifteen thirty-five."

"Do you want to go into my office?"

"Not necessary," said Officer Boulli. "I would like for you to read this description for accuracy." He pointed to a large white square on the form with his black BIC pen.

She leaned in to see the tiny handwritten statement and read the few sentences Officer Boulli had apparently written down after her phone call. "That looks accurate."

"That's good." He held out the pen. "Sign here."

Savannah signed the form and handed the pen back to him. "I found a second coded message last night. This is very serious. I'm convinced my father believed he was in danger and that I'd be at risk as well."

Pressing his lips into a thin line, Officer Boulli made a laborious effort to write a note at the bottom of the form. Then handing it back to her, he ordered, "Initial this last statement."

Savannah complied with his instructions then pointed out, "I want to emphasize that I believe this to be a very serious threat."

He slipped the pen back onto the clipboard. "I'll ensure the proper authorities are aware of the second"—he paused to make finger quotes—"coded message."

Unable to resist, Savannah asked, "Is there anything I can do to"—she made finger quotes—"help?"

"That's all for now, ma'am." He ensured that everything on the form had a response by running his finger down the list. "You've verified that you made the call and we'll let you know if anything further is required." He tucked the clipboard again and pulled a business card from a fat stack in his top pocket. "Call this number if you have any questions."

"You gave me a card yesterday." She spoke to his wide retreating back and slipped the card into her pocket.

Is that really all he's going to do? What a pair we are. He is an idiot and I am crazy.

She spent the rest of the morning guiding the class, who were all still working on creating turtle sun catchers. As she was showing Arthur how to cut a gentle arc for one of the turtle legs, the shop phone rang. "Jacob, could you get the phone for me?"

With a pale face, he turned around to look at her feet. "I don't use the phone."

Savannah's brow furrowed into multiple creases. "What? Of course. I understand. Don't worry at all. Amanda, can you get the phone for me? I'll be right there." The phone continued to ring in the display room.

"Yes, ma'am." Amanda launched herself into the display room and picked up the phone. "Webb's Stained Glass. How may I help you?" Silence was followed by, "Yes, sir. She's tied up teaching a class at the moment. Can I take a message?" More silence. "Of course, I'll bring her to the phone right away, sir."

Amanda leaned into the classroom. "It's a police detective from the downtown station. They want to talk to you very, very urgently."

Savannah placed Arthur's glass on the worktable and sped into the display room. Amanda handed her the phone and Savannah placed her hand over the phone receiver and mouthed *Keep things moving*, then nodded her back into the classroom.

"Good morning. This is Savannah Webb."

"Miss Webb, this is Detective David Parker from the St. Petersburg Homicide Division. As a result of your call yesterday and your confirmation earlier, I'm sending Officer Boulli back to interview you and the students that were at Webb's Glass Shop yesterday. Is it possible to have them come back to the glass shop today?"

"But Officer Boulli was here this morning," she said through a clenched jaw.

"Yes, he was. There was a . . . a miscommunication in the focus of that interview." The detective sounded annoyed, though not, Savannah thought, at her. "He needs to complete the interviews as quickly as possible to make up for lost time. I apologize for any inconvenience." His voice was soothing and Savannah reckoned that he was sincerely sorry.

"Sure. The class is continuing, so everyone is here who was in the shop yesterday when we found Hugh. Is that all right?"

"That's perfect, Miss Webb. Is this afternoon around two a good time?"

"Yes, sir. Fine."

Savannah hung up the phone and just stood there. *Did my call make them pay attention? Did they find something?* She entered the classroom, cleared her throat, and waited until she had everyone's attention. "That was the St. Petersburg Homicide Division. They are sending Officer Boulli back. He wants to talk to all of us this afternoon."

Right at noon, as the rest of the class left for lunch, Savannah motioned Jacob into the office and Amanda followed. Savannah had a sinking suspicion that Amanda would not be kept out of this. She pulled the onion skin sheet out of the notebook and laid it on the clear center of the desk and smoothed it out with her hands. "This is the second cipher."

Amanda bristled. "What do you mean second cipher? What's going on?"

Savannah sighed and reluctantly nodded to Jacob. She didn't want more people involved in this situation, but Amanda's curiosity was relentless. She would keep asking until she had answers—and she might unwittingly ask the wrong people. "You can tell her now."

"Miss Savannah got a frightening note from Mr. Webb. The note said, 'Savannah, if you find this, I've been murdered and you are in danger.' That is scary."

"Murdered? Mr. Webb told you he was murdered?" Amanda's voice pitched high as she looked from Savannah to Jacob and back to Savannah. Amanda was suddenly unusually pale. "I told you something was not right."

"Yes, you did. Given the stellar performance of our clueless Officer Boulli, I'm going to follow along with Dad's clues to see if they reveal why he was killed . . . at least until the police start listening."

Amanda harrumphed and crossed her arms. "I wouldn't count on Officer Boulli being able to find his own backside with a flashlight and a map. If there was ever a clear case for Robocop, he would be the example that could completely cinch the deal. What does Officer Bumble think about the note?"

"Amanda, honestly, don't make me regret telling you about this. Officer Boulli's boss is a Detective David Parker. He's the one who called and apologized and is making Boulli return to finish the interviews later this afternoon. Detective Parker seems to be sensible but appears to be waiting for evidence before he launches an investigation that would require more resources than our current Officer Boulli."

"Does anyone else know? Is it just us three?" Amanda whispered, conspiratorially turning her head in all directions.

"I told Edward last night after I found the note and had already called the police. He thinks the city is so critically short of funds and staff, we would need clear and undeniable proof of foul play."

Jacob had been intently pouring over the sheet and turning his head one way and then the other. "I don't see a pattern."

"I was afraid of that. Amanda?" Savannah asked hopefully.

"Beats me. It looks like bugs have gotten into it and had a random snack."

Savannah's shoulders sank.

Chapter 9

Savannah stretched out her hand to greet Offi-cer Boulli who was sweating rivers under his armpits and down the back of his white uniform shirt. It couldn't be merely a result of the short walk from the patrol car into the shop. He wiped his hand on the side of his forest green trousers and shook her hand quickly. She bit off an impa-tient protest that he was obstructing vital access to a small business by leaving the squad car diag-onally blocking the entrance to the small parking lot.

"I'm Officer Boulli, I'm investigating the death that occurred here yesterday."

"Yes, you were here that morning *and* earlier this morning. Detective Parker called to say you would be back. Would you like to see the work-room where Hugh was murdered?"

"Not right now. Don't get ahead of me, missy. This is just a routine investigation into an unattended death. *I* don't think it's a murder." There was a not so subtle emphasis on *I*. "What I need first is a private space to conduct the interviews." He pulled a notebook from his shirt pocket and started flipping through multiple pages until he found something. "I was the officer on the scene"—he glanced up at Savannah—"of course, and my notes show that there is an office back that way." He pointed his pen toward the back of Webb's. "I'll use it for interviews."

"Okay"—Savannah stretched to her full height—"but first we need to pull Suzy out of there."

"Yep, that's true. Your secretary will have to work somewhere else for the next hour or so. If I can't have total privacy, we'll all have to make a trip downtown," he said, his chest inflating with a sense of his own importance.

"Suzy is one of my students' service dog." She turned toward Jacob. "Do you think you can hold her until the interviews are done or do you want to take her home?"

Jacob looked up with cheerful eyes. "I would rather hold her, Miss Savannah. I won't let her feet touch the floor." He dashed back to the office and in a wink returned to his work stool with Suzy cuddled in his arms.

Officer Boulli searched through more pages of his notebook, peering at the print and obviously searching for the list of interviews he should conduct. He finally found a list, and called, "Amanda Black."

Amanda's full lips pulled back to smile with her perfectly white beautiful teeth. "It's Amanda *Blake*. B-L-A-K-E." She walked back to the office without a glance to see if he was following.

Officer Boulli made his way behind her with a slightly dazed look.

Absolutely nothing got done in class after he shut the office door.

"Well, I'm not going in alone," said Faith, idly fingering her cork-backed metal ruler. She looked to Rachel. "We should go in together. We'll both feel better."

"You'll feel better. I'm not sure that I will." Rachel rotated the glass square on her table ninety degrees, then another ninety degrees. "But if it will make you feel better, let's go together."

"Arthur, we should go separately, but you need to just say what you saw plainly and simply." Nancy pulled a lipstick and small mirror from her purse and quickly refreshed her perfectly painted lips.

Arthur opened his mouth to speak, but didn't.

"Don't complicate things with what classes we've attended in other studios or how happy we were to start a new class," said Nancy.

Arthur nodded at nearly every word.

Nancy continued. "Don't even mention that Jacob seemed nervous. That's not for us to say."

Savannah looked at them sharply. Did Nancy think that *Jacob* had killed Hugh and her father?

The office door opened and Amanda flounced out. "He wants Arthur Young next."

"Remember what I told you." Nancy turned back to her glass cutting.

Arthur knocked over his stool, bumped into the worktable, and made his way into the office. A moment later, he reappeared to close the door on his finger. He let out a whispered yelp, put his finger in his mouth, and closed the door behind him.

Nancy fussed with her materials and tools, constantly glancing back to the office door. The rest of the class pretended to continue with their projects while straining to hear the conversation behind the closed door. When the office door opened, Nancy dropped her pliers onto her square of green glass and it split in two. Oblivious, she hopped off her stool and nearly ran Arthur over in her headlong rush to get into the office.

Arthur stood by the swiftly closed door and turned his head sideways like a puppy. He shrugged his shoulders, displayed a goofy grin, happily returned to his workstation, and sat down on his stool.

After the longest time so far, the door opened quickly and Nancy flounced out of the office, firmly shut the door, walked over to her workstation, and sat on her stool. She huffed expressively and glared around the room so furiously no one dared to speak to her.

Arthur leaned over and whispered something in her ear. She flushed bright red from her throat to the tops of her ears.

Several minutes crawled by in complete silence. No one was talking or even attempting to work, everyone just waited to see what would happen next.

The office door opened and a red-faced Officer Boulli poked his head out. "Um, excuse me. Miss Faith Rosenberg is next. Is she here?"

Faith stood up. "Come on Rachel. Let's go."

They bustled into the office and backed Officer Boulli right out of the office doorway. The door closed behind Faith.

Savannah almost felt sorry for him, but not quite. On one hand, she wanted the police to investigate. On the other hand, he had been so unpleasant, he deserved the twins' full point-blank arsenal of rehearsed and long practiced style of bickering and expertly delivered misinformation. She smiled.

After what seemed like ten years, the twins emerged with a very satisfied look, chatting conspiratorially. They walked towards their desks, took their seats, and picked up their tools as if nothing had happened.

Officer Boulli again leaned out to call, "Savannah Webb?"

She followed him into the office and he motioned her to sit in the rickety guest chair. After she sat, he plunked himself down in her dad's chair and she grimaced at the probable strain on the hundred-year-old antique, though it had probably endured worse.

Officer Boulli flipped to a new page in his notebook and slowly wrote the date and her name at the top. "Miss Webb, could you describe in your own words what happened yesterday morning?"

Thinking that it was only possible for her to describe things in her own words, she offered, "It was supposed to be the day I handed over the running of Webb's Glass Shop to Hugh Trevor. My dad, John Webb, the owner for more than twenty years, died last week." She stopped and felt the tears beginning. She grabbed a tissue from her pocket. "Hugh could have handled the whole deal. Buying the shop, staying on top of the paperwork, and calming current customers to ensure a smooth transition. He would have been the new owner. I thought that would be the best way to tie things up here so I could get back to Seattle."

"I just need to know about the guy who died here." He wrote down her statement using a unique shorthand that she didn't recognize.

Must be his personal version.

"That's what I'm telling you. Hugh had been working for my dad for a long time and he was supposed to teach this week's workshop. I couldn't understand why he wasn't already in the shop preparing for the new class. He loved teaching."

"That's not important. Just start from the discovery."

Savannah twisted the tissue and realized she was going to have to exercise a massive amount of control to keep from throttling the still sweating Officer Boulli. "Okay. I was teaching in the classroom out there and Jacob needed to get his tools from the custom workshop. It was locked, so he used his shop keys to get inside the workshop and the next thing I heard was that Hugh wouldn't wake up."

"Why was Mr. Trevor asleep in there?"

"Hugh wasn't asleep. It was Jacob who thought he was asleep. His parents didn't take him to my dad's funeral. Jacob had never seen a dead person."

"And you have?" Boulli's eyes narrowed suspiciously.

"Of course I have." She folded her arms across her chest. "My mother died when I was nine and I just buried my father on Sunday."

"Oh, that's right." Officer Boulli shifted in the chair. "Anyway, what happened next?"

"I shouted for Amanda to dial 911 and then I started CPR on Hugh, but it was clear he was gone. I am fully certified to perform CPR."

"Then the paramedics responded, right?"

"Yes. Once they arrived, we left the custom workshop and waited in the display room."

He scribbled a few notes. "When was the last time you saw Mr. Trevor alive?"

She dabbed a pinkie in the corner of her eyes. "It was at my dad's funeral on Sunday. He was one of the pallbearers. He left right after the burial."

"And now describe your movements on where you were from that point until Jacob discovered the body."

Her heart began to race. *He thinks of me as a suspect? That's insane. Well, maybe not for Officer Boulli.*

"I had a small supper buffet at my house following the graveside service until about eight that evening."

"After that?"

"After that I was alone until I opened the shop on Monday morning."

"Did Mr. Trevor have any enemies?"

"Not that I know about. He and my dad worked together on classified projects for the government during the cold war, but that was many years ago. It was something that involved the Russians, because he was still interested in any news from there."

Lots more scribbling, a deliberate turn of a page, and more scribbling. "Thanks. That's all for you. Send in the boy."

Sitting as tall as she could, Savannah objected. "I'm not comfortable having an almost eighteen-year-old with special needs fending for himself in a formal interview."

"Your comfort has nothing to do with it."

"I understand that, but you do understand that his parents are fiercely protective of him and will most certainly file a complaint if you ask Jacob a single question without their presence. I will personally direct them to Detective Parker."

"There's no reason for that attitude." Boulli stood.

Savannah stood as well, pleased that she looked down on him from at least six inches above. She folded her arms and gave him her best school teacher look.

He gathered up his notebook and pen. "This is a waste of time. That old man died of a heart attack. But if you think it was murder, then Jacob will have to be interviewed because in my opinion he is the prime suspect, *missy.*"

Savannah shouted, "What? How did you come up with that?"

"He has a set of keys and he discovered the body. Does he have an alibi? I don't know. If not, he's at the top of my list."

She left the office gritting her teeth.

Boulli stood in the office door. "Jacob. You're the last one."

Jacob turned around on his work stool, facing the office still holding Suzy. He said in a clear loud voice, "I am not required to answer your questions. I request that my mother be present for any interviews."

Savannah raised her eyebrows.

"No skin off my nose, young man," Boulli made a production of writing something in his notebook. "We have plenty of interrogation rooms downtown. I'm sure Detective Parker will be in touch with your parents."

After that, Officer Boulli spent about two minutes in the custom workroom where Hugh died before walking out the door as if he had a million more important things to do. He didn't even say good-bye, as if the irritating case wasn't worth his notice.

Savannah called Frances Underwood to tell her about what just transpired and how Jacob prevented Officer Boulli from proceeding with an unplanned interview. Being questioned by an annoyed police officer was as far from a good experience for Jacob as it was possible to be. His mother understood the situation, and firmly stated that she was going to insist that their family lawyer be present for all interviews. Smart lady.

When she returned to the classroom, Rachel was holding court, "He had the audacity to ask if I had a relationship with Hugh. Can you imagine?"

"That's not what he asked you," Faith looked over the top of her glasses and pursed her lips. "He very reasonably asked how long we had known Hugh and if we had keys to the shop."

Rachel huffed, "I thought he was trying to pin it on me by hinting that it was a crime of passion."

Faith shook her head and turned to Nancy, "What did he ask you?"

"Not very much—he practically asked me those same questions. He spent more time trying to get his pen to work than actually talking to me. He finally just grabbed one from the desk and wrote with that."

"He what?" Savannah ran into the office at full tilt. She verified that her dad's favorite wooden pen was missing. It was a gift from one of his first students. He had valued that pen. What does one do when a police officer steals? Jacob's mother will know.

The afternoon settled down after Savannah gave her overview lecture and she switched to individual instruction based on the issue or skill level of each student. As expected, Arthur and Nancy needed the most help while Amanda and Jacob were essentially completely independent.

The twins were hopelessly craft-impaired—just as Edward had said—but they were completely content and supremely practiced in criticizing each other's work and didn't require much help.

One of Officer Boulli's questions that still bothered Savannah was that she'd had to account for her movements from Sunday night through Monday morning. He was probably just following a template for questioning witnesses, but it brought home the fact in the eyes of the police, she was a likely suspect. But not the *most likely of suspects.*

According to Officer Boulli, that would be Jacob.

The bone-chilling thought was that the killer was most likely someone she knew—or that her dad or Hugh knew over the last few months.

Jacob? She looked at him with the eyes of an outsider and tried to forget everything wonderful her father had told her about him.

She walked over to Jacob and signaled for him to follow her back to the office. He was most likely to be more comfortable with Suzy in his arms. Sure enough, he immediately picked up Suzy and sat in the guest chair.

"Jacob, Officer Boulli wanted to know this and now I'm curious, but where were you on Sunday night and Monday morning before class started?"

"I was at home sleeping. Suzy was with me and my mother knocked on the door to wake me up when she left for work."

"What time was that?"

"She knocks at 6 o'clock and then I take Suzy outside."

"Did anyone see you?"

He shook his head no.

No alibi, but she absolutely believed him. Jacob did not kill Hugh. Boulli was most likely trying to upset her. And it definitely worked.

Chapter 10

Tuesday Evening

Savannah stood by the cash register so disoriented that she stared blindly at the display screen. With a start, she remembered that she had come over to shut it down. Although she had managed to complete the lesson of the day, she was still reeling from the police interviews and the realization that the murderer could be someone she knew.

I should have expected the interviews. The police need to determine if it's a case of suspicious death.

All the students had packed up and left except Amanda. She walked up beside Savannah. "After I load up my car, I insist that Edward and I introduce you to the local artists' watering hole. You can't just go home alone after all this piffle from the police. What do you say?"

Savannah hesitated. "I meant to start clearing out the office tonight and start an inventory of the shop equipment."

"Come on. It's just a ten-minute walk. Edward said he would meet us out front and walk with us."

"You called him?"

"Yep, I need to take care of Mr. Webb's famous daughter." Amanda winked and hooked her arm through Savannah's at the elbow. "You know you want to go. Besides, we can discuss that note while we're there. Please, please, please?"

Savannah thought that Amanda was a little overeager to discuss a murder case, but she smiled at her enthusiasm anyway. Her energy provided a bright spot that Savannah didn't realize she needed. She pressed the OFF button for the cash register. "You're right. Let's go."

They walked next door and picked up Edward in front of Queen's Head.

"How do you walk in those?" Savannah pointed to Edward's black, highly decorated cowboy boots.

"Vanity . . . pure vanity. When I was a kid, I always wanted to be a cowboy and live out west. I bought these boots when I got promoted from dishwasher to busboy. They were expensive, but I love them."

"What kept you from going out west to Colorado or New Mexico?"

Edward looked over to Savannah. "Brits also adore the sea. I think the west coast of Florida is as far as I'll go."

They crossed busy Central Avenue and in three

short blocks walked into a low, industrial building with a three-story addition in the back.

Savannah laughed. "This doesn't look like a brewery. It looks like a factory or distribution center."

Amanda gave her a light punch to the arm. "Bingo! That's exactly what it was."

Edward tilted his head toward the gravel lot next to the building. "They made specialized industrial pipe here and held their inventory in the warehouse. There are still some pipes out in the car park."

"How long has this place been here?" Savannah looked around the brightly furnished new brewery. How nice that it was so close to Webb's. Edward and Amanda were right to insist that she accompany them for a social break.

"It's been open about six months," said Edward, peering at the list of beers handwritten on the chalkboard behind the bar. "The owner has lots of experience with brewing beer. He's co-owner of the Bella Brava Trattoria downtown and he was always brewing beer to use in the fish and chips batter. It got to the point where they were selling that beer to local restaurants all around the Tampa Bay area. Lucky for us, he decided to make a real investment here and start a brewery."

Amanda chose one of the high-top tables made of poured concrete with gray metal stools for seating.

Edward settled onto a stool. "I like the atmosphere here. The staff is friendly and the brewed selection is always changing. I'm bringing his three most popular beers into the pub next week. Customers are asking for them."

Savannah scanned the chalkboard and found her thoughts reaching back to Seattle. Her friends had enthusiastically educated her in the subtleties of craft beer. She should call Ivy again tonight. It would be good to hear a familiar voice. "I love me a nice ale. How's the Beach Blonde Ale?"

"It's a good beer for Florida, refreshing and light," said Edward, "with just enough hops to balance out the sweetness of the malt. It's their bestselling brew."

The server walked up and took their order. Edward ordered an India Pale Ale and Amanda asked for a light lager.

"Why is it called 3 Daughters Brewing?" asked Savannah.

"The owner has three daughters." Edward turned around and pointed to a set of handprints forever immortalized in the concrete bar counter top. "Those are their handprints when the bar was being poured. It's definitely a child- and pet-friendly place. Their hours on Sundays are only for the afternoon and they're closed on Mondays."

"That's unusual. But very nice," said Savannah. "Isn't this place your competition? Just around the corner and all?"

Edward grinned. "That's the beauty of a loyal local clientele. My pub has high end British fusion service and a full bar with cocktail specialties each day of the week. The 3 Daughters is the largest brewery in Florida with a fantastic tasting room, but no kitchen. They host food trucks on most nights. We co-exist very well and my business has increased since they opened."

"What do you think about Office Boulli and the grilling?" Amanda put her neon green–tipped fingers over her mouth. "I mean the interviews."

Savannah put a finger to her lips to shush Amanda while the server placed their pints on coasters and left them with a broad smile and a "Just give me a shout if you want another."

After a long sip of her blonde, Savannah said, "It's an indication that there is an investigation under way. But is that a good thing?" She looked at her new friends. "I think this is going to get ugly. They'll be looking at someone in the shop who was working with Dad and Hugh."

"The only one who fits that description is Jacob," said Edward.

Amanda harrumphed. "That's not likely. Well, how would they describe slimy Smythe and freaky Frank? They wanted Mr. Webb and Hugh out of their way so they could complete their nefarious deals."

Edward and Savannah looked at Amanda long and hard.

"What?" She shrugged her shoulders. "I'm just saying what most of the District is saying about those two. They are obvious suspects." Amanda pounded her plump fist on the surface of the table. "It can't be Jacob."

"Well, like Officer Boulli said, if the police begin to think it was murder, Jacob would be his first suspect. What on earth would be Jacob's motive?" Savannah asked.

"Looking at it from the outside"—Edward fiddled with the stack of coasters that were scattered around on each table—"it could be that he felt threatened by some issues that makes no sense to us at all."

Amanda puffed her exasperation. "That's ridiculous. He just isn't capable. Look how devoted he is with Suzy."

"I agree with Amanda. He might be the logical suspect, but I don't for one minute think that it could be. It's not within the realm of possibility for me." Savannah realized that her passion was running away from her and took some calming breaths.

"I agree with Savannah. Edward, you're outnumbered."

Savannah looked down into the golden liquid and made a decision. "I think we have to take on the investigation before Officer Boulli makes such a hash of things, no one will be able to look for anyone *but* Jacob."

Amanda and Edward looked at each other. "We agree, but how?"

Savannah sat up straight. "We have two advantages. One, my dad apparently figured out something quite a while ago and left me a trail to follow. Two, we're clever. Between us, we know more about the District than anyone on the police force." She raised her beer for a toast. "We need to solve this case. Agreed?"

Edward raised his glass. "Agreed."

Amanda raised her glass. "Agreed."

Their glasses clinked and they each drank to their new adventure.

Savannah fingered the moisture hugging her beer glass. "So, given that none of us believe it's Jacob, who could it be?"

Edward wriggled on his bar stool. "In my mind, the one who has the most to gain from the sale of Webb's Glass Shop would be Frank. He gets the big contract and he eliminates competition in the whole city."

"I remember that the *Tampa Bay Times* covered the competition because of the age of the historic stained glass. Just how much is that contract from the church worth?" asked Amanda.

"It's about twenty thousand dollars a panel." Savannah drained the last of her beer. "That's a large chunk of change for a small glass shop. They want to do at least ten of the most important panels. Dad told me that Frank was livid that the church committee awarded the commission to Webb's."

"That's a motive, sure enough," said Amanda.

"I agree, but how on earth do we put him in the frame for it?" said Edward.

Savannah's shoulders stiffened. "Well, one thing we can do is find out where he was on the days that my dad and Hugh died. If he doesn't have an alibi, we have something to go on. If he has an alibi, then at least he is eliminated for good."

"Good thinking, but how do we do that?" asked Edward.

Amanda scrunched her violet-shadowed eyes. "Well, we could ask him."

Savannah smiled. "That's direct. Since I'm on the hook to meet with him for lunch tomorrow, I can try to find out where he was."

Amanda smiled. "Good luck with that. He's been exceptionally obnoxious, lately. Whenever he came to Webb's, there would be an argument between him and your father—almost every time."

"What was the argument about?"

"I really tried to find out, but they were very clever. They would both go in the custom workshop or the office and close the door." Amanda spread her hands wide, "Believe me, I tried to listen in on their conversation, but I have no idea what they were fighting about."

Edward drained the last of his brew. "What about Slimy Smythe?"

"Again, I have an excellent excuse to talk with him about the shop and the other owners of the block. He should be easy to meet casually since he's measuring all of us for demolition expenses."

"That's going to be the tricky one. He's one of those compulsive smartphone junkies. He is obsessed by e-mail and would check it even when he was in the middle of discussing an offer with Mr. Webb. It's distracting and annoying in the extreme." Amanda's phone pinged and she dived into one of her bags to look at the screen. "It's my mother. Why on earth did I think it would be useful for her to have a cell phone?"

Edward signaled to the server. "That's a great

plan. Let's have another round. Savannah, there's a stout I want you to try. It's a dark wheat with chocolate overtones. It carries a strong taste, but it's very well executed. Good?"

Savannah nodded enthusiastically. "Bring it on."

Edward waved to the server and asked her to bring a sample of the Brown Pelican.

Amanda's phone pinged again and she gathered her multiple bags. "Not for me. I'm a lightweight and I've got to get over to the nursing home to see my mother. You wouldn't believe how accurately she can tell time when I'm running a bit late." She dropped a ten-dollar bill on the table and waved a cheery good-bye to them and to the server.

Savannah giggled. "I so enjoy having her around. She's so funny and sincerely good people."

"Things certainly have been wildly exciting here, I must say. What do you think the police are up to with these student interviews?"

"I feel vindicated, but I still don't think they're taking it seriously. And if they *are*—it's Jacob I'm concerned about right now."

"Do you think Jacob is the one?"

"You know him better than I do, but I agree with Amanda on that score. Jacob didn't do it. He has a few quirks but they're all related to either food or his environment. What do you think?"

Edward shrugged. "You could be right. I don't know for sure, but your dad trusted Jacob, even though he apparently feared for his life. Your dad was indeed a suspicious man, but case in point, he gave Jacob a key to the back door. If anything, Jacob may be in as much danger as you are."

"Rats. I forgot to call Burkart about the finances. Remind me tomorrow, please. Where is my brain? How do you organize yourself for getting everything done?"

Edward was looking down into his beer seemingly lost in thought.

Savannah touched his arm. "I'm worried about how the investigation will be conducted by Officer Boulli. He seems distant and detached from the facts of the case. He appears to just be walking through the process. I wonder how his boss views his behavior."

"You spoke to Detective Parker for a few minutes. What's he like?"

"He seemed the polar opposite of Officer Boulli. Boulli appears not the least bit interested in preventing a dangerous situation in the shop."

"I haven't met the famous Officer Boulli. He hasn't come next door to question me even though I knew both men as well as everyone else in the District."

"If Detective Parker takes the case away from Officer Boulli, I think things could go badly for Jacob. It might be better to keep the police at an uninformed distance until we get further along with our investigation."

"Stop obsessing. We're as bad as Boulli until we get some information."

"That's a fact."

"How do you like this salty brew?" Edward pushed the sample glass toward Savannah.

She lifted the large shot glass, sniffed delicately, took a nice gulp and swirled it around her mouth.

"Hey," said Edward, "you've done this before."

Savannah tilted her head sideways, batted her eyelashes in an outrageous flutter, then swallowed the beer. Setting down the shot glass, she admitted, "I've been playing coy. I've been a beer cicerone since the week I turned twenty-one."

"Cicerone?"

"It's the equivalent of wine sommelier. In Seattle, I organized the city's beer runs. They were very much like the Bad Santa Crawl here at Christmas and the Kilted Beer Run on St. Patrick's. I also hosted a beer blog that had over five thousand followers."

"So you officially know more about beer than I do."

"Yep." Savannah nodded her head, then sipped her beer. "Officially."

Chapter 11

Wednesday Morning

On the third day of class, Savannah opened up the shop, started the cash register, and realized that Edward hadn't delivered morning coffee along with his mouth-watering cranberry scones. She didn't exactly expect him to bring her breakfast each day, but she was a little hungry and even a bit disappointed.

Stopping by the local gym had been the exact right thing to do. The boot camp training session was already in progress when she'd arrived but the instructor had welcomed her and she'd slipped into the mindless pattern of kettle bell lifting alternating with jumping jacks and the dreaded lunges. The crack of dawn class was a complete hodge-podge of young professionals, college students, and active retirees in need of a challenging exercise class.

For the first time in days, the knot at the base of her neck wasn't trying to creep up the back of her head. She'd signed up for a one-month membership to keep up her fitness level and help reduce her stress.

The door jangled and she turned with a smile to greet those delicious scones, but it was Reverend Kline stepping through the front door. He was wearing his pastoral suit of light gray over a black shirt with a black clerical collar and narrow black leather tie-up shoes. He had a folder in his hand. "Good morning, Savannah. I was passing by on my way to see the church's district superintendent and wanted to drop this brochure into your hands personally." He held the folder out to her.

"Good morning, Reverend Kline. It's nice to see you."

"How are you holding up?"

"I'm feeling a bit alone in the world." Savannah read the banner across the brochure. END OF LIFE GROUP COUNSELING—INSPIRATIONAL INTERVENTIONS IN GRIEF AND BEREAVEMENT. She held it away from her and looked askance.

"I know." Reverend Kline shrugged his shoulder. "It's a bit sensational, but it makes it easier for me to discuss grief with potential members of our therapy group. I established it about five years ago and I must take some small credit for building it into a successful part of our mission."

Savannah flipped through the brochure and looked back to him. "I'm not sure this is what I need just now. This morning, I wanted to pull the covers over my head and stay there. Luckily, Rooney needs to go out and then needs to be fed. By then, I've started the day."

"That's exactly why you need to come and join the group. Each member has been where you are now. It really does help." He scanned around the shop. "You're continuing with the business?"

"I don't think I want to talk about my father's death to a group of strangers." She flipped to the back page of the brochure and looked at the picture of kindly faces quoting words of sympathy and supportive testimonials. "Dad's biggest contract was for your replacement windows. They require specific expertise. Hugh's death has left a gap in skill and knowledge that will be difficult if not impossible to fill."

"I thought your plan was to sell the house and the shop in order to return to Seattle."

"Well, the actual plan was to sell Webb's to Hugh, but that has been completely turned upside down. I want to finish teaching the class Hugh was all geared up to handle. I feel obligated because the students signed up and paid for it way in advance. I'm happy to keep Dad and Hugh's last few commitments. They were real particular about commitments. I don't know what I'm going to do about the backlog—probably cancel them. I don't know. I haven't decided what I'm going to do yet."

"I understand. You see, those are the things we could work out in the grief and bereavement support group. What your future should be. How you should proceed." He put his arm around her shoulder and gave her a bouncing side hug. "Your dad would have wanted you to discuss these things fully. He was so proud of your achievements in Seattle at the Pilchuck Studio."

How would he know what dad wanted for me?

She nodded her head slightly. "I'll think about it. When's the next meeting?"

"It's tonight at seven in the church community room. I know you'll make good progress within the group, but first you actually have to attend."

The door jangled sharply and Edward bounced into the shop. "Good morning." He screeched to a halt. "Oh, I'm sorry. I didn't see, er, I mean I didn't know, er, you had company." He turned around. "I'll come back later."

Savannah laughed right out loud at his silly reaction. "Edward, come back. It's Reverend Kline from my church. Reverend, this is Edward Morris, owner of the Queen's Head Pub next door. He's been helping me get used to being a business owner."

Reverend Kline tilted his head and reached out a hand. "I believe I recall meeting some of your staff at Mr. Webb's funeral service. I'm pleased to meet any friend of Savannah's. I've known her all her life."

Edward stepped into the store and put the coffee tray on the sales counter. He wiped his hands on his black jeans and stood as tall as if he were wearing a tuxedo. "How do you do, Reverend Kline." Then he looked into Savannah's eyes. "Everyone needs to support Savannah in these difficult days."

Savannah swallowed quickly and then burst
into tears. *That was so kind.* She fumbled in her
jean pocket for a tissue.

Edward produced a freshly pressed white handkerchief and placed it in her hand. "Here you go.
I'd be shocked if you didn't have a few tears over
the next week or two. Right, Reverend?"

"You're absolutely right, Edward. I think we all
need to encourage Savannah in her path to griev-
ing for her father." He turned to her. "Would you
mind if I take a look at the progress of the replacement panel? It's been several weeks since I
stopped by."

Savannah wiped her eyes and blew her nose.
She nodded in the direction of the custom workshop. "No problem, Reverend. The door is unlocked."

"Is that wise?" Reverend Kline halted in the
doorway to the workshop. "How can you ensure
that the panel is safe?"

Savannah walked into the custom workshop
with him. "I didn't think about that. You have a
good point. I'll start locking the door even when
the shop is open." She lifted the white cotton
sheet used to cover the panel.

He bent over the work and peered specifically
at the solder joins, then picked up one of the
foiled pieces and ran his finger over the smooth
surfaces. He straightened and looked at Savannah. "It's coming right along. This is very good
work. It's the same quality as the ancient Russian
pieces that I've acquired for the church. Craftsmanship of this level is difficult to find. Hugh will

be sorely missed." He placed the foiled piece back on the worktable.

Savannah replaced the protective cover. "Russian pieces?"

"Yes, I've been scouting for religious icons for years. It's one of my passions to see that they don't fall into the hands of private investors who will never let them fulfill their holy purpose as spiritual inspiration."

"So, maybe that's why you helped the committee choose Webb's Glass Shop for the duplications. You have become an admirer of the craft."

He nodded absently and she followed him back into the display room where Edward was intently looking at the reverend's brochure.

"Thanks for letting me take a look. I see you've started work where Hugh left off. I'm especially anxious to see how you get on with the completion of the panel. I know how skilled you are, but the best proof will be the quality of the work. I would be very distressed if the steering committee decided to withdraw the contract." Reverend Kline patted Savannah on the shoulder and left them standing in front of the checkout counter.

"He's right," Savannah said, turning to Edward. "I'm in a pickle without Hugh."

"But your dad and Hugh taught you everything they knew about stained glass."

"It would still be a stretch to say that I'm anywhere near as good as they were. The reverend may have to retract the contract. That would certainly make Frank happy. Dad, however, will turn over in his grave."

"Of course, I heard that your dad and Frank had a falling out, but John wouldn't talk about it. Do you know why?"

Savannah's shoulders slumped and she ran a hand through her hair. "Yes, I remember when it happened. It was a clash of titans, in a way. Frank used to work here, and Dad felt strongly about giving students the best possible instruction and highest quality materials to encourage a life-long love of glass."

"Frank didn't agree?"

"His approach is to get a ton of students jammed in a class and charge them twice the wholesale price for the cheapest of materials. It's why Frank started his own shop. Dad wouldn't have it. And being each other's direct competition didn't help things after Frank left Webb's."

"And of course, John wouldn't have grassed on him," said Edward.

"What? What's grassed?"

"Grassed means tattletale or snitch. Sorry. Are you going?"

"Where? Back to Seattle?"

"No, I mean to the grief counseling group."

"Oh. I think I need to attend something. I keep bursting into tears anytime something reminds me of Dad. That can't be normal."

"It might be. That's the kind of thing you would find out if you went to the group." Edward turned to the door. "Have you called Burkart yet?"

"Shoot, I forgot again. I'll do that now."

As Edward left, she reached for the phone, but

the Rosenberg twins walked into Webb's with a million questions for her. The remaining students arrived. They were going to spend the rest of the morning continuing to work on the turtle sun catcher. The pattern was simple, but because it touched on all the steps required for copper foil–based artwork, they needed lots of help.

During the first lull in teaching, Amanda stepped up front close to Savannah. Her head tilted to one side, she whispered. "Any news from our intrepid Officer Boulli?"

Looking up, Savannah turned her back to the class, "No, I'm very pleased to say. Have you heard any rumors from the District that could help us?"

"Not a peep."

Fifteen minutes before noon, her cell rang.

"Hey, Vanna, are we still on for lunch?"

Savannah pushed down the urge to throw the phone against the wall. "Of course, Frank. As we already agreed. At noon. I'll be on the sidewalk in front of the Casita Taqueria just a few minutes after high noon."

She pressed the END CALL button on her phone screen. "That idiot just doesn't listen. My name is Savannah."

Chapter 12

Wednesday Lunch

Tucking her slim billfold into her back pocket, Savannah enjoyed walking the few short blocks through the slow-moving lunch traffic, until she spotted Frank standing near one of the outdoor picnic tables waving his hand. She pressed a sweating palm to her roiling stomach. *That man could have murdered my dad.*

"Vanna! Over here."

"Please don't call me Vanna"—she smiled her sweetest false grin and tilted her head—"or I will box your ears until they swell up like tomatoes."

"Sorry, sorry, sorry. I thought you liked that."

"Not one bit and I've told you more than once. Let me put this in words small enough for you to understand." She leaned over to his ear and yelled, "Don't call me Vanna."

"Settle down." He backed away and covered his ear. "I've apologized already. We're supposed to be friends. I've known you since you were a baby."

Savannah pressed her lips shut and exhaled a long breath. "As many people have been reminding me lately. Have you been here before?"

Frank shook his head. "Nope, too casual for me. If I'm in the mood for it, I like the New Orleans café toward downtown. The food is one hundred percent authentic NOLA and the jazz is wonderful."

Her eyebrows lowered in disgust. *What a snob without a cause.*

"I haven't either, but I've heard that the blackened shrimp tacos are fantastic. It looks like we order inside."

They joined a line inside the repurposed gas station painted in bright colors. The décor theme was a combination of a Cinco de Mayo Fiesta and the Day of the Dead Festival. There were more decorative skulls per square foot than Disney's Mexican Showcase on steroids.

A young, slim server girl behind a small counter gave them lunch menus. "May I take your order please?"

Savannah quickly scanned it, skimming down to the seafood section. "I'll have the blackened shrimp tacos, spicy, and an order of tortilla chips with hot salsa, please."

The server scribbled the order on a yellow slip of paper. "And something to drink?"

"Sure, unsweetened iced tea."

"Anything else?"

"No thanks. Just lemon."

"The lemon will be at the beverage station."

The girl handed Savannah a clear plastic cup and a brown paper bag full of tortilla chips stapled at the top. "Your order is number fifty-seven and the beverage and salsa stations are to your right. Sit anywhere you like. We'll deliver your order when it's ready. That will be six dollars and thirty-five cents."

Savannah paid and stuffed the change into her pocket. She moved down to the drinks self-serve counter.

Frank sucked in his expansive gut and stood tall. "Hello, girlie. Just bring me a fried grouper sandwich and some extra-large spicy fries."

"Sorry, sir. We don't serve fries. Will tortillas be okay?"

Oblivious, Frank prattled, "Oh, sure. A fried grouper sandwich with double the sauce and an extra-large serving of the spicy fries."

"We don't serve fries here, sir. Would you like our fresh tortillas with a spicy salsa?"

"Oh, that's weird. Sure, just make sure the grouper has extra sauce."

"And your drink?"

"I changed my mind about the Diet Coke. I'll have the Dos Equis in a bottle."

"Of course, sir." The server handed him a quickly opened beer along with a paper bag of tortillas. "Your order is number fifty-eight, sir, and we'll deliver it right to your table." She accepted his payment for the order.

Savannah stood by the beverage station, looked at the selection of empty tables inside, and led Frank to a picnic table outside as far from other patrons as she could get.

Frank plopped down sideways and hitched his legs beneath the table.

Savannah sat across from him. "If we're supposed to be such great friends, why didn't you come to the funeral? I thought you were a person of influence in St. Petersburg."

"It was personal." Frank quickly ripped the bag of tortillas wide open and dipped one of multi-colored chips in Savannah's bowl of taco sauce, then put the whole chip in his mouth. Mumbling around the chip, he asked, "Have you studied the financials of the shop yet? That was the excuse you gave me on Monday."

"That was not an excuse." She tore open her bag of tortillas and loaded one with a moderate amount of the salsa. "I've been going over the books from the past few years and remarkably, given the number of discounted classes Dad and Hugh conducted, it appears that the shop has been holding its own."

"Sheesh." Frank's eyes watered and he grabbed his beer for a huge swig. "That's a hot salsa."

"That's why it's labeled *H-O-T*, Frank."

"Yeah, I got that." He took another swig of his beer. "The classes don't make money themselves.

I make up the loss by selling supplies to the students."

"Yes, my dad told me about your methods. Anyway, adding in the custom commissions, repairs, and restoration projects, Webb's has been enjoying a nice revenue stream." Savannah fingered the sides of the sweating glass of tea, then took a sip.

She glanced up to spot Reverend Kline strolling down the public sidewalk that ran next to the outdoor tables. He stopped mid-stride. "Savannah, how nice to see you twice in one day. Hello, Frank."

Frank made an attempt to stand but couldn't get his bulk over the edge of the picnic table. He half-stood and shook hands with the reverend. "Hey, there. How's it going?"

"Are you conspiring with my prized glass artist here? I think she's going to do an excellent job with the church's stained glass replacement contract, don't you, Frank?"

Frank plopped back down. "That's what we're discussing. I think this kid should go back to her studio out in Seattle."

Reverend Kline looked over to Savannah. "She's definitely not a kid anymore. She can make up her own mind. I just want to go on record that I strongly encourage her to take over the shop and serve the community as her dad has always done."

Frank's face flushed deep rust and he took a large gulp of his beer.

"The Lord's blessings to you, Savannah." The reverend nodded a farewell and walked quickly down the street.

Savannah smiled at his overt support. *I wonder why he's in this part of town. The church is downtown and he lives in the northeast section of town.*

Frank cleared his throat. "Hey, what's with the puzzled look? What does he mean with this confidence in your stuff?"

She fiddled with the paper bag of tortillas that was slowly turning brown with oil. "Hugh was a great teacher and he was better than Dad in his ability to repair difficult pieces. We worked on so many restoration and original design projects together before I won the scholarship to Seattle." She didn't mention that she hadn't done any in years and hadn't been nearly as good as Hugh even when she was well practiced. She wanted to make Frank uncomfortable. Insecure would be even better.

"Yeah, but the shop's steady stream of custom commissions were mostly due to the experience that Hugh brought to the shop. No one was better in the entire state of Florida—no one. You don't have that resource anymore." Frank's ego seemed unfazed. He looked up in delight as a server placed his sandwich on the table, then placed a basket overflowing with three tacos in front of Savannah.

"You don't have him as a resource either. At twelve, I was a better glass artist than you'll ever be. How many projects have you personally completed lately?"

"That's not important. John would have approved."

"Why do you say that when the two of you hadn't spoken for years?"

"That's not entirely true. We finally started to resolve our differences. It was just a few weeks ago."

"I still don't understand. If the two of you were such buddy-buddies, why didn't you come to the funeral?"

"I was out of town on a personal matter."

"What personal matter could be that important?"

"I was at a . . . you know what, never mind. Let's get back to the church commission. I'm telling you, my shop can finish the panel. There's no other place in town that can do it."

"How? I just don't see it. Help me understand." She put her taco back in the basket and stared directly at Frank. She was even more curious about Frank since he wouldn't tell why he missed her father's funeral.

"All right, all right. I have an inside connection with the family that created and installed the panels. They're going to send down two of their experts to finish the panels and conduct some training as well. It will pull my studio to the top in this town."

"Pull it out of the category of student factory? I don't think so."

"You're being shortsighted. Admit that calling in the original factory will more than make up for Hugh's loss."

"Yep, I have to admit that is an excellent plan. I

wouldn't have thought of it myself." *But I have now.*

"Well, never mind about me." Frank lifted his beer. "How about a toast to our soon to be completed deal." He tapped the bottle to her still sitting glass of tea and took another serious gulp of his beer.

"We don't have a deal yet."

He spluttered, quickly set the beer on the table, and grabbed his napkin to muffle the choking cough. "Yet." He coughed again "The key there is *yet.*"

"What will you do with the glass shop if I sell it to you?"

"What kind of question is that? What do you care? I mean, after you sell, you're going back to Seattle, right?"

"I'm trying to assess my options. Besides, your offer wasn't particularly overwhelming. Things are not as I expected with the glass shop. I enjoy teaching."

The server—ALICE on her nametag—returned carrying a tray with a stack of napkins for the table and stowed them neatly in the napkin holder. "Is your order okay? Is there anything else I can get you?"

"I'll have another beer." Frank placed his empty bottle on her tray. His eyes narrowed and he looked across the table at Savannah. "Why would you want to stay?"

"That's my business and none of yours." She pressed her lips into a thin line.

"There's nothing for you here."

Savannah raised her eyebrows. "Like I said, things are more complicated than I thought they were going to be." Edward's green eyes rushed into her mind. "Definitely more interesting."

Determined to enjoy her meal despite Frank's irritating remarks, she sprinkled more salsa on one of the messy, overfilled tacos and bit into the perfectly cooked and spicy shrimp. She savored that bite. "Wow. There aren't many places in St. Pete that can actually pull off seafood tacos. This one hits the nail on the head."

"I don't like shrimp."

She tucked into the dish like she hadn't eaten in years. "One more time, Frank. What are you going to do with the shop if I sell it to you?"

He had just taken a huge bite of his fried grouper sandwich. He mumbled, then lowered the sandwich, reached over to the napkin holder, grabbed several, and wiped his mouth. "I just don't see why you're concerned with that. I have given you a fair offer. I need a decision, now."

"Sorry." Savannah munched her taco noisily to drown the annoying buzzing that was Frank. She was determined to enjoy her meal no matter how much guff he dealt.

"Hey, I've been trying to reach you." Gregory Smythe stood next to their table, hands locked behind his back, rocking back and forth on his heels. "Your wild-haired student, Amanda I think it was, said I could find you here. She didn't say you were lunching with my competition." He threw a nasty look directly at Frank.

Savannah turned her head up. *Walking around in public wearing a cream suit with a bright teal shirt and he calls Amanda wild?* She swallowed quickly, swiped her mouth, and planted a customer smile on her face. "Good afternoon, Mr. Smythe. This is a private meeting. I apologize for the inconvenience, but we need to schedule a time to discuss our business in private. I'm quite busy with the stained glass workshop." She nodded over to Frank. "I also have other business matters to manage."

Frank raised his eyebrows in an excellent Spock impression. "You heard her. She's discussing the matter with me. Get lost."

"Don't make a fuss, Frank. I'm not convinced that your offer is in my best interests either."

Gregory Smythe adjusted his Betty Boop tie, then looked down at Savannah. "This is the real estate business. The early bird gets the sale. When may I discuss my offer with you? Can we meet later this afternoon?"

"I'm teaching this afternoon."

"How about this evening?"

"Fine. If you insist, how about meeting me at the Queen's Head Pub at six? Do you know the place?"

"Yes, I'll be there." He looked at Frank. "I'll be ready to counter any reasonable offer." He turned on his heel and strode noisily down the sidewalk.

Is everyone I know going to find me here? I need to get back to the shop.

Frank leaned over the table. "Come on, Savannah. You've got to give me an answer. You seriously can't be considering this slime bucket as a buyer. He'll tear down the whole block and there'll be nothing left of Webb's."

"And you're planning on closing down Webb's and taking all my clients. If you do that, I may as well sell it to Smythe. I've said it out loud—I'm not ready to decide." She took the last bite of her taco, stood, and placed the napkin in the serving basket. "It's too soon after Hugh's death. Things are not going as I planned at all. I'm not ready to say yes, but I'm not ready to say no either. Sorry, but that's the way it is. You'll just have to deal with it."

I forgot to give her a tip and I won't leave it for Frank to claim that it's from us both. Members of the District support each other.

She pulled the change out of her pocket, popped into the front door of Casita's, and stuffed the dollar bills in the tip jar beside the cash register. As she walked back down Central Avenue, Frank was still working on the tortillas, both his and hers.

A few blocks later, she passed the glass shop and went next door into the Queen's Head Pub. Parked right next to the street leaned Edward's Indian motorcycle. She opened the glass door and stepped into an eclectic mix of British Traditional Georgian furnishings meets everything needs to be painted white décor. It worked. It was cheerfully disrespectful of all things royal. She loved the plaster casting of the Queen mounted above the cash register against the wall behind the bar—a bar with an actual brass foot rail.

As she perched on one of the bar stools, she realized that not only was she looking for Edward, she was very much looking forward to seeing him. When she saw him come around to the bar from the kitchen, his broad smile lit up those beautiful green eyes.

"Hey, what a nice surprise. I didn't think you were ever going to visit me."

I like everything about that. She smiled her brightest. "Buy a girl a cup of tea?"

"Sure. Do you want to try my latest attempt at Earl Grey?"

"Sure, am I the first victim—I mean customer?"

He nodded. "You were right the first time. See, the problem is that I don't like Earl Grey, so I keep trying to make a tea that I like. But it's not working."

"I confess, I absolutely loathe Earl Grey. I have friends who won't drink anything else, but there it is. I'll have what you drink in the afternoon."

"I've already got a pot brewed. Be right back."

He returned with a traditional brown betty teapot and a white mug. "Try this. I've already added some honey." He set down the mug and poured a rusty red tea.

She tasted the brew. "Mmmmmm."

"It's an African Rooibos tea with a strong taste but no caffeine. It's my afternoon choice."

"It's good."

She took another sip, "I've invited Smythe here at six o'clock to discuss his offer for Webb's. Will you be here?"

"Yes, certainly."

"I think it's a good opportunity to get enough information out of him to determine if he has an alibi that we can investigate. You know, where has he been? What might be at stake if he doesn't get everyone signed up? Anything we can find out."

"Good idea. Do you want to be the good cop or the bad cop?"

She smiled. "Good cop, of course."

Chapter 13

Wednesday Afternoon

After lunch, the class tackled one of the most difficult tasks for new students—choosing glass to use in the design. The green glass for the turtle had been supplied for their cutting practice, but they could choose the glass colors for the rest of the sun catcher panel. Savannah led them into the display room and pointed to the open faced vertical shelves that held three sizes of glass sheets.

"It's time to select the remaining glass so you can complete your turtle sun catcher project. The lowest shelf holds the full-sized 24x48-inch glass panels that are ordered directly from the manufacturer. The shelf above holds sheets sized no larger than 24x24 inches. The top shelf of vertical slots holds the smaller pieces of at least six inches square."

Savannah motioned for the class to gather in front of the open shelving, "Now for the best two hints about selecting the glass you want to use for your project." She pulled out a piece of opaque blue glass from the middle shelf. "Hint number one. Be careful. The danger is not limited to the piece you're trying to look at. The danger is in the edges of its neighbors. That's what will cut you. Arthur"—she grinned at him—"be careful. We're running low on Band-Aids."

"Watch out for your neighbors." Faith giggled and poked her sister in the ribs using short, little jabs.

"Stop that." Rachel blocked her sister with a practiced elbow. "Only one of our neighbors is nice to us. Not many people will even talk to us anymore."

Savannah spoke a little louder. "Hint number two. The glass is arranged by color in order from clear glass on the far end to black glass on this end. The patterns are placed in the slots according to the most dominant color in the glass sheet. If you keep your colors near the same tonal value, in other words, light goes with light, dark goes with dark, the entire work will look much better. In short, try to keep it simple."

She placed the glass piece on a large, industrial light box that sat on a large worktable next to the checkout counter. She switched it on. The low buzz of fluorescent tubes accompanied the slender smell of burning dust. It flickered wildly, then stabilized to a soft white glow.

"The light box shows you how the sunlight

would shine through this piece of glass. So, as you're choosing different colors and textures, check the way they look in combination. Go ahead and pick out your pieces. I suggest a medium panel for the major color and one or two small pieces for the accent or secondary colors.

"Please remember to switch off the light box after you've selected your glass." She switched it off. "The bulbs are rather expensive and have to be special ordered. Go ahead and make your selections and remember to try lots of combinations."

"Oh, how I love this part," said Amanda as she began pulling various glass pieces out of the medium rack. She held them up toward the light coming through the front windows. "I think I'm going with a yellow, orange, and purple theme." She selected three transparent panels and arranged them on the light table, then flicked the switch and the fluorescent light shined up through the light box to illuminate each piece. "How's this?"

Savannah looked over her selection. "I love this color palette, however, you have a complication here." She ran her finger over the middle piece of glass. "The orange has a texture, or basically a bumpy pebble-like surface, on one side. If that's what you're going for—great, but it will make the copper foil and soldering steps a little more difficult to apply and achieve smooth edges because you'd have to accommodate for the uneven gaps between the pieces of glass. Are you sure?"

"Oh, yes. This is just the look that I want. Besides, if I run into trouble, you'll help me, right?"

Savannah smiled. "Of course. Let me measure this up and price out your glass."

Before she could start, Arthur had chosen two panels that were from the same slot in the medium rack. "Are these okay, dear?"

Nancy sidled up beside him. "That's just beautiful, dear. It will match the bathroom décor perfectly, honey."

"Good choice," said Savannah. "Those complementary shades of green are all the same type of smooth glass. The sun should come through beautifully and there's a bonus. They are relatively easy to work with."

She stepped back to give her students time to deliberate color and texture in their own space. She heard the bell on the door and turned to see Edward walking through with an old-fashioned thick white mug in each hand.

"It's time for tea, m'lady. Can you take a little break? I hope so. This is my afternoon special blend. It is not Earl Grey."

Savannah toned down the huge smile she felt stealing across her face. "Yes, please."

He ducked into the office and Savannah followed. "What did you find out about Frank?" Edward handed one of the steaming mugs of tea to Savannah. "He has a perfect motive and has been seen arguing with your dad for months."

Savannah took the tea mug and brushed Edward's fingers, causing a flutter deep down in her.

Ignoring it, she inhaled the gently rising steam and sipped. "What's this one?"

"It's a mild white tea with a hint of lavender. Just what you need. It's calming and restorative."

"Where do you get these fabulous teas?"

"There's a local tea shop down on Beach Drive called Hooker's Tea. I get batch quantities from the owner and he occasionally features one of my blends. It's a nice hobby. When was the last time you walked around downtown? St. Petersburg has become quite a cosmopolitan city."

"I haven't been down there in years. Dad and Hugh took me out to dinner the last time I was here a couple years ago. It's like a European village. I've missed so much. Sadly, I usually just flew in for a quick visit and then turned around back to Seattle."

"You're going to be surprised and I'm the one who wants to surprise you. Let's have breakfast followed by a long walk downtown."

"I'm so distracted right now."

"How about on Sunday? You don't have classes. Say yes. Yes?"

Savannah masked her rising blush with another sip of the tea. "Breakfast? I love breakfast. It's my favorite meal. That sounds perfect."

She turned around to gaze out the windows of the shop. "Back to your question. No. I did not find out anything about Frank. He's definitely hiding something because he got touchy and changed the subject when I asked him why he didn't come to the funeral. He was pressing me pretty hard to sell the shop to him and go back to Seattle."

She glanced toward the custom workshop and thought about the large panel awaiting completion on the worktable. "I'm not sure that I'm up to this job. It might be better for the reverend's church panels if I turn it all over to Frank."

"That's nonsense. You're talking rubbish."

"Edward, be nice."

"You don't need nice. You need a reality check."

"But, I'm—"

"I've heard it all from John. You got a bleeding scholarship at Pilchuck Studios in Seattle. That studio is so famous they only dole out one a year. One. A. Year. There were thousands of applicants. Your dad and Hugh taught you everything they knew. You are perfectly able to complete the panels. Don't be daft, luv."

Savannah smiled. "That's nice of you to say, but I'm of two minds about continuing."

"Jacob is amazing. He's a big help and John said he was coming up to speed like no one he'd ever taught."

"Right. I'm not thinking straight about this. I appear to be feeling sorry for myself."

"You wouldn't be normal if you didn't."

"I do need to hire a part-time worker to cover my lunchtimes. Rooney needs me to spend some time with him and I need a break from the shop."

"What about Amanda?"

"Amanda? I thought she worked full-time at the nursing home."

Edward shook his head. "Nope, she works part-time, day or night, I'm not sure. Primarily, she's her mother's caregiver so it's a good way to check up on the quality of care, but it isn't yet a burdensome occupation."

"Would she really want to do both?"

"She would love it. She's been taking classes here for a couple years now, probably so she has somewhere to go that isn't full of folks who are dealing with terminal sickness. I don't know of anyone who cares as much about Webb's Glass Shop as she does. Well, except for Jacob."

"I think that's a great idea. She would be great with customers as well." *Am I crazy for hiring someone when I'm just planning on leaving? Do I actually want to stay? I worked my way up to a joint exhibit in Seattle. Am I going to give that up, can I?*

Maybe not, but she had to solve the murders before she left town, for her own safety and Jacob's.

"I'll ask her," she decided, "though it may be very, very temporary."

The front door bell rang and Savannah walked out into the display room to encounter two women dressed in white coveralls. "What's going on! Has there been a chemical spill in the neighborhood? What's wrong?"

"No, nothing like that." said the taller woman. "Are you Miss Savannah Webb?"

Savannah nodded.

"I'm Sandra Grey, forensic investigator for the city of St. Petersburg and this is my assistant, Loraine Marshall." She gestured back to a younger, shorter version of herself. She held out a small white business card with quiet authority.

Savannah took the card and ran her finger over the crisp embossed St. Petersburg Police Department icon and noticed the same icon on the sleeve of their coveralls. She looked up. "Why are—"

"We're here to search the workroom where the body of Hugh Trevor was found."

"Oh, I see." *They're taking this seriously now. Who is their prime suspect? Should I be worried?*

"We'll need complete privacy. We ask that you please do not enter the room while we're collecting evidence."

"Which is the room?" said Sandra, waving her hand between the custom workshop door and the entry to the classroom.

Savannah pointed to the custom workshop. "It's there. Hugh was found in that room. It contains an extremely fragile and expensive stained glass panel. Can I help?"

"I'm sorry. That's not permitted."

"It's worth thousands of dollars and contains some very rare cathedral glass. It would be difficult if not impossible to replace any damaged pieces at this point."

"We've worked around valuable works of art before. Don't worry. We'll be very careful around the panel."

"I'm not worried about the panel. I'm worried that you might cut yourselves. There are shards everywhere. They can cause serious injury if handled improperly. Are you sure I can't help you?"

Sandra started toward the door. "We'll take extra precautions. Thank you very much for the warning."

"When can we have the workshop back?"

"We won't be here long."

"I've got a competitor who would love to take this vital contract away from me if he can prove to our client that I can't deliver."

"We'll be as efficient as possible. If we need your help, I'll ask."

She and Loraine walked over to the custom workshop and tried the door. It was locked.

Loraine nodded her head to Savannah. "On second thought"—she sent Savannah a friendly wry grin—"you could help out by unlocking the door."

Savannah grabbed her dad's set of keys and found the one to the custom workshop. She unlocked the workroom and opened the door wide.

Sandra nodded her thanks. "By the way, we'll also need to take fingerprints of everyone who has been working at Webb's and also all of the students who have recently taken classes. We'll do that right after we've finished in here." Sandra and Loraine stepped in and closed the door with a sharp snap.

Savannah felt Edward right beside her. He whispered in her ear. "I think this means that they believe you."

She whispered back "Yes, and I think this also means that we should be worried. Very worried."

Chapter 14

A fter the forensics ladies had taken everyone's fingerprints, including Edward's, Savannah had dismissed the class and poked her head into the custom workshop. It was completely undisturbed and not a single piece of *The Last Supper* was out of place. It was impossible to tell what they had accomplished, except that Hugh's coffee cup was missing.

They must have taken it.

She closed up the shop, chuckling at Jacob asking in complete seriousness if they wanted Suzy's prints as well. Walking next door, she entered the Queen's Head Pub for the second time. On her last fly-in fly-out visit from Seattle, the building had consisted of a derelict abandoned gas station of the 1950s variety. Now it was the hot spot for British Fusion cuisine. The transformation was amazing. Edward had kept all the architectural details and embraced the vintage feel of the building.

Even though she was a bit early, she spied Smythe precariously and loudly perched on one of the bar stools with a bottle of Bud Light in front of him. He was smoothing and adjusting the fit of his Betty Boop tie to perfection for the selfie he was taking.

He's in a British pub with an opportunity to taste authentic ale, but no—he's drinking a Bud Light. It's official. He's a jerk.

Shaking her head, she walked up to the bar and pulled out the bar stool that was snuggled up right next to him. She dragged it at least two feet away from him and perched with her heels resting on the bottom bar of the stool.

He turned to her at the sound of the stool scraping on the polished cement floor. "Hey! Thanks for meeting me. What would you like to try? You could order a sampler if you want to taste their imported beers. Apparently they specialize in British ale."

Savannah looked over at the long row of taps behind the bar. "No thanks. Not a sampler. Maybe some other time." She turned to the petite buxom blond bartender wearing a NICOLE name tag. "I'll have a pint of Guinness, please."

Nicole nodded and pressed a pint glass over the cold rinse fountain, then tipped the glass to the proper angle and pulled the brown liquid with its creamy head to about two inches from the rim. She set it aside to settle and smiled at Savannah. "Welcome to the Grand Central District. Edward says you're here from Seattle. That's a long way."

"Thanks, Nicole. It's a long way in distance, but not so far in culture. A lot of things here remind me of Seattle."

Nicole smiled to reveal a dimple in her left cheek. "Not the weather."

"No, not the weather." Savannah laughed. Turning back to Smythe, she asked, "So, how long have you been in town?"

He wiggled to a marginally less uncomfortable perch. "I've been here a couple weeks scouting the candidate property opportunities in and around the Grand Central District and the Midtown area just south of here."

"By a couple weeks, do you mean more than two?" Savannah noticed that Nicole was gently topping off her Guinness and placed it on the beer mat in front of her. Lifting the cool glass, she admired the color, then took a short sip quickly followed by a thirsty drink of the rich, dark ale.

Smythe took another sip from his bottle of Bud Light. "Yeah, well, I guess it's really more like a month. But back to business, how much longer am I going to have to wait to get a contract on the shop?"

Why do I find this disgusting? He's only doing his job. Oh, I remember. His job is disgusting.

"Where are you staying? At the beach?"

"No, no, too pricy. Corporate limits, you know. I'm at the Hollander Hotel near downtown. I negotiated a great weekly rate. Do you have an answer to my question?"

"You'll have to do better than Frank Lattimer." She took another sip of the Guinness. "He's given me an almost fair offer and he won't be tearing down the whole block for yet another huge super store."

"That's an emotional response, not a business decision." His voice jarred her nerves with a whining tone. "Whatever you decide, the rest of the owners will follow. I've again talked to most of them when I surveyed the buildings for estimated demolition costs and they want to know what Webb's is going to do before they sign anything."

"A responsible business owner evaluates all aspects of a decision and takes into consideration the health of the community."

"That sounds a bit naive."

"Naive or not, that is something my family has held close to our hearts for decades. My dad started this business over thirty years ago. My grandfather ran a motorcycle repair shop here nearly fifty years ago."

"You are not your dad or even your grandfather," said Smythe.

"Did you even attend my father's funeral?"

"No, I didn't. I've never been to a funeral and I'm not starting now."

"So then where were—"

"Hello chaps. What are you two conspiring about?" Edward appeared by their table and stood tall between their stools with his arms folded. He looked at Savannah and then at Smythe and then again at Savannah. "Have you sold Webb's Glass Shop to this worm, yet?"

Smythe stood up, his bar stool scraping on the floor like fingers on a chalkboard. Standing, he was no taller than when he was perched on the bar stool.

Edward furrowed his brow and looked at Savannah. "You didn't tell me you were coming here to meet Smythe," he lied smoothly.

Savannah suppressed a smile. He was taking the bad cop routine in stride.

Edward tilted his head down to Smythe. "Nicole told me you were here."

Smythe blurted, "Hey, it's not like this is a date or anything. Don't get riled up. We're talking business. I'm not trying to take over your turf."

Edward held his hands palms up. "Savannah isn't *turf* as you so politely put it. You have to look at things from my point of view. I'm deeply interested in what happens between you two. I've put everything I've got into this place and the business is beginning to enjoy a large following. My whole heart and soul goes into running this pub, you know"—he pointed his thumb at Smythe—"in the same block this bloke wants to buy up and put me out on the street and probably out of the country."

Savannah smiled at Edward. "Excellent point. I don't have anything to hide in my dealings with Smythe here, and since you have a stake in this, why don't you join us. Let me buy you a pint."

Edward smiled. "Thanks for the offer, but as I said, it's my pub. You don't need to buy." He grabbed an empty bar stool and placed it between her and Smythe, making a small triangle. He perched one leg onto the stool and glanced behind the bar. "Nicole, a cold Stella Cidre would be very welcome." He turned back to Savannah and Smythe. "Now, catch me up, please."

The real estate developer grabbed his Bud Light and dragged his screeching bar stool as close as possible to Savannah. He looked pointedly at her. "We were discussing a fair offer for Webb's Glass Shop in light of supporting the wishes of the other business owners on the block." He stretched his collar and smoothed his tie down along its entire length.

Savannah gave a sideways look at Edward, then turned to Smythe. "So, in the month you've been here, you've gathered the future wishes of everyone in the Grand Central District and you believe it is their desire to demolish all the shops and turn the space into a super store?"

Edward looked at Smythe. "You've been here a month? Why didn't you contact our district association when you arrived?"

"I just told Savannah—" His voice began to shake so he cleared his throat. "I just told Savannah that I was investigating another location in the Midtown neighborhood. It seemed very promising, but in the end, I just didn't think that neighborhood could support a super store." Betty Boop got another smoothing adjustment.

"I thought you had talked to my dad quite some time ago," said Savannah.

"No, it was only about two weeks before"—he

cleared his throat again and took another sip of his Bud Light—"before his heart attack. Things would be a lot simpler now, if he were still alive."

Edward leaned forward between Savannah and Smythe to place his downed cider on the bar. He signaled Nicole for another by pointing to his empty glass. Nicole showed that dimple and took the glass.

Savannah scrunched her face. "I don't understand. Why does that make things simpler?"

"Oh, didn't I tell you? Your dad had agreed to sell and also convince the others. It was a handshake, but basically a done deal." Betty Boop got another full adjustment and several smoothing strokes down the full length of the tie.

"That's rubbish." Edward stood and looked down on the red-faced Smythe. "He would have told me. Why are you lying?"

"Look," Smythe croaked. "I'm not going to discuss my business practices or," he looked over to Savannah, "personal whereabouts here in public. I've got to go. Savannah, I've made my position clear. After you've come to the right decision, give me a call when you're ready to deal." He handed her another business card. "I've prepaid the tab, so enjoy yourselves on me." He scraped the bar stool back and quickly left Queen's Head.

Savannah motioned for Edward to use Smythe's stool and appreciated his long, lean grace in such close proximity. "That was certainly not what I was expecting."

"Not what I thought at all." Edward reached

for the cider that Nicole placed in front of him. "How much lying would you need to do to—"

"If Dad was going to sell, Smythe wouldn't have poisoned him."

"Yes, but the other explanation is far more chilling."

"What?"

"That he was lying his butt off just to keep off the list of possible murder suspects."

"Then for the record, he's at the top of my list." She drained the last of the Guinness. "We need to see where he was when Dad and Hugh died."

"How do we do that?"

"I don't know at the moment, but I'm going to figure it out."

"Brilliant," said Edward. "I'll brainstorm as well."

It feels good to have people helping me. Savannah fingered her empty pint glass. Her eyebrows lifted. "Wow, this was almost as good as the Guinness in Dublin. It's better than I expected by a long shot."

Edward smiled. "You have exceptional taste in beer."

"That's another reason I think Smythe might be lying."

"What reason?"

"Who drinks Bud Light in a British pub? Liars, cheaters, and killers. Oh my."

Chapter 15

Wednesday Evening

Savannah parked the van in the church lot. She automatically pulled up against the hardy oleander bushes into the same parking space her family always used. It felt surreal that she was the only one who would be looking out for it. Like her dad, she usually arrived early to any appointment or event.

She recalled that he always said, "For me, on time means I'm late." She felt uncomfortable that she had arrived a bit late, quite a bit late.

The funeral was only three days ago, but it feels like an eternity . . . and also like a moment ago. I'm back too soon. Things are going too fast.

Glancing at her watch, she realized it was already twenty minutes until eight. The 7:00 PM Grief and Bereavement Counseling meeting had to be well under way and practically ready to end.

After talking to Edward and running home to take care of Rooney, she had completely misjudged her timing.

She hurried down the stairway just right of the entrance and walked softly down the tiled hallway. It was a nervous, spooky dark because several of the overhead fluorescent bulbs were burnt out.

Savannah stood outside the community room and looked through one of the windows in the double door. About fifteen members sat in folding chairs arranged into a circle with Reverend Kline a little separated from the rest of the participants.

The slim man sitting to the left of the reverend was reading something aloud from a red leather journal he held open across his knees. "Mostly I see her in the kitchen pulling dishes from the dishwasher and telling me about our plans for tomorrow."

This is ridiculous. I'm not ready to read from a journal. I'm not ready to write *in a journal.*

She thought the best thing to do was to talk to Reverend Kline for a few minutes after the meeting broke up. She backed out of their sight line and watched as the next person began to read from another journal.

I'm really not ready for this. Why would Reverend Kline think I need this kind of help? I'm a little emotional, but certainly not crippled. I've got bigger things to do. I need to find out who killed Hugh and my dad.

Not wanting to eavesdrop on another recital, Savannah took the stairs up and walked slowly down the sanctuary aisle, recalling the large crowd that had been there on Sunday afternoon for her dad's service. Frank had been conspicuously absent.

She stepped up to the altar and realized that the Russian icons hanging just below the north window were a different set from the ones she remembered hanging there during the memorial service. She had a clear memory of them because that was where she'd focused her eyes to avoid looking at the coffin.

This collection was very faded with large cracks running through the figures. Most of the delicate gold foil had worn away to just a few stray flecks.

I guess the reverend rotates the collection.

She returned down the aisle and stood underneath the beautiful stained glass *Last Supper.* It was dark outside and the streetlight wasn't angled properly so it was difficult to make out details. Even in the poor light, she could tell that the craftsmanship was superb. The solder joins were practically invisible and the painted segments stunning. It was easy to lose herself completely in the glass. She recognized the seed of fear in her stomach. *What if she couldn't replicate this exquisite panel?*

She made a mental note to come back during the day to get some reference photographs. Although there were already a pile of them in the custom workshop, she preferred to make a personal study of a commission piece.

She pulled out her phone and took a quick reference photo, forgetting that the flash would fade most of the detail until she saw the washed out image blink onto her screen. *How am I ever going to find someone to help me do this? Ugh. Maybe Frank's idea of hiring someone from the original company who might be ready to move south to St. Petersburg might be the best approach. That would annoy him. Enough reason to try it.*

Her watch said two minutes past eight when she heard the noisy chatter of the group breaking up and making their way up the stairs. The sounds were getting closer and the tinkle of their companionable laughter was more than she could bear.

It's too soon.

Anxieties gripped her and accelerated the beating of her heart. She rubbed the center of her chest.

It's too soon.

She took a last glance at the timeless beauty of *The Last Supper. I'll be back when I'm ready. I promise.* She bolted out the door like a cat that suddenly discovered it was in the wrong room.

Pulling away in the van, she looked back at the entrance. Reverend Kline had walked out behind her. He stood on the bottom step with one hand on his hip and the other waving her a farewell. She felt a moment of relief. He didn't look disappointed at all, even though he had wanted her to come.

He's trying to tell me it's okay. That's good.

Driving home took only a few minutes, but her thoughts returned to the nagging question of finishing the panels. Maybe she should trust her skills as much as her friends did. She should also trust in the selection process for her scholarship.

Savannah tossed her keys into the Craftsman-style pottery bowl on the table by the front door. At least Rooney hadn't sounded his intruder bark. But he didn't run to greet her either. From the central hallway, he eyed her with a steady sullen gaze and returned to her dad's bedroom. She heard his nails clicking on the wooden floor as he turned three times and plopped down on the small pile of T-shirts still beside the bed.

There would have been no question of him sleeping in the bed with her dad. That was rule number one in the Webb household—no sleeping with the pets.

It was a bit early for the last walk of the day, but she felt restless and couldn't settle to television. She stepped over to the built-in bookcase beside the fireplace. A shelf had been dedicated to puzzle mysteries—Agatha Christie's *The Clocks*, Umberto Eco's *The Name of the Rose*, and the complete works of Arthur Conan Doyle.

She absently ran her finger along the spines of her dad's first-edition collection of novels by Dan Brown and beside each one was an advanced review copy released a few months before publication. She grabbed the one that was sticking out a bit, *The Da Vinci Code*, and opened to the title page.

"To John, thanks for your help. I couldn't have done it without you. Your cipher friend, Dan Brown."

She pulled out another and it also had a personal inscription. Curious, she flipped to the acknowledgment pages, but there was no reference to a John Webb.

I wonder how Dad helped. This collection must be worth a mint.

She wandered back to the sofa, but wasn't able to get into the novel. Casually reading a novel seemed frivolous so soon after Dad and Hugh's deaths.

The second cipher was once again resting on the dining table next to her morning coffee cup. She picked up the onionskin and then put it back. No one could figure it out, but they could continue investigating without it . . . she hoped. At least she had plenty of excuses to talk to Frank and Smythe. Hopefully they would give her something to go on. *The world and its problems can wait. I'm not ready to go further with this.*

She rinsed the cup in the original porcelain farm sink and put the kettle on to boil for some strong mint tea. *Maybe that will calm my nerves.* She took her brewed cup over to the couch and tucked her feet beneath her. How many evenings had they sat this way and talked about her day in school and his day in the shop?

Not enough in her view. Not enough. *I should have come home a lot more. I regret it.*

The phone rang and the caller ID displayed KLINE. Her head drooped and she automatically ran through a hundred excuses. Maybe she should let the answering machine take the call.

Do the right thing. Answer.

She picked up the cordless phone. "Hello, Reverend."

"Good evening, Savannah. Did I see you in the parking lot tonight?"

"Yes."

"What happened? Why didn't you come down for the meeting?"

"I'm not sure, but I suspect I'm not ready to talk to strangers about things."

"Even if this group of strangers are kind and supportive?"

Savannah walked down the hallway to stand in her dad's bedroom doorway. Rooney lifted his head from the floor to look at her.

"Even so. It's too soon for me. I need a little more time."

"I understand that you feel that way, Savannah, but those feelings are likely making the grief worse for you. If you meet with us, you will feel less isolated."

"I'm—"

"Please don't make a decision yet. How does a private meeting sound to you? Just a few meetings until you're comfortable. How does that sound?"

"That doesn't sound so scary."

Rooney had laid his head back down on the floor. She felt the wisdom of a dog's patient wait.

"I think that would work for me."

"Good," said Reverend Kline.

She could hear pages flipping.

"I have a free half hour on Friday at two-thirty."

"Not this week. I'm teaching an all week workshop. It's in session from ten to four each day."

"I'll move a few things around and you can come by after your workshop ends tomorrow. It will be a quick private one-on-one session. I don't think you realize how much help you need."

I'm not a baby. I'm doing fine. "Okay. I'll be there, but I can't stay very long. I have to let Rooney out for his run. I appreciate all the trouble you're going through to help me. Thanks."

"It's my job and my joy. Bless you, Savannah."

She replaced the phone in its charger stand and picked up Rooney's leash. "Time for a walk." She shook the leash and made a real effort to put some cheer in her voice. "Let's go, boy."

Rooney got up and poked his head out from the bedroom door to look at her. He walked toward her so slowly it looked like he was slogging each individual foot through neck-deep mud.

She clipped the leash to his collar, stooped to take his head in her hands, and looked into his amber eyes. "I know how you feel, Rooney, but apparently, life goes on. And we need to go on with it."

His tail barely wagged twice.

They went out together dragging the weight of the universe behind them.

Chapter 16

Thursday Morning

A westerly weather front swooped in overnight and turned into a dark, dreary impromptu downpour. Savannah struggled to hold her umbrella against the gusty winds while unlocking the back door of the shop. Her head stayed mostly dry, but her jeans were soaked and her sneakers were damp and squeaked like ducklings on the floor.

Folding up the umbrella and shoving it in an old crock by the door, the rain stopped in typical Florida fashion. She recognized an odd feeling that things were not as they should be. The shop was quite dark because of the rain, but it didn't feel right. "Left of center" is what her dad used to say. Switching on the light, she could see that her stacks of business papers had been moved. She always kept her paperwork aligned to an exact square with precise right angles. These stacks were a tiny bit askew. The second from the bottom desk drawer had not been completely closed, too. She stiffened. Someone had been in there looking for something.

Her throat tightened. A shiver ran down her spine to the heel of her damp shoe. The thought of someone pawing—no not pawing, but rather meticulously searching through the desk left her feeling vaguely dirty. She heard a tap at the front door.

"I'll be right there, Edward," she said loudly, just in case the intruder was hiding in the shop. "Coming over to bring me coffee is so nice." She ran to the door and unlocked it as quickly as her shaking hands could manage.

"Why are you yelling?"

"Someone has been here searching through the desk." She locked the front door, grabbed his upper arm, and dragged him back to the office.

Edward struggled to keep the tray steady to avoid slopping coffee everywhere. "Hey, be careful. I don't want to wear the coffee. What's the matter?"

She pointed to the desk. "See, someone has searched through my papers."

Edward was silent for several long seconds. "I don't see anything. Did you get any sleep last night?"

"Argggghhhhh!" She stretched her hands up into fists. "I can't believe you don't believe me.

Well, yes, I do believe you don't believe me. I wouldn't believe me if I didn't know how I keep things organized in here." She turned, then plopped down suddenly in the office chair and put her head in both hands. "I think I'm going crazy."

Edward pulled one of the sliding work trays out of the desk and put the coffee tray down. "Okay, I believe you." He turned around. "Let me make sure the searcher has gone."

Savannah could hear his footsteps tromping through the shop as he checked behind cabinets and opened all the doors. She sat at the desk and straightened the paper stacks, minutely adjusted the contents of the drawers, and shut them completely flush. It was silly, she knew, but nevertheless it made her feel better.

"All clear. It's just us." Edward pulled up the side chair and sat. "So, basically, someone *very* carefully looked through the papers on the desk. Why?"

"Good question."

"Here, drink up." He handed her the coffee and leaned back in the chair. "Some caffeine will help with the thinking. Who has keys?"

"Hugh had a set. I have Dad's set, and Jacob also has a set. I think that's it, but I haven't been around much in the past few years." She took a long, deep drink of the coffee. "The logical culprit is Jacob, but I can't figure out why he would search the desk."

They stared at the pile of papers.

Unless he's the killer.

Savannah shuddered and immediately dismissed
the idea as a natural consequence of sleep depriva-
tion and anxiety.

Even if he did have it in him to kill someone—
she couldn't imagine he did—Jacob loved the
place and the work too much to jeopardize the
people who had brought him there. No, it could
never be Jacob.

A tapping at the front door startled them. Savannah stood. "That must be Amanda. She's enthusiastic. She's starting to come in earlier and
earlier."

"She would make a great assistant office manager. Have you asked her yet?" Edward gathered
up the cups and tray as he spoke. "She needs the
money, you know."

"Not yet."

Edward looked down at her with a serious
look.

"Okay, okay. I'll ask her right away, but she's
going to need a lot of training." She went through
the classroom and the display room and unlocked
the front door. "Good morning, Amanda. You're
nice and early today for such ugly weather." She
held the front door open for her.

Amanda bustled in with her various bags and
stained glass board. "Good morning. I hope this terrible storm front will pass through quickly. The rain
keeps Mother awake at night. I don't know why, but
we finally got her settled well after midnight last
night and then she woke up at five bright and
cheery and called me to ask when I'm coming

over to see her. It's extremely annoying." She put her burdens on the workbench and perched on the stool. "What's going on?"

Savannah walked over to the door of the office. "The office has been searched and I'm a little freaked out about it."

"Did they take anything? Is anything missing?"

"I don't think so. I had pretty much sorted through all the papers and everything looks like it's here. I'll double-check everything later, though."

"What could anyone want?"

Savannah shrugged her shoulders. "It could be someone who wanted to find the offer letters from Frank and Smythe."

"I can't imagine either of them capable of a tidy search," said Edward.

"Desperation might provide enough incentive for either of them to search very carefully. Either one of them could have done this," Savannah said.

Amanda nodded her head toward the custom workshop. "What about the panel?"

They waited for Savannah to unlock the door. "I can't tell if anyone has been in here. I haven't sorted through things here, so I don't know if anything has been moved." She lifted the cover over the panel. It was just as she'd left it. "The panel hasn't been touched. I would know if it had been disturbed. I checked the panel after the forensics team finished their investigation. That's a relief."

They left and went back to the display room. "Well, this is new." She picked up a small white note that rested on the cash register display screen. Written in square block letters in black ink was

SELL WEBB'S
GO BACK TO SEATTLE!

"Well, that narrows it down to literally everyone. Frank, Smythe, me, either of you . . . anyone could have written that." Savannah said as she looked over to Amanda and Edward.

Amanda said, "You have to tell the police that you've been threatened."

Savannah sighed. "You're right. I'll give them a call. But, you know this might be something positive."

"What could be positive about a burglary and being threatened?" Edward waved a hand to the note. "This is a serious threat."

"It means we're getting close and someone is nervous. Nervous enough to risk a burglary charge." Savannah paced around in a small circle. "How can we find out more about Gregory Smythe and Frank Lattimer?"

"Lattimer?" Amanda's voice pitched higher than normal. "Did you say Lattimer?"

Savannah stopped pacing. "Yes. What about it?"

"One of the resident old ladies in Mom's nursing home is a Vera Lattimer."

"Yep, this is a small town. Frank's mother is named Vera and she is the right age to be in a nursing home. I remember meeting her when I was a kid. But there aren't loads of older ladies named Vera. It wasn't a very popular name. It's got to be her. When are you due to work there?"

"My official shifts are Sunday morning and Thursday evening. But since Mom lives there, I can come and go as I please—and I do."

Edward held his hands up. "Hey, what are you two thinking?"

"I'm thinking of visiting Amanda's mother and then looking up an old friend. Vera Lattimer used to stop by the shop when Frank was working here. She might remember me and I can find out where Frank was last week."

Amanda high-fived Savannah. "Awesome plan."

"Let's get ready for class."

Edward mouthed a *See you later* and escaped back to the Queen's Head.

As they walked back to the classroom, Savannah inhaled a quick breath. "Amanda, I've been thinking. It occurs to me that I need some temporary help here in the shop. Is that something you might be interested in doing to help me?"

Amanda squealed with delight, swooped over to Savannah, and embraced her with a full body hug. "Oh, I thought you would never ask. I would love, love, love to work in the shop. Can I start now, right now, please? Tomorrow would be fine, as well, but today is even better."

"Today would be great. I've got to start getting home to have lunch with Rooney. It would be good to take over from my neighbor who has been letting him out. I can only pay you a little above minimum wage, but you would get all your supplies at wholesale prices. Fair warning, new assistant office manager—this may be very temporary. Good?"

"More than good!" She clapped her plump hands together like a child anticipating ice cream.

The front door jangled. Savannah checked her watch. It was still too early to start the class.

"Vanna. Hey, Vanna."

"Good morning, Frank. You have the memory of a goldfish."

"What?"

"I thought I was pretty clear at our meeting yesterday that I want you to call me Savannah, not Vanna. Why are you here anyway? I'm not ready to discuss an offer."

"I want to get this wrapped up as quickly as possible. You know by now that my offer is fair."

"I think your idea of fair is a good deal lower than my initial assessment of the value of Webb's."

"We disagree there. I have some risk factors that you should consider. Maybe even some personal risk factors that might make a real difference in your decision. Is there anything I can do to speed things up?"

"No, there's nothing you can do." She lightened her voice a tone. "By the way, I know you didn't get to Dad's funeral, but when was the last time you saw him?"

"Oh, it hasn't been very long. I can't remember the exact date."

"Days, weeks, months?"

"Nope, just don't remember. My memory isn't as good as it used to be. Are you sure there's nothing I can do to help you decide?"

"In fact, nothing is the best thing you can do to help me. I'll know by the end of the week." She grinned her best customer smile, led him by the elbow toward the door, and opened it. "Definitely by the end of the week."

Frank stopped abruptly. "How is the work on the church panels coming along? Who have you got working on them? It's not just you and the kid, is it? It's a large and important project and you've been away a long time."

"I've got a class starting in a few minutes."

"Now really, you don't want the reverend to have to cancel the contract, do you? That would really upset him to start legal action against you, one of his flock."

"Frank, I said I would give it serious thought and that's what I'm doing." She placed a firm hand flat on his chest and pushed him slowly but definitely out the door. "I'll have a lot more to say at our next meeting."

The twins walked up to the door and fiercely glared Frank out of the way. They barged in by angling their work through the door and on into the classroom. Frank got the message. He silently waved, got in his car, and drove away.

Shortly, Nancy and Arthur Young followed the twins into the shop, and when Savannah entered the classroom Jacob was already in his seat.

Yep, he has a key to the back door all right. Could someone have borrowed it from him? Or did the intruder take the keys off Hugh after he died?

"Is Suzy settled?"

"Yes, Miss Savannah."

"Good morning everyone. This will be a fun lesson, I promise. Today we learn how to apply a thin strip of copper foil to each of the individual pieces of glass. The foil comes on a roll with an adhesive backing like a roll of tape. After that we apply the first layer of solder to form a solid panel. But first, let's make sure that your cut glass pieces are in the right place and fit together snugly."

Savannah walked carefully between the tables. Jacob and Amanda's projects were aligned precisely within the template. "Good work. That's really nice cutting."

She looked over Nancy and Arthur's sun catchers. "Just a little wiggle room here, Arthur." She fingered one of the edge pieces. "This will interfere with the border if it's not straight. There's almost always some room for adjustment within the body of the piece. Unfortunately, this is a little too much out of tolerance. By that, I mean the piece is too big or too little. It's best to replace it with another piece." Arthur nodded and prepared to cut yet one more.

"Let's see how you've done, Nancy." Savannah

pressed the pieces against each other. "See, this is what I mean. This piece is a little long, but its neighbor is a little short so that basically works out. If you like the look, keep it. If you don't like it, trim a little of the bigger piece and cut a new smaller piece."

"Actually," said Nancy, "I like the asymmetrical look of it as it is. It makes it refreshingly different from the run of the mill artwork."

Savannah moved to the twins' worktable and looked at their fingernails. Her stomach sank. They were all painted. How on earth would she be able to tell them apart now?

The twins had placed their sun catchers toward the middle section of the shared workspace so that their pieces reflected like a mirror. Their tools were bookended to the outside edge of the worktable.

"Interesting. Did you make them mirror images because Faith is left-handed?"

"Faith is the left-hander and I'm the right-handed one. It was the only way our mother could tell us apart," said Rachel. "But not everyone catches on to that. You're observant."

"Vital skill in the glass business. Thanks." Savannah looked at their work and fingered the glass pieces to show them how much a few of them were not fitting the pattern well enough to start foiling. "Rachel, if you re-cut this piece"—she placed her finger on one of the central squares—"the whole panel will fit more snugly. It will be easier to solder if the gap between the individual pieces is smaller."

She leaned over Faith's piece. "You've at least two pieces to recut to make a better fit." She fingered an inside piece and one of the edge pieces. "This inside piece is too small and leaves too much slack. Also, if you replace this edge piece with a new one, the border will fit smoothly around the entire panel. It will be much easier for you."

"I only have to do one." Rachel did a little dance jig. "You have to replace two."

Faith flushed red and puffed out her chest. "We're not done yet. In the end, mine will look better than yours. That's the way it always goes. You take an early lead and then I blow right past you."

"What do we do with the leftover glass?" Nancy held up two small bits of her glass, speaking over the twins.

"I'm glad you asked." Savannah grabbed a small dish that was underneath the instructor's worktable on the storage shelf and held it up. "This dish is an example of glass mosaics. All your leftovers can be used up in creating this ancient form of art. The Romans loved their mosaic floors. When you're a little more experienced, you can do more complicated things. Personally, I make kiln-formed earrings."

Savannah left them to it and popped into the office for a few minutes. Sometimes the students made the best progress when the instructor wasn't hovering. Reaching for one of the cards that Officer Boulli had left, she dialed the number, waited for the machine, and punched in his extension.

"Officer Boulli."

"Good morning. I want to report a break-in at Webb's Glass Shop. This is Savannah Webb."

"You again?"

"Yes, Officer, me again. Someone broke into the shop, searched through the papers in the office, and left me a threatening note."

"Okay, okay. Hold your horses."

She could hear him shuffling papers and, based on the loud smack of the phone dropping and the muffled cursing, he apparently knocked over something.

"Okay. Just give me the details and I'll write up the report."

She described her discovery and he assured her that someone would be around to collect evidence.

Dollars to donuts he forgets to report that note to anyone, she thought as she hung up the phone.

She patted Suzy on the head and refreshed the water in her bowl. At the desk, she quickly turned on the computer, opened the browser, and logged into the geocaching database. Searching through the nearby sites, the list displayed her dad's geocache at Crescent Lake. Scanning down the table, she found the title had a line struck through the middle of the words.

She clicked on the title and read the entry displayed under the label CACHE ISSUES. "This cache is temporarily unavailable. Read the logs below to read the status for this cache."

She scrolled down to the log section and a note written using her dad's member name indicated "Until further notice, this cache is temporarily disabled." The date of the log entry was several weeks earlier. She exhaled deeply. The date wasn't early enough to eliminate Smythe as a suspect. In fact, it looked like it was just after he'd arrived in the area to begin his search for a possible location for the Big Value Store.

Logging off, she pulled out the sheet of paper she had been using for calculating the net worth of Webb's Glass Shop. As a small family business, she was quite surprised at how well things were situated. She had known that Webb's was making solid money in the past months, but it seemed as though her dad had been building up the business for years to reach numbers like this.

No wonder Frank was so keen to press his offer. His bid was at least a hundred thousand dollars under its financial value. Smythe's was higher, but still well under the true value.

Returning to the classroom, Savannah demonstrated the process of grinding the cut glass pieces using safety goggles and a little hockey puck–like pusher to press the glass edges against the grinder wheel without grinding her fingers.

She stepped aside. "Who wants to try first?"

"Me, me, me." Amanda raised her hand high.

Savannah tilted her head. "Yes, ma'am. Watch out that you don't take too much away. You can't put it back on."

Amanda ground her piece perfectly. *She has*

been hanging around here quite a bit. That was not the grinding effort of a newbie.

"Amanda, that's a professional job. Why are you taking this class?"

She ducked her head, "Confession time. I've been hoping to get a job here. I love glass and I love this shop. I hope to teach one day. Thanks, again, for giving me a job here. I'm so over the moon."

"I'm glad you're excited, Amanda. But just remember it might be temporary," Savannah responded.

Amanda nodded her head in acknowledgment as one by one, the remaining students stepped up to the grinder with varying levels of success. For once, Arthur didn't put his fingers in danger, though Nancy's professionally manicured nails came a little too close to the wheel for Savannah's comfort.

Ducking into the office while everyone had a turn at the grinder, she meticulously finished sorting and filing all of the paperwork on her dad's desk.

As far as she could tell, nothing was missing from the burglary, but that didn't mean that something disappeared from the stacks that she hadn't gotten to yet. It was also possible that an important paper or even an entire folder could be missing from the filing cabinet. At least she had finished her cleanup, but still felt frustrated about the entire situation. Shoulders slumped, she returned to the classroom.

"Okay. It's time for the copper foil demonstration. Each of you has a package of foil in your kit. Place it flat on your work board and pin it so that it won't unroll. Not so tight that it won't release the foil, but loose enough so that you can pull the foil toward you a few inches at a time."

She walked around the classroom and adjusted some and praised others.

"Okay, we're ready to foil." She picked up one of Amanda's pieces. "Gather around so you can see."

There was a shuffled rustling of movement.

"I can't see," said Rachel.

"Here, stand next to me." Faith pulled her sister by the elbow.

"Good. Take one of your glass pieces"—Savannah held the small square of glass—"and place it on the foil strip about one quarter of an inch from the edge."

She picked up a small tool that looked like a miniature paint roller. "This is called a burnisher and it is used to press the foil solidly onto the glass. This is an extremely important step to—"

The phone in the office rang.

Savannah continued. "—ensure that the solder will adhere smoothly. Now, it's your turn. I'll be right back to check your first foiled piece." She smiled and ran to answer the office phone. "Webb's Glass Shop. How may I help you?"

"May I speak to Miss Savannah Webb?"

"Yes, this is she."

"I'm the managing director of Eternal Gardens where your father was laid to rest. I thought it my responsibility and duty to inform you that we've received a court order from the St. Petersburg Homicide Department to exhume your father."

Chapter 17

Savannah replaced the phone and stood completely still. That was direct confirmation that the police were now taking her suspicions seriously. The roiling in her stomach was evidence of the conflict she felt about wanting to be believed and the consequences of being believed.

She sat so heavily in her dad's chair it let out a high squeak. Focus. *This is what you wanted.*

She picked up the phone and dialed the main number for the police department. "May I speak to Detective Parker?"

"May I tell him who is calling?"

"This is Savannah Webb. It's in connection with the deaths of Hugh Trevor and John Webb."

She was connected very quickly.

"This is Detective Parker, Miss Webb."

"I've just been told that you are exhuming my father's remains for an autopsy. Is this true?"

"Yes, it is. You were my very next call. I will let you know the results of the autopsy as soon as it is finalized."

"So you think he was murdered?"

"I can't really say, Miss Webb. I'll call you when I have more information."

"Who do you suspect?"

Detective Parker paused for several moments. "I'm not at liberty to say just now. When I have something to report, I'll let you know right away. We'll be in touch."

Savannah hung up and placed the phone back on the receiver.

The class stared at her as she returned to the classroom, but she was focused on the class at hand and continued to provide guidance and answer any questions until the time to leave finally rolled around. Amanda kept a constant stream of chatter with Jacob but it was obvious that she could barely wait for the start of the lunch break today so she could ask Savannah about the phone call.

When noon finally arrived most of the students left with the exception of Amanda and Jacob. Savannah felt dazed and couldn't readily recall what she said to her students after receiving the news from Detective Parker.

Amanda and Jacob followed Savannah as she walked into the office and immediately sat down. Jacob picked up Suzy.

"What was that call about?" Amanda's words coming in a rush. "You look upset."

"Yes, I guess I am. They're going to dig up my dad for an autopsy."

Jacob looked straight at her, "That means they believe you now."

Savannah nodded her head.

"Does this change anything? Are we still going to Mom's nursing home?" Amanda's eyes widened.

"As soon as I make a call to Dad's finance manager. For some reason, I keep forgetting to do this."

Amanda looked over her glasses. "It's not like anything much is going on. I'll work on my sun catcher until you've finished your call."

"Okay, I'm going to go home for lunch. See you later." Jacob and Suzy left the office and proceeded to walk out of Webb's.

Finally, Savannah picked up the phone and dialed the number. The phone had barely rung once when it was immediately answered.

"Kevin Burkart, Financial Services."

"Hi Kevin. This is Savannah Webb. I've been meaning to call for several days now."

"Hi Savannah. I've been expecting your call. No problem. Do you want to make an appointment so we can review the financial state of Webb's? I have a meeting with another client for most of the afternoon, but I can squeeze you in tomorrow."

"Maybe next week for a detailed review, but for right now I just need to know if there was anything major that Dad had in the works. I've reviewed the statements that covered the last few months and things look quite good."

"Cash flow, expenses and earnings had been going pretty well for John and except for the loan to the Queen's Head Pub, there are no outstanding liabilities."

"Loan? What loan?"

"Oh, I thought you had met Edward already."

"I have, but he didn't say anything about a loan. How much was the loan for?"

"It's an unsecured loan for thirty thousand dollars."

"What? Why did Dad do that?" Savannah found herself standing.

"I don't know. I urged him to place a lien against the pub, but he refused. He had his way, of course. I'm only the advisor."

"Dad could be stubborn."

Kevin laughed, "That's putting it mildly. Do you want me to start preparing for the sale of Webb's?"

"I'm not sure yet. Things are in turmoil with Hugh's death and I'm trying to find my feet."

"Just let me know what you want to do. The decisions are now yours."

"OK. Thanks, Kevin. I'll make an appointment for early next week."

Savannah sat back down as she hung up the phone. She was trying to figure out why Edward had failed to mention the loan. *He's been so nice to me this entire time—the loan must be why.*

The front bell clanged and Edward called out, "Anyone up for tea? It's a new one."

Amanda followed Edward into the office, "Are there scones?"

He carried in a small tray with blueberry scones and a small ornate teapot with four tiny cups to match. "I've found a new white tea I adore called White Orchid. The flavor is delicate and the caffeine is very low."

He set the tray down on the little table and turned to Savannah, "I think I'm a suspect. Detective Parker stopped by to ask me questions about my business and if anyone could verify my alibi. Of course, I was home alone. So, nope."

Edward looked at Savannah's flushed face and tight lips, "What's wrong?"

"Wrong?" she could hear the near squeak in her voice. "Just when were you going to tell me about the loan?"

"Oh," He looked over at Amanda, then back to Savannah, "I have been trying to tell you since Monday, but—"

"Burkart told me. Really, you couldn't find ten seconds to let me know about something that major? I might have made a terrible mistake negotiating a sale."

"I'm sorry, but I didn't mean to cause any problems. It was just business—"

"I can't talk about it now, please leave."

"I'm sorry, Savannah. Let me—"

"Leave, now!" He picked up the tray and headed back to the pub.

Amanda watched the blueberry scones disappear with Edward. Her sad expression had no effect on Savannah's resolve.

"What a pitiful face," Savannah shook her head, "I'm sorry for that. Let's get a bite on the way to the nursing home."

Savannah and Amanda closed up shop and walked outside towards Amanda's car. Savannah dragged open the heavy passenger door of Amanda's vintage Cadillac and buckled up with the retrofit seat belts. "Where did you get this beauty?"

Amanda was a cautious driver and looked at the rearview mirror and then to the side mirrors and then yet another scan before answering. "This was my mom's car. She only drove it to the hairdresser and then to the Publix supermarket. It was the last car my dad bought her, so we both love it. I still take her to the hairdresser when she's having a good day. It really perks her up. But the car isn't as important as what went on between you and Edward back there. What gives?"

Savannah took a couple of seconds to compose herself before she responded, "Well, it seems that my father loaned Edward thirty thousand dollars, but Edward didn't think it was important enough to mention to me. I found out when I finally spoke to Burkart."

"Oh, wow. I understand why that would upset you. But I'm sure there's a reason why he hadn't mentioned it yet. I bet he was planning on it, Savannah."

Savannah remained mum on the matter as Amanda drove the few blocks down Central Avenue and parked near the Bodega, a Cuban sidewalk café.

They ordered at the walk-up window and carried their fresh sandwiches and drinks out to one of the sidewalk tables. The earlier rain had left the sidewalk with that fresh smell that made them want to linger all day.

Savannah sipped her ginger orange soda. "When I was in the office, I checked on the global geocache database for the one that Dad had used for the cipher that Jacob and I solved to find the onion skin sheet. Dad took the cache down for repair just after Smythe showed up to canvas the area for potential super store locations."

Amanda had just taken an enormous bite. Holding a napkin in front of her lips, she mumbled around the mouthful, "That's suspicious."

"Well, that means Smythe is still in the frame. We need to get more information about him. Maybe we could find some of his selfies on social media. Since he's always taking them, he must be posting them to some site somewhere."

"I would love to try my hand with that," said Amanda. "Who knows what might be out there on slimy Smythe. That would be diabolically fun." She looked over to Savannah. "Oh, I didn't mean that the way it sounded. I meant interesting or challenging."

Savannah smiled. "I understood, Amanda. Don't worry."

They finished their sandwiches, tossed the debris in the trash, and drove over to Martin Luther King Jr. Street North.

As they pulled into the Abby Rehabilitation Center, Amanda said, "They don't call them nursing homes anymore. The new jargon is rehabilitation center or assisted living residence. I don't think it makes any difference inside, but there it is anyway."

Savannah wondered if Amanda was feeling nervous for her to meet her mother. "How long has your mother been here?"

"Oh, let's see." Amanda looked straight ahead and then to the mirrors and then made another scan before answering. "I think it's been five years now. She doesn't have Alzheimer's, but rather it's a bit like that. She has vascular dementia. Some days are pretty good, but the worst days are when she doesn't know me."

"I'm so sorry."

"Thanks, but she's very well taken care of and I get to see her nearly every day. Luckily, she has the type that lets her enjoy the present—not one of the angry or violent reactions to her condition. I'm lucky."

Savannah was not surprised that Amanda considered herself lucky that her mother had the "good kind" of dementia.

They parked and entered through a side door.

Amanda led the way into the pleasant lounge with a low hum of television background and general chatter. "Mom's usually out here trying to find someone to chat to. It's the same conversation every day, but no one seems to mind."

The air held the typical nursing home scents of cleaning products, air fresheners, and old people. The furnishings looked well used, but not tattered. There were amazing arrangements of fresh flowers scattered around the room.

"Hi, Mom. How are you doing today?" She leaned over and kissed a small woman on her mottled cheek. Mrs. Blake was sitting poker straight in a streamlined wheelchair. She wore a purple tracksuit and a shorthaired wig of tight burgundy curls. Given the look of her neon lime sneakers, Savannah would not have been shocked if Mrs. Blake had suddenly launched out of the wheelchair and raced wind sprints around the room.

Amanda dragged up a couple chairs for herself and Savannah and they sat on either side. "Mom, this is my new boss, Savannah Webb. She's John's daughter . . . John who used to run Webb's Glass Shop. Do you remember him?" She took her mother's hand in hers and rubbed the top of the slender, blue-veined forearm.

Mrs. Blake turned to Savannah with a serenely blank stare.

Savannah smiled. "It's nice to meet you, Mrs. Blake. Your daughter is going to be a big help to me in the glass shop. She's so cheerful and courteous with my customers . . . and the other students, of course."

Mrs. Blake nodded and looked pleased. "I'm glad to meet Amanda's friends. Where's Amanda?"

"I'm right here, Mother." Amanda looked up and puffed her cheeks out in a long sigh.

Savannah stood. "I think I'll just look around for Mrs. Lattimer now."

"Go ask them at the reception counter—right through those double doors and down the hall." Amanda pointed. "They should know where she is."

Savannah followed Amanda's directions and met the harried receptionist. She was told that Mrs. Lattimer was outside at the back of the facility. She went back and got Amanda and together they walked over towards the back.

Amanda hung behind as Savannah approached the covered patio. A rather large woman in a bold blue dress was reading. She sat in a sturdy wheelchair beside a large planter full of blooming petunias of every imaginable color.

Mrs. Lattimer looked up with bright clear blue eyes. She removed her reading glasses and let them hang by a sparkling silver chair on her ample bosom. "Hello Savannah."

"You remember me?"

"Of course. Frank talked about you earlier this week. He comes to take me out to lunch on Sundays, Tuesdays, and Fridays. He's a very attentive son."

"Yes, I had lunch with him yesterday. I'm not sure he enjoyed it. Do you mind if I sit with you?"

"I'd be happy for anyone to sit with me." She held up the novel she was reading. "Most of my company nowadays is found in books."

Savannah sat in a white wrought iron chair with a deep cushion. "What are you reading?"

"One of those new thrillers full of bullets, bombs, and sex."

"Really?"

"I'm frail—not dead. This book is fantastic."

Savannah chuckled. "That sounds fun. Frank and I had lunch at the new Mexican taco place just down the street from the shop."

"Oh, we haven't been there yet."

Savannah chuckled, "I don't think he was very pleased with the place. It was quite casual with outdoor seating on picnic tables. Not fancy enough, I suppose. Where did he take you on Sunday?"

"Sunday? Let me think." Mrs. Lattimer furrowed her brow and then looked sideways at Savannah with a tiny smirk forming in her cheek. She leaned over and took Savannah's hand patting it softly. "Are you trying to find out about Frank's little conspiracy to buy Webb's?"

"What?" Savannah leaned forward. "What conspiracy?"

"Well, honey, Frank has been having a hard time lately, and although I don't think it is my place to tell you about his affairs, Frank and I disagree on this little scheme of his. He tells me everything. Well, he may not in the future, but I'll tell you. After all, you are John's little girl."

"What's going on? I don't understand."

At the strident tone of Savannah's voice, Amanda walked over to stand behind Savannah's chair.

Mrs. Lattimer noticed the movement, but continued to pat Savannah's hand. "His clever plan was to bribe the pub owner next door to Webb's. I think his name is Edward." She rubbed her temple. "Yes, Edward." She sat very still for a moment, "Where was I?"

"Clever plan?" prompted Savannah.

"Yes, dear. It is a bit underhanded, which is why I'm telling you."

"But you haven't told me anything yet. What plan?" Savannah could hear the frustration in her voice and took a long breath. *Calm down. She'll tell you in her own time.*

"Yes, the plan was to have Edward get close to you, friendly, if you will. Then Edward was to convince you to sell Webb's to Frank rather than the real estate developer."

"But—"

"He was offering to forgive a large loan that John had made to the pub in exchange for ensuring that you sold Webb's to Frank. It is a clever ploy, don't you think?"

"I'm stunned," Savannah leaned back in the soft chair. "Stunned."

She felt a small poke on her shoulder and Amanda whispered, "Sunday—where was Frank on Sunday."

"Oh, yes," Savannah leaned forward, "I really only wanted to know if Frank took you out on Sunday. I mean, since we're being so forward, was he in town?"

"Well, he didn't pick me up for lunch on Sunday. He said he had other plans, but wouldn't talk about them on Tuesday. You're such a lovely girl,

I'm sure you can get him to talk about his weekend. Just give it a try, sweetie."

Back at Webb's, Savannah and Amanda went into the office. Savannah sat in the squeaky chair and buried her face in her hands, "I can't believe that Edward would collude with Frank. I expect that sort of behavior from Frank," she lowered her hands and looked at Amanda. "I expected better from Edward."

"I'm sure that there's an excellent explanation for this."

"He could have explained it all earlier."

"Really?" Amanda lifted an eyebrow.

She pressed her lips thin. "Oh, right. I made him leave."

Amanda shook her head. "Okay, what's next?"

"We need to try to nail down Smythe. He was very practiced at avoiding answering personal questions. Edward and I just wasted our breath."

She booted up her dad's antiquated computer, and clicked on the Web browser. It was painfully slow—the operating system was out of date. It didn't even have a Wi-Fi feature—another thing that would have to change. Amanda stood beside her tsk-tsking and shaking her orange curls at John Webb's obvious aversion to modern electronics.

"Well, I know he was into advanced communications technology when he worked for the government, but in private life he wanted nothing to do with it," Savannah said.

"He also didn't need much for running Webb's."

"True. He sent orders by mail, received glass by UPS, and delivered projects personally. He didn't need the Internet. Ah, finally." Savannah entered a string into the browser. GREGORY SMYTHE, then clicked on the SEARCH icon.

After waiting another eon, the first hit returned an article in the *Tampa Bay Times* about the proposed Big Value development project. There were more hits on social media sites of a Gregory Smythe on Facebook and Twitter. Skimming down the page, she stopped on an article describing the arrest of Gregory Smythe for breaking and entering into an abandoned warehouse in the Midtown section of town.

The bell over the door jangled as the rest of the class came back for the afternoon session.

"Okay, Okay. I'm hurrying." Savannah scanned the search results. "Okay, Amanda, we finally found something. Smythe has a record. He was arrested—when?" She squinted and peered closer to the small screen. "Oh, it indicates that it was over a month ago. That was right when he began to research locations for the super store."

"Then he's probably the one who broke in here and left you that note."

"Worse than that. He's the one with the most to gain if Webb's is sold for the development project. It's also the tipping point for all the other merchants. If Webb's sells out, then the rest of the block will follow."

Amanda jumped up and down. "This is the guy."

"Hold on. All we've done is find an arrest record. That's a long cry from being a double murderer. We need a lot more proof."

Amanda still smiled. "It's a good start. Wait until Edward hears about our adventures. He'll be jealous."

"Edward? I'm not over the fact that he colluded with Frank," Savannah replied testily. "He's got some serious explaining to do."

Chapter 18

Savannah parked and entered the church through the front doors just under the gorgeous stained glass panels of *The Last Supper*. It was always a shock to see the faces and hands disappear into the plain sienna-colored glass. The lustrous-painted elements showed up from the street after dark only when the panels were lit by the sanctuary lights.

The walk to Reverend Kline's office allowed her to look up and admire the stained glass panels. As she walked up the aisle to view the row of Russian icons, she noticed that they were again different from the ones she'd noticed on Wednesday night. *There must be quite a collection if they can be rotated every few days.*

Reaching the office, she knocked on the open door.

"Welcome, Savannah," said Reverend Kline as he stood behind his desk and signaled for her to sit in the guest chair. He sat back in his red leather tufted chair and steepled his fingers, resting his elbows on the arms of the chair. "Thank you for agreeing to this one-on-one meeting with me. I can't tell you how important I think it is for you to have professional support through this trying time. How are you feeling?"

Savannah adjusted her position in the wooden chair to something a little more comfortable. She wished for a cushion to support her. "I feel stressed and lonely."

"What is the source of the stress? Is it the investigation into your father's death? I heard about the exhumation of his body from Eternal Gardens."

"Yes, that's a big part of it. Just thinking about a formal police investigation is unnerving. The realization that the culprit could be someone I know is worrisome."

"That is a troubling thought." He leaned forward and clasped his hands together. "How are the police coming along with their case?"

"That's another source of worry." She shifted in the chair again. "The officer sent out to investigate is beyond incompetent. The police have finally assigned a more senior and sensible detective to head up the investigation into Dad and Hugh's deaths."

"Have they any suspects?"

"Unfortunately, I don't know exactly. I've asked, but that's not the kind of information they're willing to share with me. They are keeping me apprised of any developments regarding Dad's autopsy."

"Any news there?"

"No, it's too soon. Officer Boulli, that's the irritating one, said that if the deaths do turn out to be murder, Jacob would be the prime suspect."

"Jacob?"

"Yes, Jacob. Isn't that ridiculous? Because of that, I've started to investigate on my own—with Amanda and Edward's help."

Reverend Kline sat straight up in his chair. "Why would you do that?"

"Dad left me a coded message. I haven't figured it out yet, but I think I can get to the bottom of it."

"That's a daring move, Savannah. Do you think such overt action seems wise?"

"It's what Dad wanted me to do. If not, he wouldn't have left the ciphers."

"Of course, of course. He was a very intelligent and brave man." The reverend paused so long Savannah thought the session was over and she started to rise.

"Sorry, sorry." He motioned for her to sit. "I was just trying to take in your situation. So tell me a little more about any other areas of tension."

"I'm tackling issues with what to do about Webb's. I had planned to sell it to Hugh—and he agreed with that—but now that's not possible. So that's a major headache. Frank Lattimer is pressing his case to buy the shop."

"And the loneliness?"

"Continuing with the class has been amazing. When I was a kid helping Dad out with some of his classes, I saw teaching as an interruption to my projects. I didn't understand how good it feels to share with others what I've learned."

"That's good."

"But it's tough being at home. I keep expecting Dad to walk through the door any minute. I am getting along better with his dog, though."

The reverend nodded. "Yes, I can see how that would be a comfort. Now, let me cover just a few basics for our first session and then we'll formulate an action plan to easily allow you to attend the group sessions. How does that sound to you?"

"Action plan? That sounds pretty formal."

"It's counseling jargon for taking some small, intermediate steps so that you feel comfortable enough to attend our weekly group. It's not magic or rocket science, merely some common sense strategies that I'm going to work with you to create. Are you comfortable with that?"

Savannah nodded.

"Good. Let's go for the first step. I want you to know the stages of grief and try to identify which stage you think you're occupying. This is based on the 1969 book by Elisabeth Kübler-Ross, *On Death and Dying*. I find it clear and easy to relate to her descriptions of the stages of loss." Leaning forward, he handed Savannah a well-used copy of the book.

"I can get my own," she said.

"Not necessary. We have been using the same fifteen copies for a long time. When you feel ready to leave the group, and the group agrees, you give it back at your last meeting."

"Okay. That's a nice ritual."

"Now, for your first assignment, I want you to read through the book and choose which stage of grief fits you right now."

"Aren't they in order?"

"People don't typically follow the stages in order, but they experience all the stages."

"And the stages are . . . ?"

"They are listed as"—he ticked them off on his fingers one by one—"denial and isolation, anger, bargaining, depression, and"—he touched his little finger—"acceptance." Leaning back to steeple his fingers again, he said, "All I want you to do this week is choose the stage that fits your feelings best right now."

"That seems simple enough."

"One step. That's all for this week and then we'll see how it goes next week." He stood up. "Can you make it at the same time?"

"Yes, I think so." She stood and put the book in her backpack.

"Let me walk you out."

As they reached the back of the sanctuary, they automatically stopped to look up at the five-panel stained glass reproduction of the classic Leonardo da Vinci painting.

Reverend Kline broke the silence, "I'm here every day and I never tire of looking up to that image for inspiration."

"The tiffany-style is so unusual for a church. Do you still offer tours?"

"Every Wednesday morning at ten. When the church was built in 1926, Payne Glassworks in Paterson, New Jersey, was commissioned to install ten windows. Three generations—all named George Payne—ran the studios over a hundred-year period, but they finally sold the business to Rohlf's Stained and Leaded Glass Studio in Mount Vernon, New York, quite awhile ago."

"It is amazing."

"We had the granddaughter of the glass artist here on a visit a few years ago. You may have seen the write-up in the *Tampa Bay Times*."

"No, I'm afraid not." She felt the burn of embarrassment flame in her cheeks. "I was too busy." She looked up the aisle and pointed at the small display of Russian icons below the window. "When did the church start displaying these?"

Reverend Kline rubbed the back of his neck. "I think it's only been about eighteen months. You haven't been here since then, but the committee approved the purchase of these rare Russian icons that are coming out of abandoned rural churches."

Stepping up the aisle to get closer, Savannah said, "I love the exquisite gold leaf accents. How do you find out about them?"

"From here and there." He eyed the exit. "Have you seen my little garden?"

"I didn't know there was room here for a garden."

"Well, there isn't really, but there's a four-by-four-foot plot back here that I'm using to teach some of our teens about gardening. It doesn't take much space to teach beginners the thrill of growing things." They walked out the side door adjacent to the parking lot. "Jacob is one of my best students."

"My Jacob?"

"Oh yes. He's very bright and follows directions right to the letter."

"Oh, that is extremely small." Savannah stooped to look at the variety of plants, from tiny to nearly full grown flowers, peppers. and tomato starts. "Why the different sizes?"

"That's my teaching method. We start them in the church basement from seed. I demonstrate the use of a small table with a grow light, then we transplant them up here to the garden. Finally, they take seeds home to plant in their own garden."

Savannah stood up and pulled out her keys. "I'm very impressed. How many students do you have?"

"Only three at the moment."

"That's a lot of work for only three students."

"Oh, but I have always been a keen gardener— even as a youngster. I consider it a real success to instill a love of nature to teens in a stress-free, competition-free, no blue ribbon for this, supportive environment. Nature has its own rhythms and cycles, yet still manages to get everything done in good time."

Chapter 19

Savannah parked her dad's van in front of the bungalow, leaned forward, and rested her forehead on top of the steering wheel. The cold fact of her dad's exhumation was a horror that sank into her muscles like a wasting disease.

I'm trying to be brave, Dad, I'm really trying.

A sharp tap on the passenger side window startled her. It was Mrs. Webberly motioning for her to roll down the window. "Savannah, dear, I'm so sorry."

"What?"

"He's just so fast and I wasn't expecting him to bolt."

"Slow down, please. What has happened?"

"Rooney has run away!"

"What? Why on earth would he do that?" A sick taste smacked the back of Savannah's throat as she visualized his sleek, gray body lying against a curb.

"I went over to check on him just a few minutes ago and he practically bowled me over scrambling out of the house. You know how fast he can run. I called, but he was going at top speed. I was going to call you at the shop when I saw the van."

"What direction did he go?"

Mrs. Webberly pointed down the street. "He ran that way. He was on the sidewalk at least. But he was running full tilt. For a puppy, he's very fast."

"Okay. Hop in and let's cruise the neighborhood. Oh, wait!" Savannah dashed inside and brought out Rooney's leash and one of her dad's shirts.

"Savannah, what a good idea."

"Okay. With you in the car along with one of Dad's shirts, it's possible we can entice him to hop in."

Mrs. Webberly hopped in and quickly buckled up. "I let myself in at about two-thirty this afternoon for a quick snuggle and to let him out for his business. He was anxious, out-of-sorts-like, but he seemed docile enough. I didn't really think he had the energy to run very far. When you didn't come home at the normal time, I went over to give him a little outing. I didn't expect him to bolt."

They drove in ever-larger circles searching the streets, driveways, and back alleys of the neighborhood, stopping frequently to shout, "Rooney, here boy!"

Not a sign of him.

The few neighbors out taking care of lawns and just chatting hadn't seen a running gray streak either.

They criss-crossed the major streets with Savannah slowing so that they could stop for a moment to look under and between cars and down along the alleyways. More than a few impatient drivers tooted their annoyance. She and Mrs. Webberly ignored them and continued to shout his name.

No luck.

After an hour, Savannah parked in front of her house again, feeling sick. "It doesn't look good, Mrs. Webberly."

"No, dear. It's not fair, I can't bear another loss," she pulled a lace bordered handkerchief from her skirt pocket and blew her nose. "I'm going to be alone here."

"What do you mean?"

"When you leave, I'll have to move in with my oldest son. He and his wife will treat me like a dried-up old lady."

"I don't understand."

"They didn't like it that Hugh and I were, well, intimate, but I think they felt confident that he would look out for me after John died."

Savannah's eyes opened wide. "You and Hugh? I had no—"

"Oh no, of course not. Hugh would have been embarrassed. He was very traditional and couldn't understand why I didn't want to get married again after my husband died. I love my independence, but I'll have to fight them for it. Let's move on, dear. What are we going to do about Rooney?"

Clamping her mouth shut, it took Savannah a moment to think, "I'll make up some flyers at the shop tomorrow and we'll post them around."

"I just don't understand why he would take off. It's not like his true nature at all." Mrs. Webberly got out of the car and went into her bungalow.

Savannah pulled the van under the carport.

She felt the heavy silence of the house as soon as she opened the door. Rooney had such a big presence. *Why would he leave?*

The phone rang and she nearly jumped out of her skin. She picked up the receiver. "Hello."

"Thank goodness you're home."

"Edward? Honestly, I don't want to talk to you at all right now. Rooney has run away and I'm just—" Savannah could hear the sorrow in her voice and took a deep breath.

"Don't worry, I —"

"I'm just back from searching the whole neighborhood for him. He's nowhere to be seen and I've really looked hard."

"Don't worry, I —"

"Of course, I'm worried. He's still a fairly young dog and it's my fault that he's unhappy enough to run away."

"Savannah! Stop talking. Listen to me. Slow down for a second. He's here at the pub with me. I heard him barking next door. He was waiting at the back door of your shop."

"Why in blazes would he go to the shop?"

"Your dad used to take him in when he was
working late on paperwork. Then they would
stop over here for a drink. Rooney was just following the routine."

"Okay. Thank goodness. He seemed more anxious than usual today. Hold on to him. I'm on my
way."

"No rush. The customers love him."

They wouldn't love what he's done with my left shoes.
She clicked the handset switch and dialed Mrs.
Webberly. As soon as she answered, Savannah
said, "He's been found."

"Oh thank the stars. I was so worried. Where
was he?"

"He's been waiting at the back door of Webb's.
I guess he figured that Dad has been working
there all this time so he went over to remind him
to come home. It's kinda sweet, really."

"Where is he now?"

"Edward has him. Rooney's busy charming all
the customers at Queen's Head."

"That's perfectly Rooney. Thanks for letting
me know so I could stop fretting."

Savannah hung up and leaped into the van,
concentrating on driving as fast and safely as she
could. She parked behind the shop and went up
the alleyway towards the front of the pub. When
she got to the street, she noticed a white forensics
police van parked in front of the shop.

*That's strange. I thought they already finished with
the forensics investigation.* She looked into the
storefront windows and saw a light shining from
around the closed workshop door. Bristling, she

unlocked the front door, making the bell shriek with the force she used to shake the door. "Is someone here?" she yelled over the jangling door bell. "Come out or I'm calling 911."

Forensics specialist Grey opened the workroom door. She was wearing an ordinary business suit in black with a white blouse and long pants, which made the white gloves on her hands look like Easter formal wear. "Don't panic. It's just me. You already gave me permission to search this room yesterday."

"Even if I'm not here?"

"I needed to check out something for a moment."

"How did you get in?"

"I checked Mr. Trevor's keys out from the evidence department. I needed the keys to his house and car as well." She shrugged.

"What about the alarm."

She had the grace to blush. "Like many people, he had the access code written across a bit of tape on the key."

Savannah lowered her shaking head, then looked directly into Sandra Grey's eyes. "But still, you could have called me. You have my wholehearted support."

"This is an on-going investigation. We will be continuing to gather evidence at the request of Detective Parker. Wherever—and unfortunately for my love life—whenever he wants us to gather evidence." Sandra took a small breath. "That was the official doctrine. I was supposed to have called.

It's what I always do. I can't think why I didn't this time. I'm truly sorry. I can see you're upset."

"Yes, it's an uncomfortable situation, to say the least. A situation that I don't think is at all possible to be prepared to handle."

Sandra smiled quietly and nodded. "Of course. I'm just doing my job, but I try not to make a terrible situation even worse for the victim's family and friends. I failed this time. I can only apologize."

"Yes, I know that and appreciate your position, really," said Savannah. "We're on the same team. I want to know who killed Hugh and my dad. Is there anything I can do that will help you?"

"You can't really help." Sandra turned to go back into the workroom. "On second thought, maybe you can. I don't know much about stained glass, but I am surprised that so many chemicals are involved in creating them. Can you tell me which ones you use so I can keep a lookout for anything out of place?"

"Chemicals? Sure, there are a few." Savannah ticked them off on her fingers. "We use alcohol to clean the glass before soldering. We use etching compounds to prime the leaded panes. We apply chemical solvents to create specific finishing effects like a copper patina. We use a variety of glass enamels for the painted portions. I think there are more, but everything we use should also be for sale in the display room."

"Hmmmmm. Those I figured out and I did check them for a match with your inventory. Could you identify this one for me?" Sandra walked over to Jacob's bench and picked up a baby food jar by the lid with her gloves. It was half-filled with a dried green herbal mixture. "What's this used for?"

Savannah instinctively reached for the jar.

Sandra pulled it out of reach. "I'm sorry. I can't let you touch it."

Savannah bent over to look at the jar's contents and shook her head slowly. "I have no idea."

Chapter 20

Late Thursday Evening

Savannah knelt down and cooed sweet praise to Rooney. She found him lapping up attention from the patrons at Queen's Head Pub and everyone wanted to pet him. Most of the regulars spoke to her about their favorite memories of her dad and it was a bit like a mini wake. In light of everything that was going on, it was nice to hear that the townspeople had such fond memories of her father.

Edward took the leash from her hand, knelt, and clipped it to Rooney's collar. He removed the temporary leash made of cooking twine and gave the puppy a rigorous scratching all the way down his back. "I'm glad to have you visit here, Rooney boy, but it's time for you to go home. Next time, make sure your mum brings you."

Savannah stood. "I'm so relieved he's okay. I

was imagining him hit by a car, kidnapped by animal testing laboratories, underground puppy farms. Everything bad."

"He probably thought you should have some company."

"More likely that he thought Dad was still here and needed to come home. I can understand why Dad would bring him along when he worked late hours. He is a great watchdog. Have you heard his bark? For a puppy, it's pretty scary."

"Yeah, it sounds aggressive, but he's not particularly territorial. Listen, Savannah, I really want to explain to you the details of the loan. Amanda called right after class and spilled the beans about what you learned from Mrs. Lattimer."

"I don't want to get into it now, Edward."

"Please, love," he took her hand and bent down to press a kiss onto her palm, "I'm begging for an audience. Let me explain."

The pleading in his smile ruined her resolve to be stern. She removed her hand, "This better be good."

"It's good. Your dad was my biggest supporter in the neighborhood. He ate here every day when I first opened. He recommended it to his students, vendors, and clients. I believe he thought of me like a son."

Savannah folded her arms across her chest, "Some son you are. Betraying his trust so quickly. And with Frank, for heaven's sake. That's disgusting. You know how Dad felt about him."

"It wasn't that way. Your dad made me a loan so that I could expand the outdoor seating to increase my cash flow. I was just barely getting by and I needed to do something quick."

"You should have told me."

"But, from my viewpoint, I thought you were selling it to Hugh then returning to Seattle. Hugh and I were good with your plan to turn it over to him and then I would pay him back as soon as I received my inheritance from my uncle."

"Why did you deal with Frank?"

"After Hugh died, Frank stopped by the shop and offered to forgive the loan if I could persuade you to sell Webb's to him." He looked down at the floor. "I'm ashamed of that, but I didn't know you then. I shouldn't have done that anyway—I was close to John and you're his daughter. It was just Frank's offer was so very, very attractive to a strapped new business owner."

She stood and looked at him.

"Say something," he pleaded. "I can't stand it."

"I'm disappointed, to say the least, but I can't ignore the fact that my dad seemed to trust you absolutely. Let me think about this."

"Fair enough. I just need a chance to prove myself to you. I'll tell Frank that the deal is off and he is on his own to try to persuade you to sell it to him."

"I don't really know what to do at this point," Savannah's shoulders drooped with the weight of the decisions she would need to make shortly. Her mood was interrupted by Rooney's nose nudge. She took a deep breath and rubbed his head.

"I would not have believed how many friends Rooney has here."

"Would you like a drink?" Edward asked. "Rooney will be happy to have you stay."

"No thanks. I'm exhausted. Today had too many ups and downs. But, I'll take a rain check. Good night and thanks for the explanation."

She smiled at the happy crowd. She wouldn't have any trouble finding a new owner for him. Looking around at some of her prospects, she felt a twinge of sadness. She might not stay, and Rooney certainly wasn't comfortable with her yet, but she had gotten attached all the same.

She led him around to the passenger side of the van. He hopped onto the front seat and sat upright like an adult. He had obviously ridden shotgun before. He turned his golden eyes to her.

"What's going on with you, Rooney boy? If you're trying to drive me crazy, you've got it down pat."

He let out a mournful howl that turned into a puppy whine.

"Okay, okay. I get it. You're done with being home alone all the time."

Driving home, she thought about the small jar that the forensic specialist had found at Jacob's worktable. Sandra said the jar would go to her lab for analysis to determine what the substance was. If it was a poison, who could have placed it there among Jacob's painting supplies. Why? Who was threatened?

At home, she settled Rooney with a vigorous

back rub, some race-track puppy running in the backyard, and finally a treat. He sat perfectly still after the treat, willing her to provide another. When he determined that no more was coming, he walked slowly down the hallway, plopped down next to her dad's bed, and looked up at her.

"Yes, Rooney, I know he's still gone. We both have to learn to live without him. We have no choice."

Her treat for the evening was a cold Spencer Trappist Ale that she opened and poured into a goblet, then plopped down on the couch for some mindless television. Flipping through the channels, she paused on a show that unsettled her. It was one of those time-limited archaeological-type investigations about an ancient scroll so old it had pieces missing from the brittle document. The technology portion of the program demonstrated how the restorers used a software application to fill in the holes with likely letters to reveal the original meaning of the ancient scroll.

Savannah scrunched her brow in concentration at the image of the suggested letters showing up in the small holes. Missing letters? *How about if you wanted to reveal letters in an ancient book.* She went over to the bookcase on one wall of the dining room and pulled down the family Bible. Placing it on the round oak table that was as old as the house, she carefully opened the leather-bound holy book.

Rooney followed her footsteps from the bookshelf to the dining table and then sat, looking up

at her with his ears perked as cute as he could
manage.

"What?" She scratched him behind the ears.
"What do you want? Another treat?" He wiggled
his short tail and trotted to the treat jar in the
kitchen. "Okay, big guy. You need a reward for
not sulking." She gave Rooney his treat and spied
the backpack on one of the kitchen chairs. She
pulled out the onion skin sheet that had been
hidden in the Hello Kitty pencil box and spread
it flat on the kitchen worktable. It was a new type
of cipher to solve and spoke loudly to the seriousness of the situation. *Dad must have felt he needed
this level of security.*

Working on the idea of revealing letters that the
TV program had sparked, she felt that the onion
skin sheet would need to be placed on a page of an
ancient book. Since her mother's Bible was the
oldest book in the house, it was a slim possibility
that it could reveal the next message through the
little holes. The fly in the ointment was that it was
a large edition with more than seven hundred
pages. Rooney looked up at her with his head
cocked, trying to understand.

"You're right. This looks crazy, but I've nothing
better to do and I want to find out what Dad
meant for me to discover sooner rather than
later." She sat in front of the Bible and turned to
Genesis. The onion skin sheet was slightly smaller
than the text of Bible pages, and the holes revealed a string of nonsense letters. If she was
right, the visible letters should form words.

Looking down at Rooney, she said, "So, how

long do you think this will take me? Forever,
right?"

She looked down at Rooney. He had stretched
out on the floor with his head resting on his paws.
"You're right. This is the wrong way to do this.
Dad must have left another clue for me."

*A book he knew I would handle. Something hidden
in the Bible?*

She went to the kitchen and rummaged
through the junk drawer to find a large magnifying glass. She examined the front and back covers and spent extra time with the edges in case he
had made another hiding space. Probably not.
He wouldn't dare mess with her mom's Bible,
and he wasn't likely to use the same trick twice.
After scanning the inside front and back pages,
she put the magnifier down and propped her
head in her hands.

Back to the kitchen she went and pulled a soft
pure white dish towel from one of the drawers
and spread it out on the dining room table. She
gently placed the onion skin paper on top of it.
Using the magnifier, she slowly scanned every
square inch of the delicate document and finally,
in the lower right-hand corner she found three
tiny numbers—3 3 7.

She leaned back in the chair. "You were right,
Rooney. This has got to be the next clue. If these
numbers are references within the Bible, then
these numbers would represent the third book,
chapter three, verse seven. Let's check."

Using the indented thumb marks of her mother's
Bible, she turned to the third book of The Holy

Bible, Leviticus. She flipped over a few pages to chapter three and then ran her finger down the page to discover that verse seven was at the top of the next page.

She remembered studying with her catechism instructor before she was permitted to be a full member of the church. It was basically about offering a lamb for peace offerings and sprinkling blood around on the altar.

Carefully fitting the onion skin over the seventh verse, Savannah tried to read the letters highlighted by the holes, but some holes didn't line up with a letter. She flipped the onion skin upside down with no luck and finally noticed that one of the holes fell into the margin down the middle of the book. She confirmed that no matter how she turned the sheet, one of the holes would never reveal a letter. "Well, Rooney, looks like we're back to square one. The key book is not Mom's Bible."

She put the Bible back in the dining room bookcase and scanned the shelves for another title that might make some sort of connection. Nothing grabbed her.

Going back to the living room, she remembered the collection of Dan Brown first editions and grabbed the one that had been protruding out from the bookcase a little from the others. Returning to the dining room table, she flipped to page 337 and the onion skin fit the page perfectly. After turning it twice, it lined up so that each hole revealed a letter.

"Yes, that's it, Rooney," she shouted, startling

him into a frenzy of excited barking. "Sorry, boy, sorry." After she calmed him, she carefully copied out the cipher on a sheet of ruled paper.

O N T H E E D G E O F S P L E N D O R

Quickly, she separated the letters into words.

O N / T H E / E D G E / O F / S P L E N D O R

She looked down at the patient Rooney who looked up at her with dreamy, gilded eyes. *He's getting more comfortable with me.* "I have no idea what this means, but I do know what time it is. Let's go for a walk one last time."

Rooney scrambled up from the floor, slipping and sliding out to the living room, and tugged at the leash from its hook by the front door.

"Good dog!" She smiled and they headed out into the balmy night.

Chapter 21

Savannah stretched her long legs and her heels struck the spindles at the bottom of her single Jenny Lind bed. For a moment she believed all was right with the world. Mostly right.

Then she remembered.

She threw off the covers and struggled to sit at the side of the bed knowing that hardly anything was right. A cool nose pressed the soft skin of her knee followed by a lick and whimper.

"Good morning, Rooney. Yes, yes, I'm getting up." She gave him a huge snuggle and he tried to hop up into the bed. "Rooney! No, Rooney! You'll break it."

He managed anyway and Savannah giggled uncontrollably at the sight of a dog almost as big as her bed wriggling like a little puppy.

Taking his head in her two hands, she said,

"You've forgiven me for not being my dad? Have you? I hope so because I've fallen in love with you."

She sped through her morning routine and was just about ready to leave for work when she saw the Dan Brown first edition. She grabbed the soft, well-worn dish towel still on the dining room table, wrapped it around the book, and placed it carefully in the large compartment of her backpack.

She drove to the shop and was soon unlocking Webb's Glass Shop preparing for the fifth day of class. She pushed the ON button and the cash register started its boot-up routine then flashed, blinked, and the screen turned blue. Panic tightened her shoulders and stabbed into the back of her neck. She leaned out the front door, but there was no Edward in sight. "Okay, Crabby. It's just us."

Pushing the switch to the OFF position, she counted out, "One alligator, two alligators" all the way to fifteen just to make sure that all the bad electrons had scurried away to cause havoc elsewhere. She pushed the switch to the ON position and gentle whirring noises announced the beginning of a normal boot-up process.

The door jangled as Edward walked in with a tray of coffee and scones just in time to catch Savannah giving herself a high fist pump.

"Edward, the cash register had a blue screen meltdown, but I challenged it to a dual by using the big OFF switch."

"Let me see. Most times it's just lazy."

He peered at the screen. "Nothing wrong here. It looks happy. Good job."

"Can I begin to hope this will continue to be your gift to world peace?"

His brow crinkled. "World peace."

"The world should be continuously protected against an uncaffeinated woman who has ready access to powerful glass-breaking tools."

"I am suitably cautioned and now very cautious." He put the tray on the counter.

"Why do you come in so early? The pub doesn't open until eleven thirty."

Edward handed her a huge white cup. "Here, have a cappuccino. It's when I get my paperwork done. You know, the vendors, orders, and deliveries routine. Also, we installed a monster of a refurbished espresso machine that makes everything you never heard of. I'm trying them out on you before I serve paying customers."

She took a tentative sip. "Oh, wow! This one is gorgeous. It is so rich and smooth. Why the monster machine?"

He pulled over one of the stools and perched on it. "It's another way to generate an income stream out of the pub."

"Why? Are you worried?"

"Like most of the small businesses around here, I'm struggling. Not failing by any shot during the high season, but I'm trying to stabilize our cash flow."

"Is this something I should worry about, I mean, does this mean you can't pay back the loan?"

"I'm not willing to let any opportunity escape. I've got everything wrapped up in the pub. It won't fail for lack of effort"—he tilted his head a bit—"but it's something you should check out. Who did your dad use for financial information? It's on his statements, right?"

"Dad's longtime financial advisor is Kevin Burkart, who he trusted implicitly. He double-checked the financials independently, but I found a current spreadsheet with more financial information on my father's computer desktop. I've only been through the last few months' paperwork and financials. I have no idea how the shop does seasonally or even over the course of a year. Since I'm not that great with numbers, I'll have to depend on Burkart to calculate whatever monthly trends show up in the data."

"Hmmmm. Sounds very businesslike. I thought you were only interested in selling out as quickly as possible."

"Well, that's something a prospective owner would need to know, anyway. I've begun to think a bit differently."

Edward stood up. "You mean you might stay?"

"Might. Yes, it's possible, I might stay."

The door jangled, followed by, "Good morning, lovebirds." Amanda shouldered the door out of her way and bustled toward the classroom.

Savannah felt a flush creep across her cheeks. She lowered her eyes. *It's too soon to think about anyone else so soon after breaking up with Ken—way too soon.*

"Not quite, Amanda." Edward looked quickly to Savannah.

Amanda looked at the door to the custom workshop. "Hey, what's that?"

Edward and Savannah turned to look. On the door was a wrinkled sheet of copy paper taped to the door with four strips of tape, one hastily placed in each corner.

Savannah's heart slammed into the wall of her chest. Written in red dry erase marker was

> *TWO MURDERS SHOULD BE ENOUGH*
> *ARE YOU NEXT?*
> *GO BACK TO SEATTLE*

Amanda shrieked, "He's been back. He's been in here. Ughhh!" She wiped down her arms and shook out her hands. "This is an intrusion of monster proportions."

Edward pulled out his cell phone and took a picture of the note. "This looks very much like the same writing as the first one you received. This means we're getting close."

"So why don't I feel so good about that?" Savannah asked. "I'll have to call this one in to the police, as well. I had hoped to have some results by now, but I don't."

"You have to call it in. You know it's the right thing to do," Edward said as Amanda also nodded.

"Yes, I know, but I don't have to be happy about it. I'm so not happy about it." She huffed in disgust. "On a high note—good news. I solved the cipher last night."

"Oh, that's fabulous. What did it say?" asked Amanda.

"And that's also the bad news. It's confusing. The message reads, 'On the edge of splendor.' It doesn't make any sense to me at all." She looked at each of them in turn. "Either of you? No? Okay, I'll show it to Jacob. Maybe he will know."

Edward ducked his head and gently took the drained coffee cup from Savannah's hand. He looked into her eyes and grinned like the chimney sweep in *Mary Poppins*. Placing his index finger beside his nose, he said, "Not quite." He left.

Savannah shrugged and followed Amanda into the classroom where she positioned and repositioned her bags and boxes around her worktable.

"Amanda, what a funny thing to say. We're not lovebirds. What was the idea?"

"Oh, I just wanted to make a little joke. Edward has been a little weird lately and he needed to get shaken up."

"He looked like he thought it was funny."

"A little imbalance is good for everyone."

"We've had enough imbalance lately, and it's not the good kind. Besides, he makes wonderful coffee and I don't want anything to interfere with that. Aren't you early?"

"Oh, yes. I was thinking that you probably need to give me some training on the cash register so that you could see to Rooney at lunch."

"Goodness, what a terrific idea. Thanks. Let's do that before the rest of the class shows up."

As she turned, something on the bulletin board caught her eye. "Hey, Amanda, look at this poster for a stained glass conference held in New Orleans. The dates were last week."

"Sure. That's been up there for a couple months. Why?"

"Did you notice who was teaching one of the workshops last Sunday?"

Amanda peered closer at the speaker advertisements on the poster, "Oh my goodness. One of the speakers was Frank Lattimer of Lattimer's Glass Shop. If Frank was in New Orleans, he can't be the killer."

"Afraid so, but we need to confirm that."

"It would be super easy for me to call the conference organizers and ask about Frank."

"Yes, but it just so happens that I know an attendee." She pulled out her cell phone and punched one of the recent numbers. "Ivy? This is Savannah."

"Hey, girlfriend. What's up?" Her roommate was perky, as always.

"Weren't you at the New Orleans conference last week?"

"Yeah, it was fantastic. I learned a lot at the lectures, but even better I now have a passion for chicory coffee with beignets. Why?"

"Did you attend a lecture with a Frank Lattimer on Sunday?"

"Uh, yep. It was lame. He didn't bring anything new to the conference and I walked out after about ten minutes. I wasn't the only one. It was a mass exodus. That had to be embarrassing for him. Everything else was stellar. Too bad."

Savannah groaned. If his lecture was that bad, it explained why he didn't want Savannah to know where he was last week. He probably thought she would be more reluctant to sell to him if she found out that he was currently being criticized within the glass conference circuit. "Thanks. I needed to know. I'll call you later on." She ended the call.

Amanda looked as depressed as Savannah felt. Frank wasn't the killer.

Savannah was trying to teach Amanda how to properly start the cash register, but they kept losing focus to talk about the investigation.

Amanda looked up from her tablet. "Has Smythe come by to see you again? He's been stirring things up around here pretty badly. Sully, one of the antique dealers at the end of the block, chased him out by waving a poker at him until he drove away."

"That's hilarious." Savannah stooped down and began tidying the papers underneath the counter.

"Sully doesn't hear very well and basically thought that Smythe was casting a curse on his store. Now Sully is trying to hire the owner of the occult bookstore to cast a spell to get rid of the effects of the evil red wand. It was quite a ruckus."

"Back to the alarm system. I don't expect you to lock up, but in case it goes off for no reason, you just punch in *W E B B* on the keypad and press the RESET button."

"Cool. That's easy. That Smythe is truly an obnoxious man. I can't believe his company has any notion how rude and vile he treats his prospective sales opportunities."

"Well, maybe when your job is to buy up people's lives, you need to be obnoxious in order to convince them that they need to sell and that it's the best thing for them."

Amanda put her hands on her ample hips. "I don't trust that man farther than I could throw him, but he has a horrible job to do."

"That's a creative way to look at it," Savannah said. "What I don't yet know is how far he would go to sign up the owners after Dad refused to cooperate. I think it's time to really dig in to his past and alibi. He's our only lead now."

Amanda rubbed her hands together. "Oh, yeah."

The door jangled to ring in the students of the class.

Chapter 22

Rooney wriggled a warm welcome to Savannah's lunch visit. On their walk, he sniffed his favorite trees, and while a distracted Savannah was checking e-mails on her phone he was able to roll in the rotting remains of a squirrel.

Unable to seriously scold him for her inattention, she took him around the back of the house. He stood shaking but willing while she wet him down, applied shampoo, and scrubbed him with a brush to put a dent in the stink. *Short hair is a good thing*. Finally, after repeating the ordeal twice, she hosed him off, let him have a really good shake, and then a final roll on a large beach towel she tossed around him.

When they stepped back into the bungalow, the house phone was ringing. Savannah picked up. "Hello."

"Miss Savannah Webb?" a deep male voice spoke.

"Yes." She drew in a breath ready to interrupt the rehearsed script of a political campaign or charity plea.

"This is Detective David Parker of the St. Petersburg Police Department. We spoke on Tuesday."

"Yes, sir. I remember."

"Good. I have the results of the autopsy performed on Mr. John Webb. I regret to inform you that the examination indicates that your father was poisoned. The cause of death was not a heart attack."

Savannah plopped down in one of the kitchen chairs. "Can you say that again?"

"Yes, Miss Webb. It appears that your father died of a toxic substance. The poison used mimicked the symptoms of a heart attack and his death was mistaken for that. It's the same poison that caused the death of Hugh Trevor. We are investigating both cases as suspicious deaths."

Savannah drew a deep breath. *I was right and now they believe it.*

"Miss Webb? Hello? Do you understand?"

Savannah swallowed and concentrated on sounding calm. "Yes, Detective Parker. I understand."

"Are you all right? Do you feel faint?"

"No, no. I am stunned, actually. Although it's what I have been expecting, it's much more unsettling to hear it officially."

"That's understandable, Miss Webb. I understand that you called in a death threat left to you by your father."

"Not a threat. It was a warning." She switched the phone to her other ear. "I'm wondering why no one came over to collect it."

"That's all changed now. Please let the forensic team have the message and if you can, please don't touch it."

"What was the poison?"

"Sorry, I can't tell you that just now. The lab is still narrowing down the components. It wasn't a typical toxin."

"What happens next?"

"I've been assigned as the officer in charge and I'll be keeping you informed about the progress of our investigation into the death of your father. I'm arranging for a detailed search of his home. I expect that to occur within the hour. The glass shop has already been searched by forensic specialists."

"Yes, I've already met the specialists. They were very considerate, but focused on their task. I'll stay here until they arrive and make sure they have whatever they need. Then I'll need to get back to work."

"Excellent. That will be helpful."

"I'll also have my neighbor, Mrs. Webberly, standing by in case you need more information about the neighborhood and my dad."

"Is she next door?"

"Across the street. She'll be over to take care of the dog."

"I'll advise the team. If you have a minute, I

also have a few questions. I understand your permanent address is in Seattle."

"Yes, I'm working as a glass artist for one of the glass blowing studios."

"Good. It would be a great help if you could send me documentation on your whereabouts over the last two weeks."

"My whereabouts?"

"Yes, I'll be thoroughly questioning everyone who knew Mr. Webb and Mr. Trevor."

"Oh, certainly. Of course. How do you want this information?"

"You can e-mail the specifics to Officer Boulli in care of the homicide department. I'll be in touch shortly. I understand you have received his card—at least one."

"Several. In fact, he's quite a problem as far as I am concerned. I have no confidence that he will be able to handle even the smallest of details associated with this case. I don't want anything to do with him at all." Savannah hung up the phone and walked back to the living room. She knelt on the floor and gave Rooney a smothering hug. "Rooney, buddy. They're taking me seriously, now. I hope they solve this quickly, but I have to admit that it's chilling now that it's happening."

She made a pass through the house, straightening up the bathroom and kitchen as if she were expecting company. She rummaged through her backpack and pulled out the manila folder she'd used to organize her travel documents. Yep, her boarding pass was still there. That's good evidence. Pulling out her billfold, she extracted the last gas station slip from her neighborhood in Seattle to prove that she was there when her dad died.

Never in a million years would I have thought I would need an alibi.

A little less than thirty minutes passed, and a City of St. Petersburg Forensics van pulled up and parked on the street in front of her house.

Rooney exploded in angry barking. Savannah ordered him to sit and stay. She was very pleased when he meekly obeyed.

Two tall men in white coveralls carrying large black toolboxes were standing on her doorstep. Their youthful faces were calm and serious. They took one look at Rooney and both stepped back several yards down her sidewalk.

After they looked at each other, the one with the mustache stepped forward half a step. "Good afternoon, ma'am. I'm Forensic Specialist Richard Kyle and this is Forensic Assistant Jimmy Marshall. We're here to conduct a search of Mr. John Webb's property. I believe Detective Parker advised you that we would arrive this afternoon."

"Yes, he called earlier. I'm John Webb's daughter, Savannah." She opened the screen door, but they stood there looking at Rooney. They didn't move.

"Could you secure your dog? We can't come in until he is either out of the house or caged. Insurance issues, you understand."

"No problem. I've got a traveling cage. Hold on just a second and I'll put him in it." She led Rooney to the spare bedroom and tucked him up in the cage. She grabbed one of the T-shirts that lay on her dad's bedroom floor and filled a small dish of water. Putting them both in the cage, she returned to the calmly waiting specialists.

"He's in his cage now. You can come in." Savannah let them in and gave them a short tour of her dad's bedroom and the third bedroom that he used as his home office.

They opened their toolboxes in her dad's bedroom and one of them began taking flash photographs of the entire room. After a few minutes, it was obvious they had settled in for a meticulous examination of her house.

Savannah felt a growing pressure to get back to the glass shop. Amanda knew about stained glass, but she might take it upon herself to begin teaching the class, and she was just not ready for all of that just yet.

Besides, Savannah couldn't really see that she could be any help here, and it was probably going to be a slow-moving drawn-out process. She grabbed the car keys out of the ceramic bowl, then went across the street to see Mrs. Webberly.

"Oh my goodness, Savannah. This is unbelievable. I never thought that this would be happening to anyone I know. What do you want me to do?"

"Nothing difficult really. Just keep an eye on things. Rooney's in his traveling cage, so he's fine."

"Right, but he'll need to be let out shortly."

"Even as a puppy, Rooney is good for at least two hours. If they're still searching at that time, come on over and tell them that you're taking

Rooney for a walk. Make sure Rooney is calm and comfortable. Make sure you clip on his leash." She turned to go but turned back. "Oh, also go ahead and answer any questions they might have about Dad. They might also have a few questions about the neighborhood. Or anyone who knew Hugh. Really, they should interview you."

"Shouldn't I ask you first?"

"No, I trust your judgment and I want to be as cooperative as possible. Whatever information they want, I don't want any delays in getting it."

"That's wise, dear."

"See if you can figure out if they find anything important. If they do take anything away, go ahead and sign for it if that's what they want you to do. Then make sure the house is locked up after they leave."

"Certainly, my dear. I hope this isn't too upsetting."

"It is definitely upsetting, but we need answers. Call me when they leave." Savannah turned, walked back across the street, and started up the van.

Chapter 23

Friday Afternoon

Savannah returned to the shop through the back door. It was a relief to step back into her comfortable world surrounded by chattering students and shattering glass.

She gave Suzy a little scratch under the chin, then plopped her backpack down in the side chair. She glanced at the computer screen on the rolltop desk. More e-mails to deal with. She was going to have to take a few minutes to deal with her dad's suppliers soon. Instead, she scooted through into the classroom. "Hi, Amanda."

"Welcome back." Amanda looked up from her project. "Did you have a nice lunch?"

"Um . . . not really."

"What? Did Rooney get away again?"

"Nothing like that. Detective Parker called

from downtown and told me that Dad had been poisoned just like we suspected Hugh had been."

"Bless your heart." Amanda put down her tools and gave Savannah an awkward suffocating hug. "So, we were right."

"Yes, we were right. The police want to know where I was when they were poisoned."

"No way."

"Yes, way. Luckily I have my boarding pass and a gas receipt to prove that I was in Seattle. How was everything while I was gone?"

"No problems at all." Amanda looked back to her project. "I like this."

Jacob looked up from his project. "Miss Savannah. I leave early today. It's my gardening class. Reverend Kline teaches me about plants."

"No problem, Jacob. He told me about the class. I can always help you with your project later. Besides, you're way ahead of everyone else. Your ability to focus is a great advantage."

"My gardening class with Reverend Kline is every Friday afternoon. He teaches me about plants that are good and bad to eat. We have lots of oleanders at my house. They're very common in Florida and every part of the plant is poisonous."

"How do you get to the church?"

"Reverend Kline comes to get me." He looked back to the office where Suzy lay curled and started to inhale deeply in great ineffective gulps.

"Jacob, what's wrong?"

"He-he-he doesn't know about . . ."

Suzy stood up and began to bark in a short staccato yip.

"Jacob." Savannah clasped him by his upper arms and looked directly into his eyes. "What's wrong?"

He looked away quickly. "In-in-hale . . . er." He couldn't catch his breath.

"Inhaler. Where is it? Your backpack?"

He shook his head. "Suzy." He pointed to her blue service backpack.

Suzy had come over to sit right beside Jacob's feet, looked up at him, and placed one paw on his leg.

Savannah stooped down to Suzy and ripped open the Velcro pocket on the side of her service vest and snatched the inhaler. She turned to Jacob and placed it firmly in one hand and wrapped his other hand around it, as well.

He popped the cover off the inhaler, pumped the medication twice, and then inhaled. The next breath was calmer and the one that followed was deep. He inhaled and exhaled two more deep breaths and everything began to settle.

Savannah put a soft hand on his shoulder and looked into his eyes. "Are you good?"

He nodded yes.

She patted his bony shoulder. "Reverend Kline will have no problem with Suzy. Is that what you're worried about?"

He nodded yes.

"He has a large congregation and I've seen some of his parishioners with service dogs. So Suzy will not be the first he has met. She's so adorable, he would like her even if she wasn't your helper. Don't you agree, Amanda?" Savannah nodded her head and lifted her eyebrows as a signal for Amanda to back her up on her explanation.

"Of course, he'll love Suzy. Don't you worry about that at all."

Savannah bent over without looking directly into Jacob's serious eyes. "I'll bet your mother has already notified Reverend Kline. Regardless, I will call the reverend and explain all about her, all right? I'll call just as soon as the class settles and everyone is working."

The bell jangled and the rest of the students returned to resume the class.

"Let's just have a quick review of good soldering safety." Savannah looked directly at Arthur. "Make sure the iron doesn't touch anything but the tip of the coil of solder. The calmer you are, the smoother your work will be. It's a good lesson in stillness." She looked directly at Amanda. "Carry on."

After ensuring that everyone was safely soldering, Savannah slipped back into the office and dialed Reverend Kline.

"Reverend Kline, United Methodist Church."

"Reverend, this is Savannah Webb. I understand your gardening class with Jacob is later this afternoon."

"Good afternoon, Savannah. Yes. I should have mentioned it when you were over earlier. How can I help you?"

"Jacob now has a service dog. She's a lovely little beagle named Suzy. He was concerned that you might not want her to accompany him to his gardening lesson. He actually had a panic attack and Suzy alerted us that he needed his inhaler."

"His mother called earlier and told me that it will be necessary for Suzy to stay with Jacob at all times. I'm perfectly comfortable with service dogs."

"I thought you would be, but I wanted you to know about his concerns."

"Thank you, Savannah. That is considerate. No problem, though. I'll be by to pick him up at three this afternoon."

She hung up the phone and returned to the classroom. "Everything is all set for three o'clock, Jacob. Reverend Kline knows about Suzy and he's cool with it. It's no problem at all."

"Arthur was the first one I've ever heard of to be burned by a spool of solder," said Amanda, standing over Nancy to watch the bandaging of his hand.

Savannah opened her mouth to remind the woman that she wasn't allowed to provide first aid in the shop but decided not to bother.

"He's always first to get hurt. I didn't know the spool could get that hot." Amanda shrugged.

Nancy's face flushed and her lips pressed into a thin line. "He just doesn't get all this yet. He's a software wizard, but we all need to develop our artistic nature. Even in the face of harsh criticism." She shot a furious glare at Amanda.

"Faith, you airhead! You're using the wrong solder. You need to use the sixty-forty tin to lead ratio for tacking and the fifty-fifty ratio for the final layer," said Rachel.

"I'm not the airhead in this class." Faith looked pointedly at Amanda. "You've got it wrong again. Savannah said that we use the fifty-fifty first for tacking and then the sixty-forty last so that it takes the patina better. Right, Savannah?"

Savannah sighed. At least they were arguing about technical issues and not whose art was better. "Rachel, Faith is right this time. We use the fifty-fifty first . . . to take advantage of its higher melting temperature. It also solidifies more quickly and spreads out more. Then we use the sixty-forty because it tends to form rounder, higher beads, which makes it ideal for copper foil projects. It also stays liquid longer, allowing for more rework time, which is handy for smoothing out areas that need touching up."

Savannah noticed that Jacob was stuck in an obsessive cycle of checking his watch, walking to the office door to pat Suzy on the head then returning to his worktable where he'd pick up the soldering iron, drag the hot point across the wet sponge to clean it, replace it in its holder, and readjust the pieces in his project. After letting this go on for several cycles, Savannah tapped him on the shoulder.

Jacob jerked away as if her finger had been a hot poker.

"I'm sorry. I didn't mean to startle you. You look like you're ready to start tacking the pieces together with solder."

"Yes, Miss Savannah."

"Have you soldered before?"

"No, Miss Savannah."

"I know how you feel. It's tough to get started, but I promise that you will enjoy it. Let me help you with tacking your first spot."

His shoulders relaxed and he stepped aside while small smiles played hide and seek across his face.

"We're going to start from the inside and work our way out, so these two pieces are where we'll start." She pointed out the two innermost adjacent glass squares. "First, I use a short stubby brush and dip it in the wax-type material called flux and coat the spot lightly. The flux changes the properties of the metal so that the solder will bind."

"I can't tell that it's there."

"Okay. This is a clear flux. We have another kind of flux that has a red tint. Let me get that one for you."

She went to the display room to select the flux and the door jangled as Reverend Kline entered.

"Reverend, aren't you a little early? I thought you would be here at three. It's only two thirty."

"I was in the area and thought I might drop by and see if he was ready. I know it agitates him to deviate from his routine."

"Let me check." She returned to the classroom.

"Hey, Jacob. Reverend Kline is here early for your gardening class. Would you like to go now?"

"It's not three o'clock."

"He will wait for you. Is that better?"

"I want to go to my gardening class at three o'clock."

"Very well. I'll tell him. Here's the tinted flux."

She exchanged the flux containers and returned to the display room.

"He's not yet ready to leave. I'm sure it will be better to wait. If you could come back, say, in about twenty minutes, I'm sure this will go much better."

"I understand perfectly. I'll be right across the street to visit with the owner of V and V Antiques. He's a major source for those Russian icons you've been admiring. I'll be back a little later."

Savannah returned to Jacob and opened the small tin container of tinted flux. "Now, here's one of the secrets of good soldering. Take your time to apply a thin but complete coat of flux where you want the solder. That way it builds the bond evenly and the solder will flow onto the copper foil smoothly. Watch."

Savannah put a small amount of flux on a bristly brush and stroked it gently on the copper foil. Then she picked up the soldering iron. "I don't really have to remind you that keeping your equipment clean and orderly is important. I've seen how neatly you keep your paint supplies." She looked closely at the silver tip of the iron. "It's vital that you get used to the temperature of the iron and one of the best ways to keep it stable is to keep it clean." *I could use some stability in my life right now.*

"This is how I finish a soldering step." She brushed the tip across the surface of the moist sponge, jabbed the soldering iron point into the cleaning metal coil pad several times to remove any remaining solder, then replaced the soldering iron in its holder. "By finishing each soldering operation with cleaning the iron, it gives the iron time to stabilize to its selected temperature. Then you'll always know how the iron will behave in its interaction with the gun, solder, flux, and copper foil. The neatness and cleanliness of all four is a major factor in the quality and resulting stability of the soldering.

"By letting it set in its holder for a minute or more, it should be back up to the perfect temperature." Savannah took up the spool of solder in her left hand, then uncurled a length of solid solder about six inches. It stuck stiffly out of the spool like a silver twig. She smoothly pressed the hot iron down through the end of the solder twig and the solder drop adhered to the flux in a smooth bead that bridged the copper of the two pieces.

"This is what your solder tacks should look like." She stepped back so that everyone could see the example.

Amanda leaned over to look closely. "That's as good as the panel in the custom workroom."

"Thanks. That's important to me." Savannah raised her voice and looked at the students. "Now it's your turn. After you finish your first one, call me over. I'd like to see it in case we need to correct your method."

As they all returned to their workstations, Savannah walked over to the first aid kit, removed a small Band-Aid, and slipped it into her pocket. She stood next to Arthur.

He dabbed the innermost join with flux, picked up the soldering iron, and poked it into the wire mesh a couple times. Then he touched the tip with his finger. "Ouch!"

Savannah rolled her eyes.

Chapter 24

Officer Boulli sauntered at the pace of melting frozen yogurt into Detective Parker's office waving a yellow sticky note stuck on the index finger of his left hand. "Hey, did you want to see me?"

"Excellent use of your vast detective skills, Officer." Parker looked up from his PC. "I've called your office, your cell, sent you an e-mail, and even texted you. What do you think?"

"My desk PC is being upgraded."

Detective Parker frowned. "And that means . . . what exactly?"

"Well, they took mine away and you know the phones are all tied into that."

"The text?"

"I don't know why that didn't come through." Officer Boulli grinned ear to ear and sat in the nearer of the two small chairs in front of the detective's desk. "Technology is great, right? What's up?"

Detective Parker took a deep calming breath to keep from reaching across his desk and tearing Officer Boulli's face off. *Whatever possessed this guy to want to be a cop?* He thought he had met every personality type possible, but Officer Boulli was the prize example of an unsuitable cop in the most cliché-ridden television show ever produced.

Reaching for the only folder on his desk, Detective Parker fished his reading glasses from his front shirt pocket, put them on, and opened the folder. "This is why I was trying to reach you this morning. The toxicology report has come back on Hugh Trevor."

"The dead guy at the glass shop, right?"

Parker lowered his head and looked over his reading glasses. "Yes, Officer, the dead guy. What can you tell me from the report?" He closed the folder and handed it to Officer Boulli who opened the folder the wrong way first, turned it around, and began to read the summary.

"Poisoned? He was poisoned?"

"As it says." Parker stowed his glasses. "So what is our next step, homicide trainee, Officer Boulli?"

Missing the irony completely, Boulli pulled himself tall in the chair. "We need to catch the killer."

"Good. Yes, that is the final goal, but before that?"

"Interview suspects?"

"Right. Who are our suspects?"

At the wide-eyed look of terror in Officer Boulli's face, the detective abandoned the next series of pointed questions as functionally hopeless. "If you had been keeping up with the case, Officer, you would have received the e-mail that reported the results of the fingerprint analysis on the coffee cup found at the scene of the murder."

"Yeah, but I—"

"The only fingerprints on the cup, besides the victim's, belong to Jacob Underwood and Edward Morris."

"Yeah, the bartender and the crazy kid."

The detective lowered his head and shook it in depressed resignation. Before exploding, he took a deep breath. The situation was politically charged because Officer Boulli was the captain's nephew. The captain insisted that this goof was a genius in solving mysteries. Such things were meant to build character . . . or drive you crazy. This one was driving Detective Parker crazy.

He spoke slowly. "Jacob Underwood has a specific condition called Asperger's syndrome. He's developmentally different, not crazy. Sometimes these kids have an intelligence level that is off the scale."

"So what?"

"So I'm saying that he might look and act different, but it's possible that he's smarter than anyone you have ever met."

At that moment, Sandra Grey, one of the forensics specialists, tapped a polite knock on the office doorjamb and leaned in. "Excuse me, but I thought you might like a preliminary report on our examination of John Webb's house. It's still a draft, but there are some interesting developments." She looked over at Officer Boulli. "Of course, if you're too busy right now, I can come back." She pulled her head out of the office.

"Wait." As he stood up, Parker admired the effect of her professionally tailored suits. They added stature and an image of power to her petite frame. It couldn't be easy to thrive in the very male world of law enforcement. "Please, I'm desperate for some intelligent enlightenment . . . unofficial, of course." He walked out into the hallway with Sandra, closing his office door behind him.

"How are you doing on your quest to rid the department of Officer Boulli?" she said in a quiet voice. "We're counting on you, you know."

"It's painful, but I'm determined. Still, the massive amount of documentation I have to collect ensures that only the most deserving are actually sent packing. However, I think this case may be the final straw needed for submitting the termination paperwork."

"Why this case?"

"He's settled on a suspect that I believe is totally innocent, a young man named Jacob Underwood," he looked at her expectantly.

"Underwood?" She raised her eyebrows, "Judge Underwood's son?"

Parker nodded.

"Well done! She'll filet him nicely and wrap up the remains in paperwork."

"That's the plan. In the meantime, I can investigate the more likely suspects."

Sandra smiled, "I knew you were working behind the scenes. Who?"

"There are several likely leads. One is the pub owner next door with financial issues who has borrowed a large sum of money from John Webb and might have had an issue with Hugh Trevor as well. There's also the glass shop's main competition, Frank Lattimer and finally, a property developer from out of town, Gregory Smythe. Now, please, cheer me up quickly with that summary."

"Just a few observations that will be thoroughly covered in my report." She grinned until her eyes crinkled.

"Of course."

"In a nutshell, the only other fingerprints in the house besides Mr. Webb, his daughter, and neighbor are Jacob Underwood's and an unknown person."

"Jacob is a friend of the family."

"Yes, but both Jacob's and the unknown's fingerprints were on the loose tea canister on the kitchen counter. I've sent the canister contents to the lab for analysis."

"So, both victims were poisoned by tea."

"It appears that way at this point. There was a similar jar of herbs at the glass shop. I'll give you a call when the toxicology reports are complete." She gave him a little punch to the arm and walked briskly down the hallway.

He smiled, opened his office door, then sat at his desk. "It appears we have a viable suspect."

"Who?" asked Officer Boulli, still holding the closed file folder.

"Jacob Underwood. He's attending a workshop at Webb's Glass Shop and appears to be a friend of the family."

Parker plucked the file folder out of Boulli's hands and placed it in the lower right-hand desk drawer. "I want you to pick him up for questioning."

"Arrest the kid?" Officer Boulli took his notebook out of his shirt pocket.

"Yes, Jacob is a minor . . . although in Florida, there are no special processes—which by the way, you should already know. As a courtesy, call his parents and tell them so they can be involved."

"Yes, sir. What time should I pick him up?"

Detective Parker glanced at the open calendar application on his PC. "You need to make sure the parents have plenty of time to get to the glass shop. Let's go for three this afternoon."

"Yes, sir."

"Officer, I want you to listen very carefully." Detective Parker stood and made sure that he had Officer Boulli's full attention.

"Sir?"

"This is your final chance. If you can't get this right—calling his parents, meeting them there, bringing him in for questioning and properly processing him—I am recommending to the chief that you not be permitted to continue in this department. In fact, I will recommend that you won't be permitted to continue employment with the police department in any capacity. Is that clear?"

Officer Boulli stood, apparently recognizing the language as part of the termination process. He turned a gray-tinted face to the detective, swallowed, and finally cleared his throat. "Yes, sir. Perfectly clear."

Chapter 25

Savannah snapped off a stem from the ugly aloe plant that grew in a plain terra cotta pot in the front window of the shop. It was lopsided and grossly misshapen from years of being used as the immediate healing topical for soldering iron burns.

She cut the stem down the middle with an X-ACTO knife and spread the two halves wide. She squeezed it firmly, smeared the seeping goo from its inside edges onto Arthur's tiny burn, and applied a Band-Aid onto Arthur's left index finger without bruising either Arthur or an anxiously hovering Nancy.

"Now, see what you've done?" Nancy planted her hands on her hips Superman style. "How can you play the cello with that? Are you determined to stay in third chair?" She heaved an exasperated breath and sat back down at her workstation whispering under her breath.

"I remember from our first day, Arthur, you play the cello," Savannah was concerned.

"Well, not very well, but yes."

"Nonsense, Arthur." Nancy patted him on the knee. "Tell them."

"I've been—"

"He's been appointed to second chair in the cello section of the Florida Orchestra," Nancy blustered over her groom's shy voice. "We just heard last night."

Savannah turned to Arthur. "That's wonderful. Congratulations. More reason to be very careful in here."

Tack soldering resumed with little trouble and finally all were able to pick up their projects and hold them up to catch the afternoon sun. Savannah was thrilled at the diversity of color and design within the tiny group. *I've been underestimating the value of teaching. I thought Dad was wasting his time. I was wrong. Completely wrong.*

"Now is the time if you need to make substantial changes," she said. "It's not hard to de-solder and rework the piece at this point. After this, it will be much more complicated.

"The reason you might want to consider a bit of rework would be if the pieces don't sit next to each other well. Basically, they won't hold together after the next stage of the soldering process if that's the case. That will make the piece weak and it may not be structurally sound enough to hang on a chain by its own."

A police siren blared down the street and two flashing vehicles pulled up in front. A cold shiver ran down Savannah's back. *Is someone else dead?* Without a beat, she made sure everyone was in the room. The door jangled fiercely to announce the arrival of Officer Boulli and a woman police officer. They stood in front of the cash register counter in the display room.

Officer Boulli stood well in front of the woman with both thumbs tucked into his belt. "Miss Savannah Webb?"

Savannah felt her brow crunch tight. *He already knows me. Does he really need to ask again?*

"I'm Officer Boulli. We spoke earlier." He took out his ID and showed her the badge and card.

"Yes, Officer Boulli. This is the third time we've met. I expect to receive a friend request to your Facebook page any time now."

A look of mild confusion swept over his face, but he shook it off. "Do you have a student named Jacob Underwood here in the shop?"

"Certainly. He's right here." She stepped back to let Officer Boulli see into the classroom, and a knot formed in the pit of her stomach. "What's the problem?"

"I'm here regarding your case, Miss Webb. We are picking up Jacob and taking him downtown for questioning regarding the poisoning of Hugh Trevor and John Webb. We have notified his parents and they are meeting us here in just a few minutes. Where is he?"

"What?" Savannah felt ice form around her heart. "You can't do that. Why would you do that?"

"Miss Webb, this is simply a part of any investigation. We can question anyone and take anyone into custody that might be a risk to himself or to others."

The young woman officer walked into the classroom. "Jacob, you must go with me into custody. Do you understand what that means?"

Jacob's eyes opened wide and all color drained from his face. "I have to take Suzy with me." He looked at Savannah with pleading eyes. "That's what my mother says, Miss Savannah. Everywhere—even custody."

The bell jangled a sharp ring as Jacob's mother pushed the door open and her platform heels broadcast her determination to protect her son. She walked into the classroom, neatly sidestepped the policewoman, and placed a manicured but not lacquered hand on his forearm. "Jacob, slow breaths. Stay calm. I'm here." She was dressed in an expensive dark navy-skirted suit with a red and white patterned silk shirt. She was calm and controlled. "Who's in charge here? Why are there two police cars waiting outside flashing their lights? There's no need for that sort of vulgar display. Everyone here is behaving in a perfectly civil manner."

"They're taking Jacob away for questioning," said Savannah, aware that her voice was high and trembling. She cleared her throat. "I was told that you had been notified and were on your way."

"I was lucky to get here in time. The call was only five minutes ago." She gave a look to Officer Boulli that would shrink a giant. "My name is

Frances Underwood, juvenile court judge for
Pinellas County. You had better follow every pro-
cedure with extreme precision. Be acutely aware
that I know more about law than you ever will."

She looked at Jacob, stood next to him, and
put her right arm slowly and gently around his
shoulders. "Suzy and I will be with you the entire
time."

Frances again turned that chilling look at Officer Boulli. "Suzy will be with Jacob for the entire
time. He will remain calm and not need medication if you let her stay with him. If anything else
happens and it upsets Jacob because of you, I am
prepared to do everything in my considerable
power to make sure you won't do it again."

"We have to take the dog?" Officer Boulli pulled
and reseated his truncheon, then rested his hand
on his service revolver. He sighed deeply and
muttered loud enough for everyone to hear
plainly, "It's never simple."

He glared at the female officer. "Take Jacob.
Take the judge. Take the dog. Just get them downtown so we can start a proper interrogation." He
stomped out the door and nearly banged the bell
off its hook.

Frances nodded. "Jacob, let's get Suzy. It's best
if you leave everything else here. We want to keep
things as uncomplicated as possible. This nice policewoman is going to take care of things properly."

The female officer smiled. "Thank you, ma'am.
That's very helpful."

The policewoman bundled Jacob and his mother
into the back of her patrol car. She carefully

checked that all were seated and buckled in and that Suzy was safe in Jacob's arms. They drove away.

Edward walked into the shop. "What the bloody hell is going on?"

Savannah looked at him. "They've taken Jacob downtown for questioning."

Edward blurted, "What?"

"I'm not sure, but I think they are going to charge him. Boulli believed he killed Hugh. I don't know what they think about Dad yet." Savannah looked at Jacob's vacant workspace and felt true frustration.

Edward raised his hand and brushed back his hair. He looked into Savannah's eyes. "What are we going to do?"

"We've got to follow Dad's ciphers and find the real killer."

Chapter 26

After what seemed like a hundred years, Edward left and everyone returned to the classroom in silent single file. They sat at their worktables and tried to make more progress on their sun catchers.

Reluctantly, Savannah tidied Jacob's work space, put his tools in his canvas carryall, and tucked it under the worktable. She held his project up to the light, admired the precise solder joins, then placed it on his working board and made sure his project was pinned securely. *I don't understand how Officer Boulli thinks Jacob is a viable suspect.*

She walked over to the twins' worktable. Rachel had smeared great gobs of flux across the entire piece. "This is a little too much for the purpose and will interfere with the smooth appearance that we're trying to achieve."

"I told you that was too much flux." Faith leaned over to point the soldering iron at her sister's glass.

"No waving the soldering iron," snapped Savannah. She caught Faith's arm in mid-gesture and gently pushed it toward the soldering iron holder. "Keep that in the holder if you're not actually using it."

Nancy was watching Arthur like a hawk, ready to pounce at the first misstep. Savannah looked at Arthur's progress and imagined what the upset might do to him. She expected to see a hot mess and maybe have to treat a few more burns.

She cleared her throat. "I'm sorry. This is simply not going to work. I'm too upset to teach and that means it's not safe for us to continue class today. Let's all clean up and start again tomorrow."

When that had been accomplished, she said good-bye to the newlyweds and the twins, but asked Amanda to stay behind. She went into the office, opened her backpack, and took out the novel and the sheet of onion skin. She brought them back to the classroom and opened the book to page 337 and lined up the holes.

"What on earth is that?" Amanda leaned over the workbench.

"The cipher I showed you and Jacob earlier fits over a page in this novel to reveal the clue. I've asked Edward to come and help us get to the end of the trail. It may clear Jacob. Can you help?"

"Absolutely. It just can't be Jacob. He wouldn't hurt a fly. Literally. I've seen him shoo flies outside like a cowboy and catch lizards just to carry them outside rather than kill them. That's way more compassion than I have or anyone I've ever met has."

"Have you found out anything on Smythe? Do you know where he was during Hugh's murder?" Savannah asked.

"I signed up as a follower to his Twitter feed. It felt sleazy, because I really, really don't like that slime bucket, but it turns out that he, unfortunately, was absolutely elsewhere during the times Mr. Webb died and when Hugh was murdered."

"Where was he?"

"He was back in Atlanta attending a week-long diversity training seminar. He kept tweeting how useless it was. He was driving back on Monday morning after spending the weekend at his condo. He takes a picture of every meal he eats and posts it to his Twitter feed. I guess after prison food, you would appreciate the small things. He's not the one. Disappointing, I know, but he's not the one."

Savannah looked into Amanda's sad violet eyes. "Then we have one more person it isn't and one more reason why the police think it's Jacob. We have to work harder."

The ring of her cell phone made Savannah jump, the display showed Judge Underwood as the caller. "What's happening?"

"The police are preparing to question Jacob, but I wanted to tell you that Officer Boulli came by and told us that the forensic specialists matched Jacob's fingerprints to the coffee cup that Hugh used on that Monday morning. He wasn't supposed to tell us and now Detective Parker is furious with him."

Savannah said, "But it can't be Jacob."

"The essential problem is that he has no alibi and Boulli can't get beyond that. My husband and I leave for work at six every morning. Jacob gets himself up and fed, then walks over to Webb's. That's why I have the best defense lawyer in the state with me. But anyway, I wanted to tell you that this idiot officer told us that Hugh and John died from the same poison. I wasn't sure if they had told you."

"Detective Parker called this morning to tell me. He seems competent."

"That will be refreshing. This may take some time because there's no hard evidence and fingerprints on a cup in a common workroom do not a murder make. The district attorney will want a confession."

"If there's anything we can do for you, let us know."

"Thanks. I've got to go. It looks like your detective is ready to start the interview."

"Thanks for the call. I truly appreciate it."

Edward rushed into the shop and went directly into the classroom. "How's it going? Is there any news about Jacob?"

Savannah put away her cell and felt a frown appear. "His mother called. The police are planning to question Jacob. She's hired a top-notch lawyer. She was angry and worried, but she's a judge and knows the ins and outs of the process."

Edward perched on a work stool. "Why is she worried?"

Savannah pulled a stool from the next table and sat beside him. "Apparently, they found his fingerprints on the coffee cup that Hugh used early Monday."

"But they worked in the same area. That doesn't mean anything."

Savannah raised her hand in a stop signal. "There's more to it. She says Officer Boulli let it slip that the poison that killed Hugh was also used on Dad. The facts are that he has a key to the shop, his fingerprints were on the cup, and he has no alibi for early mornings. The forensic lady found a baby jar full of an herb mixture tucked in with Jacob's paints in the custom workshop. I'm willing to bet that it contained the poison. It makes a compelling case. I'm worried."

"What's this?" Edward peered down on the sheet of onion skin spread out on the worktable. "It looks like bugs have chewed this up."

Amanda piped up. "That's what I thought, but look at this. It's way, way cool. I've never seen anything so clever. It fits onto a page in one of Mr. Webb's Dan Brown books to reveal the next puzzle. I'll bet he was a consultant for the puzzles in those books. Mr. Webb was a clever man. He was, wasn't he?"

Savannah felt a flush of pride at the compliment. "Yes, but I'm afraid he may have been a bit too clever to leave me a puzzle that I can't figure out. He was always right next to me and ready to guide me to the solutions when we worked on them when I was a girl. This is an entirely different sort of code."

Edward looked into Savannah's eyes and spoke softly. "The stakes are quite different, as well. Why didn't he leave a message in the will or with me or just make it clear in the first puzzle?"

"He was a very proud man, remember? And paranoid along with it. If he wasn't sure enough to have the killer arrested or charged, he wouldn't have trusted anyone."

"We need to figure out what he was trying to tell you. If there's any chance to clear Jacob by solving this puzzle, we must do that. Now."

"Right, let's copy out the letters that are revealed one more time and see if that will click something for one of us." Savannah printed the letters on the whiteboard at the front of the classroom. She stood back and inserted slash marks for word separations.

O N / T H E / E D G E / O F / S P L E N D O R

Amanda propped her chin in the palm of both hands. "I can't think of anything." She turned to Edward. "Anything?"

His eyes turned serious. "This could hold the solution to the murders. It's a paralyzing thought." He looked toward Savannah. "Did your dad solve these kinds of puzzles in his work under this kind of pressure?"

"I think he did. He was an amazing man, but

he would have known that I would need to have a simple puzzle rather than something too obscure."

"Good." Edward stood. "Let's try to relax and concentrate on obvious meanings. The phrase 'Edge of Splendor' is curious. What can we make of that?"

"Could it mean the edge of the bay? He used to take me to see the sunrise on the water over by the arbor on Coffee Pot Bayou. It was a Saturday morning ritual. While we were watching, he would say, 'What a splendor of light' during the rising of the sun. Then we would go get breakfast."

"Okay. Would he have hidden a message there for you to find?" asked Edward.

"I can't think of anything." She slumped onto a stool. "Wait, it could be the arbor. That was also one of his geocache locations that we would check when we were there. What time is it?"

Amanda looked at her Mickey Mouse watch. "It's only four-thirty. Guys, I am petrified at the thought of Jacob spending the night in jail. What if they won't let him keep Suzy!" She pulled a tissue from one of her many bags and snuffled into it.

"Focus, focus. It's only a short drive. Let's take the van. We can be there in a few minutes." Savannah pulled the keys from her pocket. "We'll lock the doors, set the alarm, and come back here with whatever we find."

Edward shook his head. "Look. I've got some arrangements to make at the pub. I'll make some calls so I can have the evening off. I can't leave the crew short-handed. I'll be back in two shakes."

"Deal," said Savannah. "We'll meet up at the van."

The trip to Beach Drive took a bit longer than Savannah remembered. The traffic was heavier during the evening commuter hour, so it was more than twenty minutes later before they were parked and standing in front of the tall white arbor with its substantial base of Spanish style columns that supported a wooden trellis. A mature twisted bougainvillea plant was in front of each pillar and the thick vines wound up the trellis with a heavy canopy of red blooms.

"Amanda, will you keep a lookout? One of the cardinal rules of geocaching is to make sure no one passing by sees where the caches are hidden. Just yell out that someone is coming and we'll back away and wait until they pass."

She nodded and began looking up and down the sidewalk as Edward and Savannah cut through the grass toward the structure.

"The cache is over here." She led him over to the bottom of one of the large white columns that gave the structure an old world look.

"Someone's coming," whispered Amanda at near conversational volume. "There's three of them. Just hold off."

Edward quickly took Savannah's arm and planted her against the column and began to nuzzle her neck. "Camouflage is quite fun," he mumbled into her shoulder.

She giggled. "And you call this convincing?"

He pulled his head back and looked into her eyes. Then he kissed her with quiet passion and tenderness.

Savannah forgot that it was a ruse and returned his kiss with unexpected warmth,

"All clear." Amanda looked over. "Hey, do you think you can start concentrating? Really, some people have great difficulty concentrating on the task at hand. I find it extremely annoying myself to be prepared to work and look what you two are up to. Really!"

Savannah felt as scarlet as the ever-blooming canopy of bougainvillea blossoms and pushed down the passion that Edward had awakened. Stooping down, she cautiously reached her arm into the multiple branching trunks—careful to avoid the two-inch thorns that make the flowering plant a trespass deterrent.

"Here it is." She pulled out a small box and stood. With Edward and Amanda blocking the view of the many walkers that constantly passed on the sidewalk, Savannah opened the box to find only a new logbook and a pencil. The logbook was blank except for a congratulatory note from the owner. She stood there a moment, then her shoulders slumped. "This can't be right. There's nothing here that could take us further."

Amanda nudged her over to peek into the box. "Are you sure? Nothing?"

Savannah turned the box over and over in her hands. "I've got it wrong. I'm not going to get this figured out in time."

Edward put his arm around her shoulders in a side hug. "Stop that kind of talk. It's not the right solution, but we still have plenty of daylight. Let's get back to the shop and take another look at the puzzle."

"Of course. I'm so anxious. I'm not considering how obscure this hint is for us." She tucked the cache back under the bougainvillea plant. "I guess the pressure of trying to get Jacob out of jail is affecting my thinking. I'm sure that he was meant to help uncover the solutions. Dad was training him in code breaking. Not a comforting thought."

Chapter 27

For the tenth time in as many minutes, Detective Parker checked the status of processing Jacob. It was irritating beyond belief to let Officer Boulli bumble his way through the minimal steps required for preparing a juvenile suspect to be questioned. He shook his head and checked the status again. It had been over half an hour already.

The documentation would be important for the day when he could finally recommend the inept officer be fired. It would probably be easier to arrest the real murderer, and at the bureaucratic level, definitely quicker.

Unfortunately, since Jacob had access and any number of opportunities to poison the two glass artists, Parker needed to quickly eliminate him as a suspect to refocus the investigation on searching for the real killer. Collecting documentation on Officer Boulli was one of those serendipitous opportunities he couldn't let pass. A chance like this one might not come his way for months if not years.

"What is the problem?" Officer Boulli looked down at Jacob. "This is a police station, boy, not a pet parade."

They were standing in front of a small postal type window and Jacob was holding Suzy and looking around her, down to Officer Boulli's shoes. "Sir, I need to take Suzy outside."

"What? No way. I need to get you through this processing bull so I can start the real questioning. All you have to do is empty your pockets."

"I don't carry anything in my pockets."

"What? That's impossible."

Jacob's voice rose a little higher and he began to breathe faster. "I don't have anything in my pockets."

The officer behind the window leaned over to Boulli. "What's the problem? A line is starting to build. Check his stuff and get moving."

"Sir, I need to take Suzy outside."

Ever-patient Suzy looked at Jacob and whimpered a short whine.

"This is important. Suzy needs to go," Jacob insisted.

"Okay, already. Take off her pack and check it in."

"But I can't—"

"Yes, you can." Boulli pulled at the Velcro straps that held Suzy's service pack on and pitched it through the window." Sending a hard look to the property officer behind the window, he asked, "Are you good now?"

"Thank you, Officer. He's processed and in the system." Shaking his head, the property officer tucked Suzy's pack into a large bag and labeled it JACOB UNDERWOOD. He added the date and the case number muttering all the while, "That man has no sense, no sense at all," and motioned for the next in line.

Officer Boulli trotted down the hallway dragging an agitated Jacob with him. Jacob was struggling to keep upright while holding on to Suzy cradled in both arms. They finally arrived at the end of the hallway and Boulli held open the door to the outside.

Jacob placed Suzy on a small patch of grass that faced Central Avenue just a few yards away. Suzy performed, shook herself thoroughly, and returned to sit beside Jacob, who instantly scooped her up into his arms.

"Let's go," urged Officer Boulli. He looked at his watch. "We're late."

"Late?" echoed Jacob. "Late?"

"Yeah, very late. We should have been done long ago." Officer Boulli led the teenager by the arm down the long hallway.

Jacob stood stiff in his tracks and nearly pulled Officer Boulli over.

"What the—" Boulli uttered as he regained his bulky balance and looked to see that Jacob was having difficulty breathing. The officer released his grip and Jacob set Suzy down and sat down beside her still struggling to get enough air.

"What? What's the matter?" Boulli yelled down at Jacob.

Suzy moved close to him and placed a paw on his knee.

Jacob scooted backwards to lean his back against the hallway wall. "In"—he took a tiny breath—"hale"—another breath—"er"—another breath. His lips were taking on a slightly blue tinge. He puffed out a forced breath and struggled to say, "Inhaler."

Suzy looked up with pleading brown eyes.

"Oh, your inhaler. Where is it?"

Jacob's eyes were beginning to droop. "Suzy's pack."

"Crap, crap, crap." Officer Boulli sprinted as fast as his bulk would allow down the long hallway and back to the property window. Gasping, he pushed the people in line out of the way and leaned his head into the window. "I need the dog's pack." He panted like a steam engine. "Hurry. It's got a medicine in it."

The property officer raised his eyebrows high, reached for the bag, and pulled out the pack. "Here. You had better hurry." He shoved it through the window and the sweating Boulli grabbed it.

The trip back down the hallway extracted the last vestige of fitness from him as he staggered the last few feet and dropped the pack at Jacob's feet.

Jacob lifted his head and pulled his inhaler out of the pack and puffed it quickly. He exhaled long and inhaled another puff.

Boulli was sweating profusely and leaned against the wall trying desperately to get his breath.

As he stood there recovering, Jacob calmly stowed the inhaler back into the storage pocket and fastened the pack around Suzy. Lifting her back into his arms, he stood patiently beside the panting officer. "I'm ready. Can I see my mother now? She said she would be waiting for me."

Nodding wearily, the officer led the way down the hallway and turned into the corridor where the interview conference rooms were located. He opened the largest one, motioned for Jacob to sit at the table in the center of the room, and collapsed into one of the chairs along the wall, sweating like a beached walrus.

In his office, Detective Parker clicked the status tab once more and it indicated PROCESSED for Jacob. "Finally." He retrieved a file folder from his desk drawer and marched quickly down the hallway to the part of the building that contained the interview rooms.

Jacob's parents and lawyer were sitting on the plain industrial metal chairs that lined the far hallway just outside the entrance to the interview room. Like the chairs in a hospital waiting room, they simply couldn't provide comfort no matter the design.

Detective Parker walked over and they immediately stood like soldiers awaiting orders. He extended his hand. "I'm Detective David Parker in charge of the case involving Jacob."

Jacob's mother stepped forward and shook his hand. "Good afternoon, Detective Parker. We may have met, but you don't look familiar. I'm Judge Frances Underwood, Jacob's mother." She gestured to the pale man standing next to her. "This is my husband, Ben and our lawyer, Mark Howard."

"Ma'am, your name sounds familiar." Detective Parker's eyes narrowed. "Should I know you?"

"I'm not sure we've crossed paths, but I've been the chief judge for the Sixth Judicial Circuit's Juvenile Division of Pasco and Pinellas Counties for the last fifteen years."

Detective Parker shook Ben's hand while still looking at Judge Underwood and in his mind saw his quick in-and-out questioning of Jacob fly out the window. "I don't think our paths have crossed." He shook hands with Mark Howard. "Obviously, I can skip the brief instructions about how the process works."

Judge Underwood smiled tightly. "Please continue as if I were just an ordinary parent."

Nodding, Detective Parker motioned for them to sit and he took the chair next to her, leaving

Ben and Mark to lean forward to hear what he
had to say. Parker smoothly recited the information he usually gave to a suspect's family at the
start of a major case.

"Succinct and well delivered, Detective Parker,"
Judge Underwood admitted, if stiffly, when he
was finished. "I'm happy that we can continue."

Detective Parker nodded. "I assume you would
prefer to be present during our interrogation of
Jacob?"

"Yes, absolutely."

A familiar tension began to knot its way up the
back of Detective Parker's neck. "If you'll follow
me, he's just down here." He led the way into the
hallway of interview rooms around the corner
and held open the third door on the left. He
stepped back to let them enter the room.

Jacob stood up instantly with Suzy in his arms.
He looked down at his shoes. "Mother, I didn't do
anything wrong. I didn't hurt Mr. Webb. I didn't
hurt Mr. Trevor."

Judge Underwood hurried over to her son, but
didn't embrace him, as society would have expected. She lightly rested a hand on his forearm
and bent down to look into his eyes. "I know,
Jacob. I believe you. We need to find the truth.
Right?"

"Yes, Mother, we need the truth."

She spun around to the lounging Officer
Boulli. "I've never heard of an incoming suspect
taking this long to simply turn over *no* possessions
to the property officer. You realize I made sure he

had no possessions. What took you over thirty minutes to check in at the property window and walk half the length of this building?"

Detective Parker was delighted with Officer Boulli's answer.

Chief Juvenile Judge Frances Underwood—not so much.

Chapter 28

Savannah, Edward, and Amanda returned to the shop and gathered around the classroom worktables once more.

Amanda looked down at the Dan Brown novel and up at the whiteboard. "So far, all we're doing is proving that Jacob is the only one who could have killed John and Hugh. Maybe we should just leave this to the cops."

"I'm not giving up. We haven't completed the code so we don't have all the information yet. Savannah paced back and forth in the front of the classroom before light dawned. "Wait. Dad called the panel in the custom workshop *Splendor*. It was on the invoice for the stained glass project." She headed to the custom workshop to look at the panel.

Amanda followed. "Do you think he meant the

panel that they were working on for that big contract?"

Edward shrugged his shoulders, following them. "Well it's possible, but why would you think that?"

Savannah flipped on the lights and the large panel lay out like a patient ready for the doctor to complete a lifesaving operation.

"It's just a hunch, but it makes sense that he would have a clue here in the shop so that he could make sure it was available to me." Savannah gently ran her hand across the smooth surface of the panel. Most of the individual pieces were spot soldered. The more recent pieces were held in their place within the panel with small metal pushpins. "This copy panel is going to be as beautiful as the original."

Amanda crossed her arms across her chest. "Everything in here is *splendid*!"

Savannah felt her frustration. "Yes, but he called *this* one *Splendor* on his invoice."

Edward circled the table. "Well, if this is it, there must be a message at the edge."

Savannah looked over at Hugh's workbench. "Maybe Dad wrote something on the metal frame that finishes the panel."

She found the metal pieces at the back of Hugh's workbench and laid them in place around the edges next to the panel. "Everyone, take a framing piece and see if you can find anything."

They bent over them, ran fingers over all the edges looking for solder dots or hidden papers and Savannah shined a flashlight across all the surfaces in case a message could only be revealed that way.

"Nothing." Amanda looked at Savannah, "Now what?"

Edward leaned over the nearly finished panel. "It is splendid, isn't it?"

Savannah stepped back and tilted her head. "Hey, there's a technique I used in painting class to get a different perspective of my work. I need a mirror." Without waiting to hear anything from the others, she went into the display room and returned holding a twelve-inch square of mirrored glass. Turning around, she stood with her back to the panel and held the mirror up high so that she could look at it in reverse. "Sometimes, what you need is a change in perspective to pick out the problems in your painting."

She angled the mirror to point at the bottom edge of the panel. "This lower border looks odd." She put the mirror aside. "Hang on. I took a picture of this when I was in the church on Wednesday night." She pulled out her phone, flipped through her photo gallery, and peered at the picture, trying to see details through the discoloration caused by the flash. "Look! This is slightly different from the one downtown."

"Let me see." Amanda peered over Savannah's shoulder to look at the photo on the phone. "Can you send that to your computer so that we can make it a lot bigger? Your phone screen is too tiny."

"Sure." Savannah tapped a few buttons and

they heard a small beep from the office computer. "Come on. Let's take a closer look."

She sat in the creaky desk chair and Amanda pulled up the side chair. Edward huddled over the rolltop desk sheltering the display. The photo opened and they looked at the top and bottom edges.

"It's a little hard to see," said Savannah, "but it does look different from the one in the workroom. I'll print just the border out in color and let's compare." She clicked the PRINT icon and the printer fired up in a whir and ejected a piece of paper.

Amanda snatched the print, dashed into the custom workshop, and walked around to the bottom of the panel. "Yes! You were right. It's quite different in a subtle way. It's a perfect duplication except for the last two rows of squares in the bottom edge."

"Yes, but what does this mean?" Edward asked.

Savannah moved them over. "Let me see if it's one of Dad's codes." She peered at the two squares that were different, then grabbed a pencil and drew them on a yellow sticky pad. "Let's put this up on the whiteboard and see what's what."

Back in the classroom, she drew the glass border and stepped back to look at the illustration. She studied the lines for a few long minutes. "This reminds me of something. It's tickling the back of my mind, but I'm just not remembering it."

"Is there a record of the types of codes you and your dad used during the sessions?" Edward asked.

"That would at least allow us to eliminate some codes."

Savannah thumped the front of her head. "No, there's no record. As part of the game, he made me memorize them. A major element of his games involved not keeping written evidence of either the code used or the final solution."

Amanda squealed, "Oh, that's so fantastic. He was training you in case he needed to leave this situation in your hands for solving. Yes, he was clever."

Paranoid is more like it. Savannah squeezed her eyes tight and rubbed her temples. "All I have to do is remember which code he is using." She stood still. Her only movements were the fingers making small circles at the sides of her head. "I remember that we talked about the code games the last time I spoke to him on the phone. He mentioned them very casually. He didn't ask if I remembered them or anything . . . just asked if I remembered when we played the code games."

"What about listing the ones you remember?" Edward prompted. "That might give us a start."

Savannah erased the board clean and held the marker poised over the surface. "Okay, here's the names of ciphers that I remember." She turned back to look at them over her shoulder. "I was quite young.

"The Maritime Signal Flags. I loved this because we read them off the boats when we walked around the waterfront. Some of them were rude. Then the Semaphore Flag code which we played when we were at either end of Crescent Lake. That was fun.

"It can't be either of those. But there was one more that these symbols remind me of." She paused for a few seconds. "Got it. It's called the Pigpen Cipher. It reminded me of the comic strip character. Sometimes it's called the Freemason's Cipher. There are many ways to vary it, but this is the one we always used and how the letters are interpreted." She wrote it on the whiteboard below.

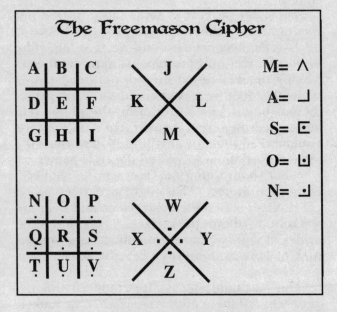

"This one works as a series of symbols within those four images. So for working out the code along the border, this is what we use. If I wanted to code the word MASON, you can see that it would look like this. Savannah wrote down the letters and their symbols beside them.

"Good." She stepped back. Now let's put the border images up as well. She took pictures of the border with her phone, sent them to the shop computer and printed them out in color. As each image printed, Amanda brought them to Savannah and on the right side of the board, she taped them up in two rows—the top border over the bottom border.

"Now we're ready to solve this puppy." Savannah stood in front of the whiteboard with her hands on her hips. "First, we transfer the symbols on the top border." Turning to Edward and Amanda, she said, "Make sure I don't copy a symbol wrong. We can drive ourselves crazy with just one small transposition error."

One by one, Savannah decoded the border symbols into a long string of characters below.

⌐⌐Ⴞ⅃Ⴊ⌐ⅢⴄⵕⲞⴖⲞ⌐⌐Ⴊ⅃Ⴑ⅃<⅂⌐⌐

"Okay, let's transfer the symbols on the bottom border. These are so tiny, no one would ever think of this as a message."

ⴖⴞⴞ>⌐⌐Ⴊ⅂⅂ⴞ▽⌐⌐

"Now, let's translate them into letters." Savannah stepped back and looked at the scramble of letters. She looked back at Amanda and Edward who were staring holes into the whiteboard. "Are you seeing what I'm seeing?"

Edward stepped up to the whiteboard and took the marker from Savannah. "I think so. If you isolate the first five letters, I can get I C O N S. He wrote a slash after the *S*, separating the word from the other letters.

I C O N S / B E H I N D A L T A R
B O O K S I N T O W E R

"Oh! Oh! Oh! Let me do it. I see the words," squealed Amanda. "I can do it."

I C O N S / B E H I N D / A L T A R
B O O K S / I N / T O W E R

"What could that mean?" Edward squinted at the letters, turning his head one way and the other. He looked over to Savannah. "What was John trying to tell you with this?"

Savannah dragged her hand through her hair. "Oh, no." Her wavering voice was barely above a whisper. "It can't be—it just can't be." She looked over at Edward who didn't seem to get it. Clearing her suddenly scratchy throat, she explained. "Reverend Kline collects Russian icons for the church. Dad thinks it's Reverend Kline."

Chapter 29

Friday Evening

"I can't believe my dad thought that Reverend Kline was a threat." Savannah rubbed absently at her arms. "No one else we know matches the words in this message, but how could it be him? How *could* it be him?"

Edward glanced at Amanda who was still studying the lettering on the whiteboard. He motioned to the revealed words. "Who else is tied to icons and the church?"

Savannah shook her head. "No one I know of, but I've been away for so long. He's a reverend. I've known him all my life."

Amanda scowled. "He's human, right. Just because he's a reverend doesn't mean he isn't capable of murder."

Savannah dealt with her shock by shaking her

hands from the wrists. "I just don't understand it. What is he doing that needs to be covered up?"

"You've got to catch me up. I still don't understand the message." Edward stepped over to the whiteboard and underlined the first word. "What does *icons* mean to you and why does it point to the reverend?"

Savannah relaxed her breathing and sat on one of the student stools. "The reverend has been collecting a category of religious artifacts called Russian icons. *Icons.* He's talked about them to me several times in the space of a few days so he's obviously very passionate about them. He says he had received the church council's approval to seek them out and purchase them."

"What for?" Amanda scrunched her brow. "They're paintings, right? Just paintings. What's the big deal about religious paintings?"

Savannah rubbed her temples again. "I'm trying to remember what he said about them."

Edward pointed to Amanda, then pressed his index finger up to his lips. *"Let her think,"* he mouthed without making a sound.

There was a long pause for several minutes while Savannah stared at the whiteboard sitting absolutely motionless. "He said that his personal mission was to ensure that they don't fall into the hands of private investors who"—she paused again—"will never let them fulfill their holy purpose as spiritual inspiration."

"How does he find the icons?" asked Edward. "I've never even seen one."

"They're quite small—a bit larger than an eight-by-ten photograph. They are simple yet beautiful. By that, I mean the subject matter is uncomplicated—no background to speak of—and the painting is usually on hard wood with a gold leaf border. If Jesus or Mary is one of the subjects, a gold-leafed halo would be painted on it, as well."

Amanda shook her head. "I don't get why icons are in the message."

"It's not clear to me either, but Dad obviously felt it was important. This is the clearest message he coded. It refers to objects that could be examined or prove something. So, I think this is the last message and the key message."

"So we need to examine the icons and the books"—Edward pointed to the second message—"to find the proof we need."

"There is a rotating collection at the church just behind the altar underneath the Rose stained glass window. I wonder . . ." Again, Savannah stared at the whiteboard for a long minute. "The reverend must have a nearby source."

Edward sat on one of the student stools. "You know, he's been showing up in the Grand Central District more frequently these past few weeks. Do you—"

"Right!" Savannah snapped her fingers. "When he arrived early to pick up Jacob today, he said he would drop in at V and V Antiques." She looked at her watch. "Are they still open?"

"I'll look. They're just across the street, you know." Amanda sprinted to the front door of the shop. She grabbed the doorknob, turned her head, and yelled back, "The lights are still on."

"Perfect," said Savannah. "Let's go talk to the owner. He must know something about the reverend's collection."

Amanda opened the door and swooped across the street.

"Wait, Amanda. Wait. I need to lock up. Catch her, Edward."

He sped out the door. Savannah grabbed her backpack, quickly locked the front door, and followed them. She barely caught sight of the back of Edward entering a small collectibles shop almost directly across from Webb's.

She was only a minute or so behind them, but Amanda and Edward already had the little old shop owner trapped behind his desk all the way to the back of the store.

". . . for the last several weeks?"

Savannah heard the last part of Amanda's question asked in a rush.

The shop owner replied, "Sure, Reverend Kline is a regular customer. He's here in the shop several times a week."

"Good afternoon." Edward extended his hand, which the shop owner stood up and shook. "I'm Edward Morris, owner of The Queen's Head Pub." He motioned to Savannah. "This is Savannah Webb, new owner of Webb's Glass Shop and our impulsive chatterbox here"—he lowered his chin to stare pointedly at Amanda—"is Amanda

Blake, Assistant Office Manager at Webb's Glass Shop."

"Very pleased to welcome you back to the Grand Central District, Miss Webb." The old man held her hand in both of his when he leaned over the desk to shake hands with Savannah. "I'm Vincent Stannous the proprietor of V and V Antiques. My sincere condolences on the death of your father."

Amanda glared at them.

"Thank you for your kind words." Savannah liked the gentle old soul who looked as if he had been born in this shop and would simply fade away into its eclectic collection of old paintings, vintage suitcases, and the bric-a-brac popular more than fifty years ago. "My father and I have been working with Reverend Kline on the church's stained glass for a long time and I was curious about what sort of objects he's collecting."

"Oh yes. He's coming up on a milestone anniversary with the church, isn't he?"

"Yes, yes, that's it." Savannah looked over to Edward and nodded. "His anniversary. We'd like to get something special in appreciation for sending so much work to Webb's Glass Shop."

"That's very easy. He has a standing order to get a first look at any religious artifacts that originated in the Cold War period. He's especially fond of icons that can be traced to Communist Russia. I've also sent some families his way that want to deal with him and the church directly for their pieces."

Amanda piped up. "Is that legal?"

"As is the case with most religious art, it depends. There's a lucrative black market for relics stolen during the last days of World War II. Many rural villages were stripped of their religious icons and laws now help with their repatriation."

"How much are the lost icons worth?" asked Edward.

"Again, it depends." Vincent spread his hands out like a book. "If it's an especially fine example or from a famous artist, it can run into the hundreds of thousands of dollars. The ones with a proper and legal provenance most typically sell in the neighborhood of five to ten thousand."

The three of them looked at each other.

Savannah cleared her throat. "Thank you, Mr. Stannous. You have been very helpful. It's clear that a Russian icon would be quite a bit out of our budget. But you've given us some ideas. I think I know what to get Reverend Kline for his anniversary. We'll be back as soon as we collect a little more money."

They made their way back to the shop and re-settled themselves on the classroom stools in front of the whiteboard.

Amanda broke the silence. "I'm guessing that the icons the reverend is collecting would not be from the proper and legal provenance category."

Savannah lowered her head. "I'm guessing you're absolutely right."

"What does this mean?" Amanda picked up a dry

erase marker and underlined the word $BOOKS$ in the message.

"I'm not sure." Savannah heaved a long deep sigh. "Given what we know about how important provenance is to a collector, it could mean documentation about the icons. But I'm really just guessing."

Edward perked up. "It could be the actual proof we need."

"Exactly. Dad was one of the deacons of the church and would have had access to financial statements and accounting data. He complained at one point that it seemed he was the only one interested in the numbers."

"As a cipher specialist, he might have detected a pattern of expense that no one else would have the skills to notice." Edward looked at Savannah, "Right?"

Savannah nodded. "The reverend would have known that any patterns would catch Dad's curiosity. In fact, he might have awarded the big duplication project to Webb's just to keep a close eye on Dad."

"I agree," said Edward. "Your dad did seem a little puzzled about that because Frank's bid was lower than Webb's."

"And that would have turned on the paranoia," said Savannah. "I think if we can find these illegal icons as well as the books, we could hand them over to the police. It should be enough to implicate the reverend. Both are apparently in the church."

Amanda tossed the dry erase marker onto the whiteboard shelf. "Then what are we waiting for?"

"We have no choice." Edward handed Savannah her backpack.

"If it is real," said Savannah, "it will clear Jacob, but at the same time, be enough to arrest the reverend."

Chapter 30

Friday Evening

They piled into Savannah's van and drove downtown to the church. Savannah parked about a block away and turned off the engine.

Edward asked. "Now what, guys?"

Savannah opened her door. "Let's see if we can get inside first."

They got out of the van and stood on the sidewalk.

Edward winked at Savannah, then looked at Amanda. "Be absolutely silent. *Absolutely.*"

"Hey, you talkin' to me? You talkin' to me?" Amanda poked him in the arm. "Goof! I know how to be quiet. I just don't particularly *like* being quiet."

They walked across the street to stand on the west side of the church.

Savannah whispered, "Let's stick together and

check the side and back doors. They may be open. We don't want the reverend to see us."

Having no luck with the west side door, they tried the back door only to find that it was locked, as well. They followed the circumference of the church and came around to the front and stood on the entrance steps.

"I see lights on, but it doesn't sound as if anything is going on inside," said Edward.

"Nothing ventured, nothing gained." Savannah walked up the front steps and pulled on the heavy entrance door. The left one didn't budge, but the right side door cracked open. "Shhhh." She put her finger on her lips.

"I know, I know," Amanda whispered under her breath as the three of them slipped into the entry alcove. It was dim, but not pitch black.

Standing a moment to adjust to the darkness, they saw that the doors to the main sanctuary were closed.

Savannah whispered, "I've never seen them closed before." Edward tried one. It was locked. Amanda tried the other door and it was locked as well.

"Savannah," said Edward quietly, "you know this place best. There must be quite a few ways into the sanctuary for the choir, the reverend, musicians, whatever. Which way should we go?"

"There's a stairway from the basement up to the choir loft, at least. Let's go this way." Her voice was low and she pointed to the stairway down to the community room. "Slowly, slowly."

When they reached the bottom of the stairs, it

was pitch black. Not even the required public safety lighting was in evidence.

Amanda froze stiff in her tracks. "It's as dark as a cave down here. I'm not moving."

"Okay, hang on just a second," said Edward. "I have a torch."

"You have a what?" Amanda gasped.

"Flashlight—I mean a flashlight."

"Wait. That's a big problem," whispered Savannah. "We don't want to get caught, remember?"

Edward clicked on a small switch and the flashlight beamed a soft red down the hallway. "This is my astronomy flashlight. It keeps me from losing my night vision so I can manage the controls on a telescope."

"That's amazing! I need one of those for checking up on my mom. She's disturbed by any little bit of light and I'm even more disturbed by complete darkness."

Savannah said, "Focus, guys. We need to keep going. Jacob is counting on us and I don't want him to spend the night in custody. I can't even begin to think of the emotional consequences."

Edward moved the flashlight beam from side to side down the long corridor until they came to a stairway at the end. Savannah peeked up the staircase and could see reflected light at the top of the stairs. "There's some light up there. Must be the reverend's office. Let's go halfway up, then stop and listen. If he's typing or talking on the phone, I think we have a good chance of sneaking by."

They stepped quietly up the stairs.

"But I need that one. It'll be lost forever if I can't get to it." Reverend Kline's voice barreled down the hallway and the little posse halted stiff. Amanda started shaking.

Savannah leaned in very close to her friends. "Now that we know he's here. If he stays on the phone long enough, we're good. Try to stay at the far edge of the stairway, near the wall so a creaking board doesn't give us away."

They slipped up the stairs and were just beyond the reverend's office to the left of the landing, when they heard, "I don't care how hard this is for you. Do you hear me? I don't care one whit. Just get it for me before sundown tomorrow. Or else!" They heard a loud crack of the phone receiver slammed onto the base and then silence.

As one, they froze into place like a game of red light-green light. After a few seconds, they could hear the reverend typing on his keyboard. Savannah signaled them to continue on up the stairway.

When they turned the corner, in front of them was the access way to the choir loft. They entered from the back row. Only dim nightlights plugged into random electrical sockets lit the church. It wasn't enough, so Edward used his red light and they cautiously felt their way down the loft levels until they reached the steep stairway that led to the part of the sanctuary where the reverend presided and the ceremonies occurred.

The altar was a large structure that reminded Savannah of a kitchen island without a marble countertop. It was draped in a heavy dark velvet fabric that fell to the floor.

Amanda circled the altar lifting the drape at each corner. "I don't see any cupboards for storing the icons."

Savannah bent down to look at the altar sides. "It won't be obvious. Edward, shine the light at the corners to see if we can see an edge that is scratched or worn."

Savannah and Amanda lifted the drape over each corner and Edward scanned the wooden edges slowly and carefully. It seemed to take an eon to do the first corner.

"Nothing," whispered Edward and signaled for them to hold the drape on the second corner. After another slow search, he said, "Nothing."

As they lifted the drapery on the third corner, Amanda breathed in a deep breath. "It's going to be the fourth corner. I feel it in my bones."

Savannah felt that way as well.

"Nothing," Edward said as he finished the third corner. He moved to the fourth corner after they lifted the drape.

An absolute age passed until finally came, "Nothing."

Savannah dropped the drapery and stood behind the altar. "I don't understand. The message said the icons were in the altar."

"No, it didn't." Amanda spoke in a loud whisper.

"*Shhhhhhh,*" hissed Savannah and Edward.

Amanda crossed her arms in front of her ample

chest "The message said the icons are *behind* the altar."

"Fair point," acknowledged Savannah.

They moved behind the altar to where a small antifatigue rug looked like it was there to help comfort the reverend as he performed the sacrament and delivered the sermon. Since he stood for the one-hour service each weekday morning and twice on Sunday, the added cushioning would make a difference if he were having hip and knee problems.

Amanda and Savannah quietly lifted the rug aside and Edward used his flashlight to scan the old wooden floor.

"Thank goodness." He exhaled heavily. "Look at these small scratch marks on the floor." He knelt down and fingered the scratched board and it wiggled loose so he picked it up. "That was way too easy. This has been used a lot."

He continued to remove four more boards placing them on the worn rug in removal order. Savannah and Amanda sat down on the floor next to the small two-by-two-foot opening. Their heads bent down to see into the depths of the small pit. The flashlight revealed the edges of several thick packages wrapped in brown paper. Savannah tore at a corner until she revealed the contents. The tear in the paper exposed the golden edges of a gilded icon.

Savannah sat back on her heels. "I can't believe this. The reverend has framed Jacob to take the blame for this. Unbelievable."

"But this doesn't mean anything for clearing

Jacob," said Amanda. "There's nothing to tie the reverend to the money trail."

Edward began quietly replacing the panels.

Savannah handed him one of the boards and he quietly put it in the opening. "That's why the message had two parts." She handed him each board and the opening disappeared. We now need to find the documentation that proves the reverend poisoned Hugh and Dad."

They stood and moved the rug back to its original position.

Edward repeated the second clue, "Books in tower," then turned to Savannah. "What does that mean? There's no tower in this church."

"Right," said Savannah, "but I remember when they were talking about finishing a tower for the church's centennial celebration a couple of years ago. Apparently, there were plans to include another tower when the church was first commissioned. The congregation ran out of money and that part of the church design was abandoned in the middle of construction. Same thing happened for the centennial."

"What did they do?" asked Amanda.

"It was supposed to be several stories high and contain seven bells. The construction crew reworked the roof so that it looks like it was never there. You get to it by another staircase behind the choir loft. The tower hasn't been used for anything but storage for as long as I can remember."

"What kind of storage?" asked Edward.

"Decorations for the major holidays like the

life-sized figures of the nativity and the huge
Christmas wreaths that hang on the chandeliers."
Savannah readjusted the rug so that it was per-
fectly lined up with the floorboards. "It's this way."

They had just entered the choir loft and
reached the last row when they heard steps coming from the reverend's office.

Edward froze, then took Amanda's elbow and
Savannah's hand and pulled them behind the row
of choir chairs. He whispered, "Just keep still."

The click of the light switch was followed by a
flickering burst of light into the sanctuary. Reverend Kline made his way to the altar and pulled
over the mosaic rug. He quickly lifted the boards
over the hidden cache and removed the paper-
wrapped packages.

Amanda began to wiggle restlessly and Savannah glared at her as fiercely as an eagle ready to
kill a rabbit. Trembling, Amanda pulled a tissue
from one of her million pockets and pressed it
firmly over her mouth and nose. Savannah's eyebrows raised sky high. A sneeze would reveal their
presence.

Reverend Kline replaced the boards and rug,
then carried the packages down the aisle toward
the front door. He was halfway down when
Amanda sneezed. Through her tissue and covered hands it sounded more like the rustle of a
small mouse and that saved them.

The reverend muttered, "Rats. I hate rats." He
turned and headed out toward the front doors.

"That was close," said Edward.

After the doors shut, Savannah stood up. "Some-

one needs to follow him and see where he's taking those packages."

Amanda sniffled. "I could do that while you're
getting the paperwork needed to clear Jacob."

Savannah dug the van keys out of her little
backpack. "Give us a call when you find out where
he's going. Stay well behind him. Don't get into
trouble."

Edward said, "He's left the lights on so he's expecting to come back. Just try to figure out where
he's storing them or who he's giving them to and
then wait in the van for us in the parking lot.
We'll be out as soon as we get the paperwork."

Amanda dashed down the aisle surprisingly
silent and disappeared through the double doors
of the church.

Edward grabbed Savannah's hand again. "Now,
let's get this documentation before anything else
gets in our way." He started up the steep stairs behind the choir loft, holding her hand firmly.

She was surprised that she didn't protest or
pull her hand out of his. *This is nice.*

When they got to the top of the stairs, they
found a small light switch that lit a bare bulb
hanging from the ceiling. In front of them was a
plain closet door with a small combination lock
of the sort you put on luggage. It was hung
through a small clasp and bracket just above the
doorknob.

Savannah huffed in frustration. "Now what?"

"First, we'll try to guess the combination. If
that doesn't work, we'll get some tools to remove
the door." He released her hand and squatted

down in front of the lock. "Most people use three identical numbers so that it's easy to remember. I'll start with zero, zero, zero."

Savannah rubbed the palm of her hand. "Let me hold your flashlight."

He handed it back to her. "Good thinking." He turned the numbers. "That didn't work. Onward up the numbers."

As Savannah held the flashlight steady, Edward tried three ones, three twos, and three threes. "Oh wait, this may work." He tried three sixes, but the lock held. "Yeah, that might have been a bit too lame." He continued the series through to three nines. "Well, no luck with that. Oh, one more." He tried 1 2 3 with no luck.

Savannah said, "What's the address here? A lot of people use their street number."

"It's on the front of the church. It's 3 4 2." He dialed the number and the lock opened.

"That's just too simple. Why would he choose that?"

Edward just shook his head slowly from side to side. "It's easy to remember." He removed the lock, then opened the closet door. They stood in the doorway and looked into an awkward sort of walk-in closet with the light of the moon shining through a window in the roof.

He groped inside the wall for a light switch and another bare bulb lit the room with a weak yellow tint. He stepped into the room and moved to the left to allow Savannah to enter.

"This is much larger than I expected." She

could see the life-sized nativity Mary, Joseph, and
even a camel wedged in the back. Both walls at
the sides of the space were stacked six times high
with office-style filing boxes. Each box was labeled with a date and number. "Where do we
start?"

"You take that side and I'll take this. Hopefully
he has all the paperwork bundled together and
it'll be easy to find."

Savannah looked at all the boxes. "The message said *books*, so more than one, but no idea
how large."

As she worked her way along the wall of boxes
she lifted the top box, set it down in the small
aisle behind her, opened the lid, and checked the
contents. She got the next box, repeated the operation, and stacked it on top of the first. She
continued until she had only one box left on the
floor in front of her. After checking that box, she
replaced the lid and in reverse order, lifted each
box into its original position.

"Anything, yet?" Edward said as he replaced his
first stack of boxes into their original order.

"Nope. Not in this stack." She turned to tackle
the next stack.

She had been searching for about ten minutes
and reached into the top box of the third stack.
"Hey, look. This could be it."

She showed Edward a stack of slim brown
leather journals that were dated fifteen years ago
up to the present. The pages were written in a single hand with a page for each icon detailing all

information associated with its discovery, acquisition, and sale.

They moved underneath the bare bulb and Edward flipped through one of the journals and whistled low. "He's been doing this for a long time. This is the documentation we need."

"Great. Let's put everything back in its place and get out of here." Her phone beeped an alert for an incoming text message. She pulled out her phone and swiped to the message. "It's from Amanda. She says he's back!"

Edward flicked off the light and opened the door to shut off the hall light, but he heard steps coming up the stairway. He ducked back into the room. "We have to get out of here. He's coming back."

"Can we get out through the window?"

Edward looked up and stacked three boxes under the window and then two more in front of the three for a step. "I think these will hold me." He stepped onto the short stack and then up to the tall stack, which brought him up to the window.

"It has hinges and should open." He grunted and pushed the pull handle on the lower edge of the window sash. "It hasn't been opened in a long time."

"Hurry. I can hear him now."

"Unghhh! I . . . unghh . . . am . . . unghh . . . hurrying. There!" Edward pushed the window up and looked down to Savannah. She was frozen. "I'll get out here and you climb up here so I can pull you out."

"Here. Take the notebooks." Savannah climbed onto the tall stack of boxes just as Edward's feet disappeared over the rim of the windowsill. "I can't do this—you know that. I'll have to sneak out some other way."

He popped up and his face appeared in the window. He reached in for the notebooks, then placed them down by his feet. He appeared in the window again. "No, you can't go another way. He'll find out we have the proof."

He extended his arms inside the window again and reached for her. He held her forearms and pulled just enough to give her stability for getting through the window. They stood on a small platform on the roof of the church where it was easy to tell that this was the extended footprint of the abandoned tower.

"Follow me." Edward picked up the notebooks and used the red setting on his flashlight to pick his way toward an access stairway at the other end of the roof.

Savannah hadn't moved from the spot where she stood after being dragged through the window. Her face and neck felt clammy with sweat and her one-handed death grip on the windowsill was causing her arm to ache.

All I have to do is take a step. One step.

"Savannah! Hurry up! Come on!" Edward called to her in a raspy whisper. "What's wrong?"

"It's still my fear of heights. I can't move. I can't walk out there."

Edward took a step toward her, then pulled up short. Reverend Kline was silhouetted in the window. He reached through the window, grabbed Savannah by the left shoulder, and pulled her tight against the window. He pressed his right hand against her bare throat.

"Don't move!" He yelled at Edward. "Don't move or I'll cut her throat."

Chapter 31

Friday Evening

The icy glint of the sharp blade revealed a box cutter in the reverend's right hand. The back of his hand pressed the point against the base of Savannah's throat.

Edward put a hand out in front of his chest, "Easy, Reverend. You don't want to do that. Savannah doesn't need to get hurt over this."

The reverend pulled her tighter against the window. "You know about the icons. I can't let anyone know about them. They come to me to be restored to their holy purpose. No one can know about the icons. Give me the notebooks. Give me the notebooks and . . . and . . . and I'll let her go."

"Please stop." Savannah lowered her eyes and looked down at his hand holding the blade. "You can't think I'll be quiet now that I know you killed my dad." She twisted around slowly so that she could see his face over her shoulder. Using a low, soothing tone, she said, "Reverend, you've got to give yourself up. You can't go on like this. You're not thinking right. You need help."

"I don't need help. I'm the restorer of lost icons. I return them back to their original village churches in Russia. The people of those churches were so very grateful when one of their precious artifacts was returned to them. I would sometimes travel over there to participate in the ceremonies and blessings when an icon was restored. The celebration would last for days. I had to rescue them from oblivion. They were going to be added to private collections and hidden from the people. The icons didn't like that. They told me."

Edward took a step toward her with the notebooks stretched out in front of him. "Here are the notebooks. Take them. Take them. Let go of Savannah."

Reverend Kline pressed her even tighter into the window, the sill digging sharply into her back. "It was so easy to use the church funds to buy them back. Some of them I stole from selfish collectors. It was going very nicely until John was appointed as church treasurer. He spotted the financial discrepancies, immediately knew something was wrong and asked me to stop."

"You didn't have to kill him. He would have helped you make things right."

"He didn't understand. I tried to explain it to John, but he didn't understand how loudly the icons called to me. I could hear them cry for their homes when I found them. That's all they wanted. They wanted to go home. John didn't understand that."

He yelled at Edward. "Hand those notebooks over right now."

Edward was just out of reach in front of Savannah. "You'll have to let her go in order to take the books. Just drop the knife and I'll put them in your hand."

The reverend kept the knife at her throat. "No, no, no. That's not going to work. You give the notebooks to Savannah first. Then after she hands them over to me, I'll release her."

Savannah watched Edward inch toward her and extend the notebooks. She moved her right hand forward as if reaching for the books.

Edward halted. "Let up with the knife and I'll give them to her."

The reverend didn't move. "Give the books to Savannah. I'll release her."

"I won't hand over the notebooks with that knife so close to her throat. Be reasonable. You could slip. She could slip. Anything could happen. Just loosen up a little. That point is close to breaking the skin."

Reverend Kline slowly released his iron grip on Savannah's left upper arm and her back sprung away from the windowsill, leaving an ache and the start of a cramp. He slightly relaxed the hand that held the blade pressing into her throat but didn't let go.

"Savannah, get the books with your left hand. Reach out now."

Savannah stretched out her arm.

"Good. Thank you." Edward took a cautious step toward them. "I'm handing the notebooks over to Savannah so she can give them to you and we can go. You don't want to hurt her. You can't hurt her. You've known her since she was a baby. You christened her. You watched her grow into a young woman." He stepped closer and reached out the notebooks with both hands.

In her ear, Savannah heard the reverend's raspy whisper. "Take the notebooks, Savannah. Take them from him."

Savannah exhaled a controlled breath and gritted her teeth. *Reverend Kline is lying. He's going to keep me at knife point in order to control Edward.* "That is not going to happen, Reverend. You killed my dad."

She sharply slumped back against the reverend and blocked the knife by snapping her right forearm up into his arm then back to his forehead. She heard him gasp at the ferocity of the punch and felt a sharp pinch at her collarbone. "Run, Edward. *Now!*" she shouted louder than she believed was possible.

Still terrified of the box cutter's sharp edge, Savannah turned around and slammed the window down on the outstretched arms of the reverend. The box cutter dropped from his hand and skittered down the roof. She registered a faint clink as it fell to the paved parking lot.

He yelped in pain. "My arm! You've broken my arm." He raised the window awkwardly with his left hand, cradled his right arm, and slowly slid down and disappeared from view. Savannah could hear his moans but turned away. She needed to get to Edward.

He hadn't moved. She bent her knees and tentatively took a step toward him, but her balance was off. To recover, she windmilled her arms, but that only made it worse.

Reaching out to save her teetering balance, Savannah jerked the notebooks from Edward's outstretched hand. The unexpected pull caused him to tip over backward. His feet skittered on the tiles and he slid down the slanted slope of the church roof on his side.

Savannah froze when she saw him disappear over the edge of the tiled roof. "Edward," she whispered in a high shrill voice. "Edward! Answer me."

He replied in a tense voice, "I'm just over the edge of the roof. There's a gutter here that looks ancient, but it's holding me for now. I can't pull myself over. I need help."

By leaning over, Savannah could see his hands holding the gutters. She watched him struggling to get his chest up and over the protruding gutter.

The fear in her stomach was boiling over, but she pushed it down and put it in a place where it could boil alone. She forced her stiff legs to take a tiny step toward him. With one tiny step after another, she inched along the peak of the roof until she was even with where he was hanging.

Getting down on all fours, she crawled backwards down the sharp pitch. Slowly, slowly, slowly was the answer. Fear was what got her on the roof and moving towards Edward. She couldn't let anything happen to him.

When she had traveled down the tiles to within a foot from the edge, she reached into her back jean pocket. She pulled out her dad's Swiss Army knife, opened the ice pick attachment, and plunged it into the roof as deep as it would go. "I'm here, Edward. Hang on just a bit longer."

Interlocking her fingers, she grasped the red knife handle with both hands and let her entire body lie flat on the roof with her legs dangling over the edge of the slope. "Edward, climb up on me. I'm anchored and can take the weight."

"We'll both go down." He gasped from the effort of pulling himself up.

"No, you must trust me. I can be your ladder."

"But—"

"Do it now!" Savannah screamed.

She felt Edward's hand grab the shin of her right leg and then felt his weight shift as he grabbed her left knee.

"Now, grab my belt at the back of my waist." She tightened her grip on the knife and pressed her forehead against the roof shingles.

She felt his weight on her lower body and then the weight was gone. He was lying faceup on the roof next to her with his smile lighting up the night sky.

Panting like a steam engine, he looked into her eyes. "I thought you were afraid of heights? What happened?"

"I was terrified. But I was more afraid of letting

you fall. I wouldn't be able to live with myself if I just stood there and watched."

The police announced their arrival with sirens and flashing lights. Amanda, cell phone in hand, ran up to them, pointing at the roof.

Edward looked over. "I'm fairly impressed with the strength required for glassblowing. Woman, you are strong—really strong." His eyes opened wide as he looked at the blood soaking into her shirt. He used his handkerchief to press the wound.

"He stabbed me!"

"This will help a wee bit, but we need to get you to hospital as quickly as possible and that means getting off this roof."

"But, I can't get back up there."

"Oh yes you can. You got down here. You can get back up."

Savannah was beginning to feel that his voice was fading away into a black fog. She knew she had to move or the fog would overtake her. With the stability of his grip on her arm, she crawled back to the peak of the roof and over to the window. Through a dizzy fog, she recognized the face of Detective Parker reaching out for her.

"Let's get you down to the EMTs." Parker looked at the cut on Savannah's collarbone. "That's going to need some stiches."

Savannah nodded and let Detective Parker lead her over to the flashing vehicle. She got a glimpse of Edward and Amanda being driven away in a cruiser. "Where are they going?"

"They need to be interviewed and fill out statements so that we can press charges. As soon as you get treated, I'll be doing the same with you."

"As long as I don't have to talk to Officer Boulli, I'm good. Where's Reverend Kline?"

"He was taken to the emergency room to see to his injury."

Savannah let Parker help her into the back of the EMT vehicle. He began to walk away and then turned to her, "You know, I thought Edward was my principal suspect because his fingerprints were on the mug. I would have been very wrong."

Savannah's eyes widened, "Edward?" Then she tilted her head back and laughed. "Edward brings coffee, tea, and scones to Webb's every morning. He's been doing that for months for my dad."

"You saved me from making a career-limiting decision. I won't forget it."

Chapter 32

Saturday Morning

Sipping her cappuccino in the office at Webb's, Savannah looked at Edward over the rim. "I'm gonna need another one of these. I didn't get to bed until four o'clock this morning. I didn't know that making statements for the police could take so long."

"It was a first-time experience for all of us."

"Naturally, Rooney woke up at seven and that was all the sleep I got."

"Are you sure you're all right? Shouldn't you be resting?"

"I'm good. The EMT said I could resume normal activities. Not rescuing bar owners about to fall off steep roofs, but normal activities. He also gave me a medical kit for changing the dressing."

"Where did you learn to block that knife? That looked very smooth and practiced."

"I'm a trained glassblower, remember? That kind of upper body strength is the result of years and years of manhandling those long blowpipes with molten glass hanging off the end. I started doing larger and larger pieces at the studio in Seattle and as a result, I've been gradually getting stronger."

"But you really looked like you knew what you were doing."

"That was just pure dumb luck. It wasn't blood free as you know—my stitch count was five." She fingered the expertly bandaged compress taped to her collarbone. "It was an unexpected outcome for me as well as for the reverend."

"He deflated into a lump after you broke his arm."

"I think the pain shocked him into fully realizing what he had done. That his obsessive collecting of Russian icons was misguided and that he had killed two friends to keep them."

"He's confessed everything."

"Dad must have become suspicious when he was going through the financials of the church. I'd bet anything Dad created the ciphers first and then confronted Reverend Kline with the evidence he had uncovered."

Edward nodded, "I think John would have confided in Hugh and Reverend Kline would have known that."

"After he killed Dad, he took the time to set up Jacob. Really, there wasn't anyone else he could frame." Savannah pressed a hand on the bandage.

"It was nice to see Jacob get released while we were giving our statements."

"I think Detective Parker was very relieved that he didn't have to deal with Jacob's parents and their lawyer."

Edward laughed. "He did shake that lawyer's hand a little enthusiastically, don't you think?"

Savannah giggled and had to put her cup down to keep from spilling cappuccino all over the desk. "He was extremely grateful. Didn't you think it was funny that Suzy took a real liking to him? She didn't feel that Jacob was in any danger at all."

"Her instincts are spot on."

Amanda bolted in through the front door giving the bell an unholy shatter of ringing. She trotted back to the office, catching the last of their conversation as Savannah said, "When I was getting patched up, Detective Parker told me that you were his main suspect—that besides Jacob, your print was also found on my dad's mug."

"Me?" Edward reared back his head. "Kill John and Hugh? No way! John was so great to me. But I'll be honest, I'm so glad Parker didn't tell you that my print was on the mug until last night. You hated me when you found out about the loan. If you would have thought I had anything to do with your dad's death, I'd never have a chance with you, now would I?"

Savannah tilted her head coyly. "Who said you ever had a chance with me?"

Amanda burst out laughing, "Cut it out, you two. Savannah, tell us more! What else did Parker say?"

"He was basically about where we were in the investigation. He had eliminated Frank and Smythe just like we had and although Edward was at the top of his list of suspects, they were checking into the background of Dad's Cold War activities as well as his position in the church. I think he was probably only a few days away from finding the connection to Reverend Kline."

Edward shifted in his seat, "I'm not so sure."

"I know the detective was very happy to have the real murderer in custody and as a bonus, Officer Boulli was relieved of duty awaiting an investigation."

"What? The idiot was fired?" blurted Amanda. "I have a new respect for the city's police department. I was afraid that Officer Boulli was the norm."

"I told him my principal reason for getting involved in the investigation was because I thought Officer Boulli was so incompetent that Dad and Hugh's deaths would never be resolved," said Savannah. "It does happen, you know. No one ever finds out."

Jacob piped up as he entered from the back door carrying Suzy. "I heard Detective Parker tell my mother that because of me and Suzy, Officer Boulli would not be working for the police. Something about child endangerment. I think that means me."

"Yes, it means you," agreed Savannah. "We certainly missed you while we were trying to solve the last puzzle. You would have spotted the solution instantly. It took us hours."

"It was no fun to be a suspect," Jacob said.

"True, but to be fair to Detective Parker, you looked like the best bet."

Jacob said softly. "I was the worst bet because I didn't do the murders." He turned and settled Suzy into the dog bed. "Reverend Kline was the best bet."

"You're absolutely right, you know," said Savannah. "We all knew you didn't do anything wrong."

Amanda frowned. "Hey, did you guys spend the whole night down at the station? I finally got home just after midnight."

Edward grinned. "I'll get more coffee. It looks like you're going to need a whole pot."

"Hurry," Savannah called after him.

Amanda walked into the classroom and put her class material down on her student worktable. Savannah followed and Jacob was already setting up his tools.

Amanda's brow scrunched in a knot. "What's going to happen to the Russian icons that the reverend had in his secret hiding place?"

"They're going to be used as evidence, so they're in police custody right now. Because he bought them with church funds, it looks like they belong to the church. Knowing the other deacons, those that were stolen will be returned to their owners."

The bell jangled and the newlyweds followed the twins into the classroom.

Nancy spoke first. "What's been going on? We saw you on the news last night. What's this about murders?"

"Murders?" the twins asked in unison.

Rachel spoke quickly. "I told you this place was going to the dogs. There have never been murders in our neighborhood. Now we have had two. It's going to make the glass shop very difficult to sell. You have to disclose those things, you know."

"She hasn't said that she'll sell," said Faith.

Nancy put her carton down on the worktable. "Well, it would be crazy not to think about it. Terrible events leave behind a bad aura."

"Now, honeybee. You don't know that for certain." Arthur was finally feeling comfortable speaking to the group. "That's just what your Aunt Melda says about her hometown. But to be honest, Salem, Massachusetts, has a lot to answer for."

Amanda turned to Nancy. "Oh, I know just what you mean. It could totally affect the creativity of anyone taking classes. I think we need a spiritual cleansing."

Savannah cleared her throat, "I know you've all heard it on the news, but just to clear the air, Reverend Kline has confessed to the murder of Hugh Trevor and John Webb. He is in a terrible state and I wouldn't be surprised if they find him unable to stand trial."

Rachel blurted, "I knew it was him all along. He's been snooping around the place for weeks trying to convince Mr. Webb of something. I could never hear closely enough to tell what it was."

"One more announcement. Hugh's funeral will be held tomorrow afternoon. Mrs. Webberly said to please come to the First United Christian

Church for a memorial service followed by a supper at her house. She said that most of the business owners will be attending and you are all welcome, too. I highly recommend her peanut butter pie. It rivals anything I've ever tasted. Now let's get back to work."

Everyone laid out his or her project and Savannah was happy to see that the soldering was almost finished. In spite of all the interruptions and disruptions, she was going to finish the class on time. Her dad would have been proud.

"Okay, class. We're on the home stretch now with our turtle sun catchers. All we have to do is apply the final coating of solder on all the joins, attach the hanging loops, clean off all the flux with alcohol, and apply the final finish to protect your project."

She looked at Arthur's progress and expected to see a hot mess and maybe treat a few more burns. As she watched, he proceeded to slowly and gently form a perfect solder bead.

He looked up and beamed. "I think I've got this. I fix in my mind the way I feel when I play Antonio Vivaldi's "Spring Concerto" on my cello and my mind sends calming messages to my hand. Isn't that simply splendid?"

Savannah smiled. "Arthur, it's more than splendid. It's a secret you can use for many things in life. Well done."

The front door jangled and Gregory Smythe and Frank Lattimer blustered into the display room.

"Get out of my way," said Gregory. "I have the best offer by far. I even have the approval of my corporate office."

Frank chest-bumped Gregory. "Hey, you carpet-bagger. I'm not going to let you get away with this."

"Or what?" asked Gregory. "You're just going to close it up and take all the business to your shop downtown. Right?"

Frank at least had the grace to flush and shut his mouth.

"Stop it!" Savannah cried from the doorway. She stepped up to them and alternated poking her finger on each of their chests. "You both lose. *Both*." She turned to Smythe. "Take your Best Value Store plans and stuff them up your corporate ladder. It's not going to happen." She turned to Frank. "You can take your lousy offer and stuff it up your fancy car's exhaust pipe. I'm not selling Webb's to you so you can close it down and keep your student factory going."

"B-but . . . I'm doing what your dad would have wanted. I'll complete the duplication project and keep on teaching students." Frank's voice wound up to a shrill whine.

"Frank, what Dad wanted is not in your heart to give. Dad wanted to spread the love of glass. You just want your students' money. That's all you'll ever be capable of feeling about glass.

"Out." She pointed to the door.

"But . . ."

"Out."

He snapped his mouth shut.

She turned and pointed to Smythe. "You need to reassess your sense of community. There are several sections of town that would embrace the energy that your Big Value Store would bring them. Find them."

"But . . ."

"Out before I throw you out. I am quite strong."

Both men left shaking their heads and muttering. Savannah could just make out, "Crazy like her dad" and "Need to check back with the other community."

Amanda had followed her into the display room. "That's the way to tell 'em."

"There's more telling to do. Make a note to remind me to call Seattle on Monday. My ex-boyfriend is going to have the pleasure of a one-man exhibit."

Edward returned with enough coffee for an army.

Savannah felt a calm resolve flush through her from toes to scalp. She walked over to where Edward stood. She looked directly into his eyes, enjoying his look of alarm. "I'm not closing. I'm not selling. I'm not leaving."

She watched his face relax and smiled. "I'm staying. I'm staying here . . . in my home with Rooney and at Webb's Glass Shop with my new friends."

Stained Glass Glossary of Terms

Came Channels of U-shaped zinc used to bind glass pieces with a design.

Copper Foil Thin narrow strips of adhesive-backed copper tape used to wrap glass edges.

Flux Paste or liquid used to facilitate the flow of solder.

Glassblower Artist skilled in creating objects from molten glass.

Patina A chemical applied to came or a solder joint to change its color.

Solder A low-melting alloy used to join less fusible metals.

Slurry Semi-liquid mixture used for painting on glass.

Stained Glass Any colored flat glass or any object made of such glass joined by metal strips.

Information about Stained Glass Instruction

Signing up for a class in stained glass is an immensely rewarding and satisfying way to spend many relaxing hours with a group of interesting people. Webb's Glass Shop is based on the Grand Central Stained Glass business owned by our friends Bradley and Eloyne Ericson. The website for their business is: www.grandcentralstainedglass.com.

Find a class in your area by searching the web for "stained glass classes" in your local city or state.

You can also research the websites of major glass manufacturers for seminars, trade shows, classes, and inspiration.
www.spectrumglass.com/stained-glass/retailers
www.bullseyeglass.com

About the Jewelry

Just like Savannah, I make jewelry to compliment my outfits and to use up the leftover odds and ends of our various glass projects that my husband and I create. I post the new pieces to my Facebook fan page and the process is captured on Kensington's Hobby Reads site:
http://www.HobbyReads.com.